Ru

Sherrill Willis

My Thank You List

I wish to thank my Dad, Dave Willis, for urging me to just do it, my Mom, Rose Silver, and sister, Diane Newton, who spent many hours reading, rereading and asking "When will there be a love scene?" until I finally put one in. April Callahan and Carol Loscutoff for also reading and being my cheerleaders (and butt-kickers) when my inner-demons got the best of me. Dr. Michael Dorso helped me with medical terminology, any mistakes are mine. Steve Huber, fishing guide extraordinaire, assisted me with all fishing related scenes, again if I made any mistakes, those are mine. Prof. Eaton who assured me that I had the "write stuff" and encouraged me greatly to just keep writing! Brandy Wosika who helped me with the lyrics for the Blues song. Tammy Canady for my way cool cover, and all my FB buddies. Especially Dawn Watters who graciously edited this for me and tells me she is still puking up commas. My children for their patience while I spent countless hours writing, but now say they are so proud of me.

Thanks also go to my old DHS crew: Maureen, Kris, Kim, Deb, April, Jamie, Gail and Krissie for all their encouragement (is it out yet??) – you Women ROCK!!

I would be remiss if I didn't mention my Very Dear Friends: Janet Huber, Cindy Piasecki, June Moyer, Gretchen Bonnell, Tami Flory, Colleen Kubiak and Carol Cirilli who helped this fish out of water find love, acceptance and friendship in a little coffee shop in the Northwood's of Wisconsin. This one is for you, ladies!

Grab a blanket and get comfy, this might take a while...

Prologue – Start at the Beginning

"Oh c'mon Sydney, tell us again! It's been over a year and Suzanne never heard the whole story from you." Betty waved her dishtowel as she spoke, her brown eyes crinkling around the edges as she smiled at Sydney. Sydney took a sip from her mocha, and flung her red, curly hair over her shoulder before she responded.

"You guys have heard this story ten times. Aren't you getting tired of it?" Sydney asked, fingers drumming slowly on the large, overstuffed blue chair, her smile never wavering as she shook her head.

"Nope, and after you're done, I'll tell mine…again," Illana said, smiling as she warmed her hands around her latte, acknowledging the usual request before it was made.

"Oh all right, where shall I start this time? When I got here?"

"No, before that. Start the day you got the contract. I love the lead in!" Lucy said, wiggling back into the pale cream couch, mug of hot coffee steaming up her glasses as she sipped.

"Oh, you have to tell the part about love, remember? Do you remember what you said to us when you got back?" Amelia asked, grabbing a tissue out of her purse, knowing this part always made her cry. Lucy, who was sitting next to her, patted Amelia on the arm in sympathy and stole a tissue out of her friends purse as well.

Sydney sighed good-naturedly and said. "I'll never forget it. But that's the ending. You sure you want me to start there?"

"Yes, then go back. Start there." Betty came around the counter to turn off the open sign, and locked the door. It would be a while before any of them wanted to be interrupted. For the next couple hours, the

1

Stay A While coffee shop was closed to outsiders. The snow falling outside would keep most people away anyway. Only the regulars braved the roads in the small town of Ruby Lake, Wisconsin during a blizzard. "And no leaving out the juicier details this time. There aren't any kids around after all," Betty said as she flicked her dishtowel at Sydney's elbow, barely missing it.

"Hey!" Sydney exclaimed, moving her elbow. "Well, since it's only us girls, why not? Ok, let's see if I can remember. It was just after coming back here and I was having coffee with Betty and Lucy. I said, a few times I think, that I had never felt this way before. I couldn't eat, and when I did it tasted like cardboard, I couldn't sleep unless he was next to me and it was like living outside of my body. When it's true love, when I really knew I was in love, smells were sweeter and snowflakes looked crisper somehow. I know it sounds silly, but I could spend all day with him, just wrapped up in his voice, and the outside world ceased to mean anything. It was only him, I didn't care what anyone thought or how crazy it was. I mean we only knew each other a short time, so it appeared foolish to everyone, well, almost everyone," Sydney said, looking at Illana who smiled in return.

"I suddenly realized it was for this feeling, this intense, secure, overwhelming feeling people had written all the love songs since the beginning of time. The reason wars had been defended or won, the love for someone else is the only thing that can make people overcome overwhelming odds. Why poems and plays had been written, statues made, beautiful buildings erected. Love is everything; it's worth everything. My world had been turned upside down and he and I were the only thing that made sense. I couldn't remember where I ended and he started; we were feeling all of the same feelings at the same time."

"This is what I think is the best part about being human, it's like nothing else, love. No drug could ever feel this good. No matter how exciting other things are whether its sports, even the Olympics, or movies or games, nothing on this earth comes close to the effect true love does. I never doubted him, except the once, but even then I would have known if I had given it any thought. You know, it's been over a year and when he walks in the room there are times I still get butterflies? My God, I wouldn't trade a single minute of what led me to him because it was all worth it in the end."

Sydney tucked one foot under her leg, sat back in her chair and looked at the proprietress of the coffee shop. "Betty, can you make me another mocha? I think I'll be talking for some time."

Chapter One – The Fates Are Very Literal

"I have a delivery for someone," the flower delivery guy sang, standing just inside Sydney's cubicle. Sydney turned around and saw Ralph, who was wearing one of his trademark tie-dyed tank tops, purple and pink today, holding her favorite purple tulips Sean had been sending her every week for the last two months. She couldn't believe he had the nerve to send them today. The bastard.

"I don't want them Ralph, take them back." Sydney's green eyes flashed as she spoke through gritted teeth.

"Whoa honey, problems with lover boy?" Ralph took a step back, and covered his mouth with his hand, his eyebrows shooting up to match his blonde spiked hair.

"I so don't want to talk to you about my problem. Just take them back," Sydney looked around her desk for a spot to put her coffee cup and shoved two computer manuals closer to the phone to make room.

"Oh, wait, they um, they aren't for you, they're for Ashley Kane. Can you sign for them sweetie?" He shoved the clipboard towards her face with a smile that was all teeth.

Exhaling loudly, she grabbed the pen and clipboard to sign her damn name for the stupid flowers for the ditzy blonde who was getting married in two weeks. The one who was getting *her* favorite flowers. Bitch.

"There want me to take them to her too?" Sydney asked sarcastically as she handed the clipboard back to Mr. Oblivious.

"Oh would you? Thanks a mil, I'm *way* behind schedule. Toodles!" Ralph handed her the clear vase and then was off in his mincing walk, leaving her holding the flowers. Sydney marched over to Ashley's cubicle, slammed the flowers on the desk with a terse "These are for you," and tried to walk away. Sydney wasn't sure where the woman would put them since her cubicle was already stuffed to capacity with trinkets and what-nots. All pink. It looked like a bottle of Pepto-Bismol had exploded in her cubicle. Really, who put lace doilies on their cabinets and shelves at work?

"Oh, they're the same flowers you get from your boyfriend! I told my snookie bear how jealous I was, seeing you get them all the time, and he finally listened! Aren't men just wonderful?" Ashley asked as she stuffed her face in the flowers, presumably to smell them, her blonde hair covering the flowers like a weeping willow.

"Sure they are. As target practice." Sydney's curly red hair swung as she quickly turned to leave before Ashley could say anything else. She walked across the blue carpet down the hall and made it back to her desk only to find her best friend and web designer extraordinaire, Illana Garet, waiting for her. Great.

"Okay, you've been avoiding me all morning. Are you going to talk to me about what's bothering you, or do I have to bribe you with coffee first?" Illana asked with an impatient sigh while leaning on her best friends' cubicle wall.

Keeping her head down, she pushed past Illana to sit down. Illana spun the chair around so Sydney had to face her. Sydney's eyes were as red as her hair, and the skin around them so puffy it looked like she had been stung by a bee only to discover she was severely allergic.

"What the hell happened to you?" All impatience gone, she picked up a pile of manila folders and put them on the floor so she could sit on Sydney's desk. "You look like shit. Spill it."

"Thanks so much. I feel loads better now." Sydney took a deep breath. She looked around her cubicle, and all she could see were differing shades of blue. Light blue carpet, sea blue walls and greenish-blue cubicle walls. She again silently cursed the ex-girlfriend of her boss, John, who had stuck one toe in Feng Shui and said blue was the color of creativity. The following week the same ex-girlfriend was studying the art of Tantric Yoga, and Sydney really didn't want to think how that had affected John considering his back went out a week later and he then promptly broke up with her. Taking a deep breath, she looked back up at Illana. "I caught Sean cheating on me, in my bed no less. Oh no, he couldn't just go to his own apartment. He had to defile my bed."

"I'll kill him. And her. Who is she? Do we know her?" Illana asked, her eyes narrowed and lips pursed.

"*Him.* Yes I know him. He's the landscaper for my apartment complex."

Illana blinked her eyes and shook her head and then asked, "Who is? I thought Sean was in the hotel business?" Sydney kept staring at Illana until she got it. Illana's eyes stretched to capacity and holding up one hand she said, "Whoa, back up the train. You mean Sean cheated on you with a man?"

"Yes Sherlock, thanks for picking up on that so quickly." Sydney's breath whooshed out of her. "I still can't wrap my mind around it. What the hell am I supposed to do with this? I mean, I can't rail at him about 'What does he have that I don't have?' since it's fairly obvious." Sydney's hands flew as she spoke, and then dropped helplessly on the arms of her chair, her eyes starting to well up with tears again. "I'm really thinking of taking a vacation. Maybe I'll go to Hawaii for a week. I need a change of scenery."

Illana stood up and started pacing, which is hard to do in a five by eight cubicle. "Okay, we'll deal with this. Crying is *not* going to help. But you're right, a vacation might. I'll go with you and we can stay in my dad's house on Kauai. Jesus, Syd, I'm so sorry." Illana gave her a hug just as their boss came out of his office.

"Is...everything okay?" John asked. He looked impeccable as usual. Not a gray hair out of place and not a wrinkle to mar his dark green Italian suit. Of course, the way he was looking at the two women practically said he'd rather be fighting with rattlesnakes than dealing with a woman who had been crying.

"Yeah, just an emotional moment. You know how we girls are," Sydney said, smiling weakly.

"Is this one of those new fads going around? Getting in touch with your feelings and all that?" John asked, slowly backing up. After the Feng Shui/Tantric Yoga ex-girlfriend he was very suspicious of any fad.

"No, I won't be posting a flyer for a support group or anything. What's up?" Sydney asked, wiping the last of her tears away.

John cleared his throat and straightened his tie as he looked back and forth between the now smiling women. Shaking his head at how quickly they had changed their outward demeanor, he said, "Well, I just got a call from a guy who wants us to set up a database to go with his online business. I was going to send you. If you aren't up to it Sydney, just say so."

"Oh no, I'm up to it. Where am I going?"

"A little town in northern Wisconsin called Ruby Lake. Here's his number. I'd like you to call him and get all the details. Also, find some prices on the accommodations, the flight and a rental car. After you email those to me, I'll handle the reservations and payment for them."

John still looked vaguely uncomfortable, so Sydney decided to wait until later to get more info from him. "Sure, I'll do that first before I call him," Sydney said, taking the proffered note from John before he walked back into his office. Illana followed him and poked her head in the door.

"Hey John, we were just about to grab some coffee. Do you care if we do that first?"

"Go ahead, but do try to come back before lunch," he said sarcastically as he sat down with his back to her to reply to an email.

"Very funny. Do you want anything?" Illana asked.

"No, I'll get my coffee in a bit. Thanks." John was pecking madly on his keyboard using two fingers and didn't bother to turn around as he spoke. Shaking her head, Illana walked back to Sydney's desk.

"C'mon Syd, Starbucks is on me today." Illana stood in the cubicle doorway with her hands on her hips looking like an avenging pixie. Her black, spiked hair had orange tips this morning and as Illana narrowed her brown eyes, Sydney knew arguing would be pointless but tried anyway.

"I can't go anywhere in public looking like this!" Sydney complained, pointing to her eyes.

"That's what sunglasses are for. No more excuses. Let's go."

They walked into Starbucks and even though it was around 9:30am, they still had to wait in a line of about eight people. The sound of the frothing wand mixed with the murmur of voices and the light jazz playing discreetly over the speakers. Thankfully, the woman behind the counter was fast and no one had ordered more than one or two lattes or mochas apiece so their wait was fairly short.

"Give me a grande-non-fat-mocha, extra choc with whip," Illana demanded, digging in her Burberry purse to find the matching wallet.

"I'll have a venti Sumatra coffee; leave about an inch for cream. Please." Sydney half-smiled at the girl across the counter, who was too busy grabbing espresso shot glasses to return the nicety. Looking at Illana she was jarred back to the moment and asked the same question she had asked a hundred times, "Why do you get extra chocolate and whipped cream but order non-fat milk? Why not just get it made with two-percent like a normal person?"

Illana played along, knowing Sydney wanted to be distracted from her feelings right now. "*Normal* people do get non-fat milk, hence why I order it like that. Syd, you know I can't have whipped cream and two-percent! That would be way too many calories." Illana was clearly horrified by the thought, which is the only reason Sydney mentioned it.

"Oh right, you have so much to worry about. You're what, a size two?" Sydney asked. "You try being a size ten while being surrounded by emaciated women! Maybe I'll luck out and in Wisconsin, the land of dairy, I won't be considered fat. We can't all be skinny with long legs like some people," Sydney said, raising her eyebrow as she gave Illana the once over.

"No," Illana complained, "but thin and tall has its disadvantages too. I can't wear heels if I date a man shorter than six feet tall. Plus, you have that whole Marilyn Monroe figure going for you; at least you know what cleavage feels like without having to buy it." She waved her hand back and forth, to get them back on the subject her best friend was trying so hard to avoid. "Anyway, the topic at hand is how to use this little Wisconsin vacation to your advantage. I know you need it Syd, especially after yesterday. Not to mention all the other shit that has happened this year."

After picking up their coffees they approached the condiment bar. Sydney proceeded to add an inch of half and half and poured in what looked like three pounds of sugar to her coffee. Illana looked on in disgust. "You do realize all your teeth are going to just fall out one day, right? I hate watching you doctor your coffee. I'll meet you outside."

"Then why do you watch?" Sydney retorted over her shoulder at Illana's retreating back. Sydney joined her to walk back to work and gave some more thought to what had happened with Sean. They walked past the stately Capitol that was surrounded by all kinds of different trees, which now housed another movie star Governor, except this one still couldn't pronounce "California" right. The warm August morning air felt good on their skin, but in another hour Sydney's pale complexion would get sunburned while she stood in the shade.

"Maybe I'm just not cut out to be in a long-term relationship." Sydney said, sighing.

"Whoa girl...back up. You're not blaming yourself for this are you?" Illana asked. When Sydney shrugged her shoulders noncommittally, it was Illana's turn to roll her eyes. "My God Syd, Sean being gay has nothing to do with you! So you had a couple of bad relationships this year-"

"Four. I've had four failed relationships this year." After Sydney's interjection, they resumed walking back to the office.

"Okay, four. But I wouldn't call them 'failures' since you learned something from each of them. Look at Rick. He was cute, but a total stoner. Then there was the pretend 'I'm-the-son-of-an-oil-baron' guy, what was his name?"

"Ari."

"Right, Ari. Then there was Derek, who was married. I still say we should send a text to his wife, but whatever. I'm not sure what lesson to take away from this latest one, except not to go out any man who knows who Manolo Blanik is." Illana said, and was rewarded with a laugh from Sydney. "I think this contract in Wisconsin comes at a perfect time. You'll be able to step away, have a little break and hopefully come back with a new perspective of your life. And, we'll go to Kauai when you get back." Illana stopped in front of their building, which was asphalt gray and had the same amount of charm as the matching sidewalk they were standing on, and turned to Sydney. "Give it some time, there's someone out there who's perfect for you. It's just not the right time yet." Standing right next to her, Illana threw her arm around Sydney's shoulders and gave her a girlfriend-pep-talk squeeze. "All you have to do is find one who admires a great cook, and he'll be a goner."

"Ha! The-way-to-a-man's-heart bullshit was thrown out along with bras in the '60's. I'll be okay, and thanks for listening." Sydney reached up and patted Illana's hand in return as she pulled out of the embrace and glanced towards the glass doors.

"No problem, I'm here for you and I'll always be on your side." Illana shrugged her shoulders and added, "Who knows, maybe you'll meet your dream guy there."

Sydney smiled, but it didn't reach her eyes. "Sure Illana, just think of the new pick up line I could use: 'Hi, I have some serious trust issues since my last boyfriend turned out to be gay. Wanna go out with me?' Right, I don't think so. I have to figure out my travel arrangements, and while I'm doing that, you need to get started on making our travel plans for Kauai."

Sydney found a reasonably priced room at a place called the Tamarack Hotel, which was the only hotel in town with internet access, and an absolute steal on a Ford Taurus rental for a week. The flight would be a long one, but at least it didn't depart until ten in the morning. Sydney emailed all the travel information to John and then called the new client.

"This is Alex Greyson."

"Hello Alex, this is Sydney Myers from 21st Century Technology. I understand you'd like us to build your company a database and I'm calling to get some additional information from you."

"Hi. I thought John said he would have the database builder call. Are you his secretary?" he asked. Sydney wished she had a quarter for every time that assumption was made. She took a deep breath and mentally counted to ten.

"No, I'm the database *designer*. We women are allowed to learn about such things now," Sydney said dryly. "Anyway, if you could please describe how many people will be using the database at one time, and if you're still interested in having me come out, I'm confident I can save you both time and money." She could've cost John this contract with her smarmy comment, but in her current mood she just didn't care.

"Of course I'm still interested. I, uh, apologize for my assumption," Alex said, then rushed to say, "I assure you that you will be welcome here. Since I'm the most thickheaded person that works here, I doubt you will have any other problems. Sorry to get off on the wrong foot."

Since he sounded sincere, and totally embarrassed, Sydney let it go. "It's okay, happens all the time. Why don't you describe what you're looking for so I can get started right away? I plan on arriving Sunday and should be done in less than a week."

"Wow, sounds great! If you think - I mean if you need more time it won't be a problem."

Sydney stifled a laugh, but smiled hearing how agreeable he was trying to be. "I'm pretty sure I won't, but I'll keep it in mind."

Alex finally got unflustered enough to explain what he needed. His company, Parties Are Us, sold all the items a person would need to throw a child's theme birthday party. Since he indicated their web site had been designed by someone on staff, she didn't mention building that aspect into the contract. She did write down the web address to get an idea of what they were selling and marveled, once again, how a client could have a web site, but no database.

"Okay Alex, I think that about covers it. I'm going to transfer you to John so you two *guys* can hammer out the rest of the details." Sydney wasn't known for being subtle, but that barb was about as close as she could get. She wondered briefly what, if anything, Alex would say to John. John probably didn't mention her gender since it wouldn't have occurred to him it might matter. She wasn't at all sure John was aware of her gender to begin with.

Fifteen minutes later, Sydney could still hear John laughing and talking loudly with Alex like they were old friends. She hurriedly shot John an email with her bid amount. John opened his door shortly thereafter and waved her in. Swinging out of her chair she walked across the hall, briefly shot a smile at Illana who was walking towards the copier, and stepped into his office. Shutting the door behind her, she sat in the brown leather chair across from his desk. John leaned back in his chair, put his feet up on his mahogany desk and crossed his arms behind his head.

"You're all set. I made the reservations for the flight, car, and hotel. You can use the company credit card for any expenses while you're there. The hotel manager asked a billion questions about why you were coming and said we were lucky to get a room since there's some sort of festival going on. Anyway, Alex mentioned there was a misunderstanding of some sort but you cleared it up. He then went on and on about how his people aren't a bunch of redneck hicks and how they're very forward thinkers and so on. What was that all about?"

"He thought I was a secretary so I quickly disabused him of that notion," Sydney said with a small grin.

John smiled and said, "I'm sure you did. Do you think you'll have any problems?" Acquiescing to Sydney's smirk and raised eyebrow, he continued. "Good. I included your plane ticket and expenses into the contract and he didn't bat an eye. He also reiterated that he was more than willing to pay for an extra week if needed."

"I really doubt it'll be necessary, but I'll keep you posted."

"Do that. I'll email you the e-ticket in a few minutes along with the car and hotel confirmations. Take whatever equipment you'll need with you tonight but there's no need to start on this until you get there. I checked the on-location weather for the week. The highs will be in the upper sixties and low seventies so I'd take something warm to wear since the lows will be in the fifties. If you're done with the Olson's computer you can head out."

"Wow, it gets cold there pretty early. I guess I'll leave my miniskirts at home." John blinked in confusion, not getting the joke that she never wore anything besides pant suits to begin with. Waving a hand to dismiss her comment, she continued. "Regarding the Olson's computer, I already installed the hard drive and new video card. I just have to test it and then call them to let them know it's ready. Hey, just out of curiosity, how did Alex hear of us?"

"He's an old fraternity buddy and current hunting partner of mine. I've been after him for the last couple of years to get his business into the electronic age."

Of course he is, Sydney thought and asked, "Is there some reason you didn't tell me you two were friends *before* I talked to him?"

"I guess I could've mentioned it before, but it was more fun my way," John replied, his eyes twinkling with mirth. "By the way, Ruby Lake is where I go hunting every year in November. It's boring, but beautiful."

"Thanks for the very belated info. I'll see you in a week," Sydney said with a little laugh as she got up and let herself out as John swung back to his computer screen to research what equipment to buy with the fee she was about to bring in.

Sydney tossed her purse on the kitchen table as she walked into her apartment. Snagging a soda out of the 'fridge, she guzzled half of it before reaching her bedroom. After carefully setting the can on a coaster, she ran her hand over the smooth surface of the newly refinished cherry wood dresser. It had taken her two weeks to get it perfect, but she was thrilled with the results. Pulling her suitcase out from under the bed she neatly packed clothes for the trip.

Tracing the framed picture of her mother with a fingertip, a wave of sadness washed over her as she remembered the day it had been taken, just a little over a year ago. She had been helping her mom plant the sunflowers that would later grow six to seven feet high, and when they were done her mom had sat back on her heels to survey her new garden. Sydney had just bought a new camera and had it in her purse nearby, and shot the picture as a lark. Her mom had been wearing an old Led Zeppelin t-shirt, cut-off jean shorts and had a dirt smudge on her cheek. To Sydney, she'd never looked prettier.

Turning back to packing, Sydney thought about the past couple months. She was upset over Sean, but it had bruised her ego far more than her heart, and she wasn't about to examine that fact too closely. Losing her mom so suddenly earlier this year had fractured her daily life to the point she sometimes felt like she would never recover. She knew she would continue to feel the loss of her mom for the rest of her life, but hoped the old adage about time was true. Deep down she could admit her mom's death wasn't the only reason she needed a break.

According to her ten-year plan she had written seven years ago, she should've been married with children by now. The fact she'd failed to accomplish these two goals made her worry about her seemingly lack of ability to have a long-term relationship. *Maybe I've read too many romance novels*, she thought while rifling through her jewelry box.

Of course, she really did believe in true love since witnessing it firsthand growing up. More times than she could count she had come upon her parents kissing and exchanging "that" look as she and her sister, Jessica, had called it. Jessica would stick her finger down her throat in protest, but Sydney always thought it was sweet and looked forward to the day she too would trade "that" look with someone special. So far, her knight in dented armor hadn't shown up.

Sydney finished packing (six suits, a pair of jeans, plenty of underwear and socks, and two sweaters, just in case) and wheeled the suitcase to the front door where it would sit until she left Sunday morning. The phone rang and she glanced at the display before picking it up, and seeing who it was, hesitated before she answered with false cheer. "Hey Dad, how are you?"

"Good. I hate your caller I.D.; it throws me off every time you know it's me. I have some free time next week and I thought I'd spring for a couple of tickets to the Music Circus. *The King & I* is playing." Her dad, Graham, knew it was her favorite musical.

"I would love to, but I have to go to a little town in northern Wisconsin for the week. I'm leaving Sunday and won't be back until Saturday. Damn, I hate missing that show! I could probably reschedule if you really want to go." Since her mom died, she tried to make extra time to be with her dad, and this was an event she really did hate to miss. Her parents had been taking her and Jessica to the Music Circus ever since they were little and it was something she looked forward to every summer. There was nothing like watching a Broadway musical while sitting in a circus tent in the blistering heat.

"No, that's okay honey. Maybe we can catch *Annie Get Your Gun* the following week. So, what takes you to Wisconsin?"

"An online company needs a database and John is sending me out there to build it. I may be back sooner, but definitely by Saturday. Hey, do you want to come with me? I would be busy during the day, but we could check out the sights at night." She only asked because she knew he'd say no. If he said yes, she'd be screwed.

"Knowing you, you won't be done until nine or ten p.m. and I only have myself to blame. I understand what it's like to get involved with something and not be able to put it away. I wish I would have spent more time at home with you kids and your mom-"

"Dad, don't. We both know Mom understood and supported your work, even if it meant going away wherever or whenever necessary. Besides, she would let us stay up late and watch Johnny Carson when you were gone," Sydney added, hoping he would take the bait and not get all morose again.

"No wonder you two girls were glad to see me go! What time do you leave on Sunday?"

"I have a ten o'clock flight so I figured I would leave here about eight-thirty."

"I'll give you a lift so you won't have to leave your car there. Why don't you come over tomorrow night and I'll fix us each a steak and we can rent *Seven Brides for Seven Brothers*?"

"That sounds great Dad. I'll bring the popcorn."

"It's a deal. Too bad your sister's so far away, or we could make an event out of it. Oh well, have a good night, and I'll see you tomorrow."

Hanging up the phone, she shook her head as she sat down to write her series of lists that would keep her organized for the week. No matter how hard she tried to focus on the task at hand, her thoughts kept drifting back to her dad. She knew she wasn't the first choice in the daughter arena, for too many reasons to count. But she also knew she wasn't the only one getting caught in the undertow of sadness, and would do everything in her power to make the following night with her dad as carefree as possible.

Saturday sped by as Sydney ran a myriad of errands and it ended with her having an excellent Tri-tip and garlic mashed potato dinner and watching one of her favorite movies with her dad. She appreciated how hard he was trying to reach out to her, but old hurts were hard to forget and, not to mention, forgive. The least she could do was follow suit. So early Sunday morning Sydney fixed thin, almost crepe-like pancakes for breakfast while Graham read her interesting articles out of the *New York Times*. When he had finished reading one story about a certain New York mayor's mistress being given a political post, Sydney said she didn't see anything wrong with that, playing devil's advocate like her mom had done, just get a rise out of him. Her dad knew what Sydney was doing, but that didn't stop the explosion of disbelief from coming out of his mouth. The fact it filled in some of the hollowness wasn't lost on either of them. Sydney poured her first cup of coffee, doctored it as her dad grimaced at her and sat down at the scarred oak table.

The family dining table had the usual assortment of gouges, stains, and scratches from more than twenty years of daily use. But it also held memories. She had mentioned refinishing it a couple of months ago but her dad kept putting her off until she finally dropped it. *Maybe he would be ready next year*, she thought as she finished her coffee and followed him outside to the car.

During the last leg of her flight, the scenery as they were descending astounded Sydney. She had never seen so many lakes. She had always heard Minnesota had a lot of lakes, but now she was inclined to believe Wisconsin might have more. All she knew about Wisconsin was there were a ton of dairy farms and along with unhappy cows and cheese, and they were big on football, they had the Green Bay Packers. Sydney had thought she would be entering a place of rolling hills and farms, so she was totally unprepared for the size of the forests and the multitude of lakes.

When the small twin-engine Lear jet landed in Ruby Lake, she was equally taken aback by the size of the airport: one landing strip flanked by dense forests of some sort of pine trees. The plane taxied to the terminal and she watched in disbelief as a platform of stairs was pushed up to the door. *Well, I wanted change of scenery*, she thought. That thought led her to why she wanted to be somewhere else, and she again berated herself for being blind to some of Sean's tendencies. He never, ever looked at other women, but he did get rather chatty with male bartenders whenever they went out. She had teased him about it a few times, but he had reacted so vehemently against being gay she just thought his overreaction was funny. Now, she understood he was only protesting too much.

As Sydney and the other passengers stood up, she noticed no one was jockeying for position. So she followed their lead and let others go ahead of her before taking her stuff from the overhead. She even smiled at the male attendant on her way out, who was very cute, and probably gay. Sydney shook her head to banish the unbidden thought, and wondered if this would be a new hurdle whenever she looked at a man. Walking down the steps she took a moment to take in the surroundings. No one amassing behind her seemed to mind her slower pace. This was not Sacramento by a stretch. Even over the jet engine fuel, she could smell the strong earthy scent of the forests that encompassed her. It had been in the nineties almost every day for the last two weeks in Sacramento. Confirming the announcement of the pilot who welcomed them when they touched down, Ruby Lake was currently a brisk 55 degrees. In a T-shirt and jeans she was actually cold.

The terminal was only one large room. The focal point of the room was the single luggage turnstile, which sat in the middle. Two airline counters fronted the wall on her left, in front of and to the right of the entrance was one counter which was shared by three car rental agencies. *Illana would flip if she saw this*, Sydney thought as she made her way to the car rental counter, her black heels clicking on the dated orange tiles.

She managed to complete all the necessary paperwork just as her luggage came out. The female customer service rep from Hertz provided a map and thoughtfully highlighted the route to Sydney's hotel. Sydney didn't tell the woman she already had studied her MapQuest directions seven times during the flight. Instead, she thanked the very friendly attendant, gathered her bags and left the airport. Of course, getting the map wasn't a bad thing. Sydney couldn't count the times she had previously relied upon MapQuest, only to find out it left off a freeway off ramp, or sent her the longest way possible. She had once remarked to Illana she was sure MapQuest was manned by a bunch of crows who sat behind a bunch of computers pecking out directions with their beaks.

She checked in at the hotel, and then lugged her suitcase, laptop, and overnight bag up the stairs to her room on the second floor. Letting herself in, she noticed this hotel room was just like any other. A brownish floral bedspread covered the king-sized mattress while woodsy lamps stood sentry on the nightstands that flanked the bed. At least the full balcony afforded her a view of a river. She put her suitcase and other bag on the floor and placed the laptop bag on the desk.

After booting up the computer, she quickly showered and changed, then unpacked her belongings because she detested living out of a suitcase. If everything was hung up or folded neatly in a dresser it gave some semblance of being at home. A glance at the desktop clock radio reminded her to change her watch ahead two hours. She adjusted the hands to 9:16 pm, but her body was still two hours behind on California time so she decided to get started. She had meant to look at the client's web site Friday, but with packing and making lists, there had simply been no time.

Once it came up, the amateur site startled her. At least she now understood why they didn't have a database in place. She immediately called Illana, who answered on the second ring.

"Miss me already? How's the nightlife?"

"You're hysterical. Houston, we have a problem."

"Already? I thought you didn't start until tomorrow?"

"I *should've* started Friday, but well, anyway, here's the deal. The client has a web site I need you to look at. I just sent you an email with a link. I want to be on the phone with you when you see it." Sydney was waiting with an amused grin while Illana pulled up the site.

"You have *got* to be kidding me! There is no way to place an order online? How do these people stay in business?"

"They must do pretty well if they can pay us. I'm going to suggest, strongly, that they pull you in so we can connect the database to a completely overhauled web site. Plus, I want to be at the airport when you land." Now Sydney was smirking.

"No way, I can do it from here. Why pay both of us to fly out? And what's with the airport?" Illana's backpedaling was overruled by curiosity caused by her friend's sarcasm.

"Not telling. Having you come out here would be good for customer relations. Besides, they're willing to pay for me to be out here for two weeks, so having you come out for three or four days should be a cinch. I've already sent John an email with the web site link and the suggestion to bring you on board. Better start packing," Sydney added, her sarcasm gone, replaced by the surety of Illana's imminent arrival.

"You don't know they'll go for it. Didn't you say a staffer made the web site? Looks like he or she must have taken one Front Page class and decided to go pro. It would *not* be good customer relations to start stepping on toes immediately. How you get away with it on such a regular basis is a mystery to us all. Including John." Sydney could almost see Illana pushing her hand through her hair. Blowing air out of her pursed lips she said, "Okay, okay. I'll start on some preliminary pages and email them to you later, that way you can take them with you tomorrow. You owe me for this, Syd. Would it have killed you to look at this on Friday? You know I don't work well under pressure!" Sydney could hear Illana slamming cabinet doors. She was probably pacing too. Great.

"Yes you do. Honestly, I meant to review it this weekend but spent time with my dad instead," Sydney said, winding the telephone receiver cord around her fingers like a little girl making knots with grass.

That comment deflated Illana and her voice was laced with understanding. "Yeah, I know how it goes. I can start on this in a few. Give me your number at the hotel and I'll holler at you once the prelims are done."

Sydney read off the phone number, said thanks, and spent the next three hours coming up with an entirely new game plan to present to Alex in the morning. Illana called just before midnight and emailed the preliminary web pages. Sydney incorporated them into her new PowerPoint presentation, set the alarm for six, brushed her teeth, and packed it in for the night.

She tried for fifteen minutes to fall asleep, but it was too quiet. There was no noise at all. Until this moment, it hadn't occurred to her the white noise provided by the nightly traffic at home had been lulling her to sleep. She got back up and opened the sliding glass door to let some noise in. The night air was approaching freezing and the only sounds were from some hardy crickets and a song bird that should have been asleep hours ago. Not wanting to freeze to death, she shut the slider and turned on a classic rock station on the radio. After switching the alarm to the annoying buzzer option to make sure she'd hear it, she finally dozed off while Van Morrison sang about a brown eyed girl.

Early the next morning Sydney went over her presentation one more time, grabbed her laptop and purse, and then headed to the car. It was only 7:15 am, and since the meeting with Alex wasn't until eight, she decided to try out the little coffee shop downtown. It was called "Stay A While" and only a couple blocks away from the hotel. She started the car to get the heater going and put the laptop in the trunk. She was grateful she had a sweater and fall jacket on since it was only 49 degrees. She never liked to walk anywhere, so she was glad the frigid weather conditions justified driving to get her coffee.

She turned her car onto a pretty, tree-lined street where some of the buildings were showing their age with their peeling paint and one even had a boarded up window. But other buildings, like the coffee shop, had obviously been given a recent facelift. Stay A While had a huge plate glass window in front surrounded by brick and sheltered by a green awning long enough to hold the business name and address. Peering in the window she saw a few women sitting in the mish-mash of chairs and couches and laughing with the barista. A bell jingled as Sydney walked inside, and the laughter continued as she approached the counter.

"Oh Lucy, your poor dog! How long-" the woman behind the counter started to ask, and then turned her attention to the new customer. "Good morning. Welcome to Stay A While, what can I get you?" She appeared to be in her late thirties and wore jeans and a t-shirt. The other women, except one who was quite thin and stylish, were dressed similarly and lacked makeup. They were drinking out of pottery mugs, probably from the rack behind the counter that showed some empty spaces. Sydney noticed everyone else in the room had about the same build as she did. It was nice not to be the heaviest person in the room, for once.

"What kind of coffee do you have?" Sydney asked, not seeing the types of coffee listed on the chalkboard menu above the mugs.

"Columbian and Columbian decaf."

"Then I'll take a large Columbian and please leave about an inch for cream." The woman handed her a large paper cup and pointed to the coffee carafes on the opposite counter.

"We're pretty informal around here, so help yourself. I'm Betty," the barista disclosed as she turned to grab the cream out of the yellow refrigerator directly behind the espresso machine. "Are you just passing through?"

"No. Well, I guess I am in a way. I'm here for a week on business." Sydney wasn't accustomed to being questioned by the coffee lady, but since it was done in a friendly way she didn't see the harm in answering.

"Really? Where are you from?" By this time the other conversation had ended and all eyes were on her.

"Sacramento. I'm here to do some computer work for one of the local businesses," she answered as she poured her coffee. It smelled heavenly, not burnt like Starbucks often did.

"What business?" This came from the stylish-looking woman sitting on the couch.

"Parties Are Us," Sydney replied as she added her cream, handed the carton back to Betty, and proceeded to put sugar in her coffee. No one remarked on the amount, which was a first.

"What are you going to be doing for Mr. Lottery Winner?" asked the same woman.

"Amelia, let the woman get her coffee," Betty admonished, either not aware or not caring she had started the interrogation.

"No, that's okay. I'm going to build a database for the business. Very dry, boring stuff," she said aloud but finished the sentence only in her head with: *to everyone but me*. Sydney loved nothing more than being lost in queries and layers of codes. The four women all exchanged significant glances with one another. Betty raised her hand to stop the others.

"I'll tell her. But first let's get acquainted. Amelia's the one with a hundred questions, Suzanne's hiding behind her glasses, and that's Lucy, who has the funniest stories ever." It felt like roll call as each woman raised their hand in a partial wave as their respective names were called. "Now, Alex is a very nice guy, but you need to watch out for Annie. She'll come on nice but I swear while she brushes her teeth she also sharpens her tongue. She's Alex's little sister and he may own the company, but she runs it."

"Don't bother trying to get on her good side, she doesn't have one," Amelia said, and hid her smile while taking a sip of coffee. Two of the women nodded in agreement with Amelia.

While she wasn't particularly fond of gossiping, Sydney couldn't help being intrigued. She usually hung out with other techie people who would rather talk about the latest gadgets than about people. So this was like stepping into another world, or back into high school. So was a little surprised when she found herself sitting down on the edge of a blue and white striped cushy chair.

"Whatever you do, don't try to joke around with her. She doesn't have a sense of humor, either." Suzanne, the girl with mousey brown hair and big-rimmed glasses, slunk down further into the couch after her remark while looking around at the others for confirmation. Another round of head nodding commenced, but Suzanne still remained hunched in her chair. Sydney took a sip of coffee and, having been so caught up in the gossip session around her, was pleasantly surprised at how good it was. Apparently, she had some latent snob in her after all.

"So, I should stay away from Annie. You mentioned Alex won the lottery?"

"Yes, about eight years ago he won over four million dollars. He's a great guy, bought his whole family houses and cars and pays for his parents to go on fabulous vacations. He's not married, but God knows enough women around here have tried." Betty waved her hand to the side and said, "Okay, so that's the skinny on them, what about you? Are you married? Do you have any kids?"

"No, and no. I stay pretty busy with my work, and speaking of my work, I'd better get going. I don't want to be late on my first day. Thanks for the coffee and the heads up." Sydney gathered her things, said bye to the room at large while all the coffee ladies said goodbye and urged her to come back anytime. If she did go back, the first thing she would ask is what had happened to Lucy's dog.

Chapter Two – Attila the Bun

Sydney pulled into the parking lot where a large, carved wooden sign hung from two posts in the ground adorned with "Parties Are Us" in huge purple letters. A teddy bear grasped a bunch of balloons to the right of the lettering, a clown danced on one foot to the left, and a blue train chugged merrily across the bottom. The building's gray siding contrasted weirdly with the wooden trim, which had been painted in primary red, yellow, and green. Sydney grabbed her purse and went over the presentation one more time in her head while getting the laptop out of the trunk. She hoped Annie wasn't the one who had created the web site. The last thing Sydney wanted to do was make an enemy on the first day.

Sydney walked in and was immediately confronted by a large deer head, crowned with antlers and mounted on the wall about ten feet in front of her. On his head sat a huge sombrero, around his neck hung a lei, and next to it there was a sign that read: "Hello, my name is Bob. Welcome to Parties Are Us! Please park your antlers and make yourself at home." Sydney forced herself to walk forward to the receptionist window, which was directly under the dead animal. The glassy eyes seemed to follow her every step.

"Good morning! I'm Stella, how can I help you?" asked a very perky woman in a bright yellow t-shirt that had a smiling teddy bear stitched onto the pocket.

"Good morning, I'm Sydney Myers from 21st Century Technology. I have an appointment –"

Like a pressurized dam that finally gave way, the receptionist showed her excitement by clasping her hands together and smiling widely. "Oh you're here! Everyone is so excited! You're from California right? It must be so exciting! You're so tan; do you live on the beach?"

"Um, no, I live in Northern California, inland; the Pacific is a couple hours away."

"Oh, that's too bad." Stella's face fell for a moment, but brightened almost painfully a second later. "I'm sure you've met all kinds of famous actors though! I'll just call Alex and let him know you're here." Stella picked up the phone and announced Sydney's arrival to Alex, keeping her smile and eyes on Sydney the whole time. Sydney tried to squelch the nervous laugh that was threatening to bolt out of her throat. *Is this the way Midwesterner's view Californian's?*

Stella's tight, red curls appeared tamed by Aqua Net since they were the only part of the woman that didn't move or jiggle. She bounced out of her chair and opened the door to lead Sydney back to Alex's office at the end of the hall, introducing her to everyone as she went. Sydney had never seen so many people happy to see her. Definitely weird.

Alex came out of his office, and walked down the hallway past some dead fish on the wall. He ran a hand through his wavy dark hair, thanked Stella and turning around to go back the same way he had just come, led Sydney past the glassy-eyed fish to his office. He was just over six feet tall and had the lanky build of a basketball player, with an easy smile that revealed a dimple in his chin. He was more cute than handsome, especially with his hair pointing in every direction.

"Whew! I am sure glad to see you," he said as he shook her hand and led her into his office. After shutting the door, he said, "Make yourself comfortable. How was your flight? Is your hotel okay? Did you have breakfast? Can I get you a cup of coffee?" Alex was moving back towards the door when Sydney held her hand up.

"My flight was fine, hotel is great, I don't typically eat breakfast and I already had coffee." Alex nodded and sat down behind his desk. Another dead deer head hung on the wall behind his desk, and Sydney again had the awkward feeling she was being stared at. At least this one was dressed a little more in keeping with its natural habitat. No hat, no lei; just an odd, ever-knowing stare. As she took in the rest of his office, she noticed that there was little open wall space, most of it had been covered over by pictures of an older man, a young boy, and a teenage Alex participating in hunting or fishing excursions. Eeeew.

"I had an opportunity last night to review your web site and I have some ideas I would like to run past you." Sydney began, then outlined her plan and using her laptop, showed Alex the mock-ups sent over by Illana who had once again stepped onto the pitch in the nick of time.

"As you can see, this will give your customers the choice of buying online or calling." She then launched into her presentation and showed Alex some statistics she had printed out regarding business growth with online stores she had gotten from the marketing team back at her office. About fifteen minutes into her proposal, Alex's chocolate brown eyes had glazed over, much like the dead deer above him, and she quickly wrapped it up. "So while you consider bringing our web site creator on board, why don't I get started? Where would you like me to set up? Oh, and if I could get copies of the ordering forms and supply bills, that would be really helpful."

"You could use my sister's office, she's off this week. I wanted to, um, surprise her with the database, but I'll have to think about the web site. I'll get the forms you need; I had them around here somewhere," he said as he lifted files and other debris off his desk to look. His eyes hadn't come back to a proper focus yet, and at the mention of his sister, he had raked his hand through his hair again.

After being shown into Annie's office, Alex excused himself to find the requested paperwork. As Sydney set up her equipment, she noticed this room was bigger than Alex's; she couldn't help but wonder what type of woman his sister was. Unlike Alex's office, there was only one picture of an attractive elderly lady with her hair in a tight bun and wearing a triple strand of pearls. There were numerous awards and a college degree (Yale, no less) hanging on a wall of pride, but the rest of the office was fairly spartan. At least, that was what Sydney thought until she glanced away from her monitor and her eyes landed on the curio cabinet to the right of the huge desk. She had only been working for about a half an hour when Alex came in to find her staring (again) in disbelief at the multitude of fairy figurines that were locked up behind the glass.

"Please don't touch any of those, Annie would have a fit," Alex said worriedly. She couldn't believe she was looking at them; therefore, the jump to wanting to touch them was unthinkable. *Why would she have these in her office and not at home?*

Alex cleared his throat and said, "I talked to an associate of mine, and he suggested I go for it. With the web site, I mean." His ears turned pink at the double entendre.

"Great! I'll give John a call and see when Illana can get here. I'm sure he'll want to talk to you about adding onto the contract so I'll have him call you when I'm done."

"It won't be necessary. I agree with your proposal and as long as it's close to the base figures you showed me, I've no problem with it. Here's the paperwork you wanted," he said, handing her a stack of forms. Alex's face lit up and he stuck his hands in his pockets, "Well this is exciting, isn't it! When you're done with your phone call, I'll take you around to show you the place and properly introduce you to my team."

In less than five minutes, after John promised to fax over another contract, she took Alex up on his offer to show her around. Alex introduced her to his office staff, all of whom were wearing the same T-shirt as Stella. Sydney picked up on the fact they all seemed to be related to him somehow, well, everyone except the dead things on the walls. Nepotism aside, it appeared to be a relaxed environment in which to work. Some of the women had radios playing softly at their desks, and those who weren't on the phone were online. They all smiled and shook her hand and said how glad they were she was there. She had never seen such a happy bunch of women. *Weird.*

After meeting the Stepford clerks, Alex led her into the warehouse behind the office. From the parking lot the building hadn't looked very big and she was surprised at the vast size of the interior expanse. Inside were rows upon rows of every party item one would ever need, and then some. It smelled musty like most large indoor areas do, with the added smell of diesel fuel, and perhaps something chemically sweet like the smell of fresh stationery in Hallmark stores. Alex put his forefingers in his mouth and gave a shrill whistle aimed at the guy driving a forklift. The forklift stopped and shuddered to a halt as a living Greek God in Mount Olympus non-issue denim swung down from the high seat. She reminded herself she was at work, and to breathe. *This will be no different than the contract you had with the George Clooney lookalike, and nothing happened with him,* Sydney reminded herself. The man approaching them had muscular arms and legs, a great ass, curly tawny shoulder length hair, and a sly smile. He might as well have been wearing a shirt that said "Bad Ass", but it would have been redundant. Then he opened his mouth.

"So, is this is the computer geek? Cute glasses. Damn, I expected a nerd and here we get a hottie."

"Zeke, watch your mouth! What's the matter with you?"

"That's okay Alex, but apparently you were wrong about being the most thickheaded person who works here. I can see why you have him out here," Sydney said deadpan, while looking at Zeke over the top of her "cute" glasses.

"Yes, well, Zeke, this is Sydney Myers. Sydney this is Zeke, my little brother." Crap. This must be the younger boy from the pictures. The smug look on Zeke's face made her even more furious, but this time she wisely held her tongue as Alex continued. "I was going to have you show Sydney around, but I think it can wait until later. Did the shipment from Milwaukee get here yet?"

"Not yet bro. The dude called this morning and said it would be here around ten this morning." Zeke hooked his thumbs in his belt loops and blatantly gave Sydney the once over. Alex narrowed his eyes at his brother and shook his head.

"Great. I'll let the girls know to push back the deliveries on all the orders today." He turned to Sydney and smiled, "I'll let you get started now that you've seen the place. Zeke, I'll talk to you later." It sounded like a threat, but Zeke just winked at Sydney and walked back to the forklift. "I apologize for Zeke's behavior. He normally doesn't talk like that. I've no idea what's gotten into him."

"You don't have to apologize and I hope you didn't take any offense to what I said to him."

"Not at all. If he's going to act like an idiot, you've my permission to treat him as one. So now that you've had the three-cent tour and met my staff, do you have any questions?" At the shake of her head he remarked, "Great! I'll leave you alone so you can do your job. Thanks a lot for being here. I hope you know I'm really excited about what you'll be doing for my company." The sincerity in his eyes won her over.

"You're welcome, and I'm certain you'll be pleased by what we can do for you. I called John and he'll be faxing over a new contract for you to review. If everything's okay, Illana Garet, our web designer, will be here tonight and come in with me tomorrow morning." As Alex nodded and went back to his office, she slipped back into Annie's office and got down to business. For the next two hours she was lost in her idea of a good time: writing code and creating queries. Then all hell broke loose.

"Who in the hell is *that*? Why is she in my office? I'm not here for a couple of hours and suddenly you've replaced me?" Sydney couldn't yet see the person, but was pretty sure who it was. The volume alone gave her away as either Annie or Napoleon.

"Now Annie, just calm down. She's here to build a database for us. I just put her in there so she could close the door and not be bothered by all the noise."

"There shouldn't *be* any noise! What's with all the radios on everyone's desks? Didn't any of you *read* the policy manual? It clearly states: 'No Radios.' Should I make a sign?" Across the room, one by one, all of the radios went silent. Sydney rolled her chair back to peek out of the office window and she saw only the business web site up on all the visible computer screens. None of the clerks were smiling, and Sydney surmised Annie's absence had been the reason everyone had been so happy, not Sydney's arrival.

"What makes you think we need a database? *I'm* the one who has a master's degree in business from Yale, so before you go making these huge decisions which will adversely affect the company you should've consulted me! Who talked you into this?"

Annie stormed into her office, looking like a woman ready to do battle. Sydney was picturing a bigger woman to go along with the shrill voice but she couldn't have been more off. The woman standing in front of her was no more than 5'3" and was thinner than Illana. She wore a very outdated skirt suit, checked no less, and her bottle blonde hair was in a tight bun that looked painful. She might have been pretty, if it weren't for the scowl lines framing her mouth and creasing her forehead. And her unattractive hair-do. And her clothes. Sydney was already up and closing her laptop when Annie entered.

"Hello. I'm Sydney Myers from 21st Century Technology. Let me move my stuff out of your office and set up somewhere else. It'll just take me a minute." Sydney was putting the laptop in its case when Annie exploded again.

"You can pack up right now and leave! I won't have you here wrecking my brother's business! You just pack your things and go. I'll make sure you get paid whatever you were promised, but your services are not needed here!" The woman actually stomped her foot. Wow.

Alex stood to his full height and stepped in front of Annie. "Now you just hold on a minute. I hired her and I want her here. You're supposed to be on vacation!" He practically shouted the last part then pinched the bridge of his nose.

"I see. You thought I'd be gone so you could get this done behind my back? I would've gone, except a little birdie told me you had hired someone without telling me. It's a damn good thing I didn't go anywhere, just look what you would've done!" Annie sighed and managed some crocodile tears.

The woman deserves an Oscar, Sydney thought.

"Alex, you know I love you, but you don't have a lick of business sense. Like I've said before, you concentrate on the creative side and I'll be the brains." She reached up and patted his cheek like he was a beloved, but not very bright, child.

Not an Oscar then, she deserved to have her ass kicked.

Annie turned and shot Sydney another murderous glance. "Why are you still standing there? Didn't you hear me? I see you packed your stuff...now get out. We don't need your kind of help." Sydney just had stepped out of Annie's office as Zeke came in the building.

"I say we do. Hello sister dear, eat any small children lately?"

"Zeke, you stay out of this and go back to where you belong, in a cage." Sydney felt about two inches tall, since she had said much the same thing a couple of hours ago.

"I own almost a third of this business, and I say she stays. What do you say Alex?"

Alex put his hands in his pockets and hunched his shoulders, looking like he wanted to crawl into a cave and hide. He must have found his backbone because he suddenly straightened up and looking down at his sister, said, "I say she stays too." If spontaneous combustion could actually happen to a person, Sydney was sure they would've all been covered in little fiery bits of Annie.

"You will both live to regret this! Don't forget I was against it from the start." Annie spun on her (outdated) black stiletto heels, marched into her office and slammed her door.

Annie walked to her window and pulled down the venetian blinds. Loudly. Sydney couldn't stop herself from doing her best imitation of the Wicked Witch of the West: "And your little dog, too!"

Zeke laughed and Alex smiled, but seemed uncomfortable.

"Are there any more siblings?" Sydney asked. "I'll go get my Kevlar vest if so." Alex finally laughed, and the tension fell away as Zeke answered her.

"Nope, there's just the three of us kids. But wait until you meet our parents. Just one happy little family," Zeke said as he threw his arm around Alex's shoulders and then said to his brother, "The shipment we were waiting for finally got here, so come on out when you have a minute. That's what I was coming in to tell you. But this was way more fun than unloading. Good job, Alex." Zeke mock punched his brother in the shoulder.

"Thanks Zeke, I'll be out there in a minute. Let me get Sydney set up." Alex's nervous gaze darted around the office, trying to find a place to put her when Zeke spoke up again.

"Why don't you put her up in Dad's office? Mom and Dad aren't due back for at least a week. At least there she'd be out of Annie's reach."

"In the warehouse? That's not a bad idea; what do you think Sydney?"

"As long as I can connect to the internet and it's far away from Attila the Bun, I'm thrilled."

"What a great nickname!" Zeke laughed as did some of the staff who had heard her. Alex tried to stifle his amusement by coughing. Sydney, knowing the new name and whom it came from would get back to Annie, cursed her tendency to be a smartass and talk before thinking. Apparently, another call to John was going to be in her future. Goody.

The three of them walked out to the warehouse and Alex led the way upstairs to his dad's office. Sydney hadn't noticed the office before and was surprised she had missed it. It had long windows that ran the length of the room so you could see the entire warehouse. Alex casually mentioned it doubled as a conference room when they had contract meetings with their distributors. Alex opened the door for Sydney, but she immediately stopped after crossing the threshold. On the wall behind the desk was the most enormous deer head yet. It stuck out three or four feet off the wall.

"Wow, you guys sure have some big deer around here," Sydney said, thinking if she commented on the size of it, perhaps they wouldn't know she was terrified by the dead thing on the wall. Alex swallowed his laugh again behind a cough, but Zeke let his fly.

"That's not a deer. *That's* an elk. One Dad is particularly fond of. It took him three days and fourteen bullets to take down that bull." Zeke shook his head and pointed at the large conference table. "You can set up here at the table. There are network jacks on either side." Zeke glanced at his watch and said to Sydney, "We have to unload the shipment that just came in, but afterwards we're going to lunch. Why don't you come with?"

"Sure, just let me know when you two want to leave." Sydney felt her pulse skip under Zeke's gaze, so she busied herself by setting up her laptop. After the two men left, she decided she'd better call John and cop to her morning faux pas.

"This is John."

"Hey John. Thanks for sending over the revised contract. Alex said it would be fine."

"I know, he already faxed it back to me. Is there a problem Sydney?" John asked, more resigned than concerned.

"Well, I might've said a couple things I shouldn't have let slip this morning."

John sighed deeply into the phone. "Explain."

Sydney told him about the comment she made about Zeke, which made John laugh. Then reluctantly segued to the "Attila the Bun" comment. She listened, hoping the laughter would continue. It didn't.

"Sydney, you're my best database tech bar none. With that said, I can't have you shooting off your mouth, even when it's deserved, which in this case, it most assuredly was. I've known Annie since she was a teenager and I'm not surprised to hear she's a bit uptight. But, please Sydney, I want you to remember you are representing our company and I need you to promise me there won't be any more scenes no matter what she, or anyone else, says or does. Got it?"

"Yes sir. Sorry boss. I figured I'd better call and tell you so you didn't hear it from Alex."

"Hell Sydney, Alex would never think to tell me. Annie would. In fact, I have a message here from her. She must've left it about five minutes ago, but I was on a conference call. Good thing you got a hold of me before she did."

"This was the first chance I had, so I'm glad you didn't have a chance to call her back yet. In fact, it might be a good idea never to call her without talking to me first."

"Agreed. Go back to work and try, please try, not to be such a smartass, okay?" John was pleading, which made Sydney smile.

"You've got my word on it." Relieved that her boss wasn't too mad, she turned her focus back to work and was happily mired in creating the new database five minutes later.

"Sorry we took so long. Are you ready to go eat?" Alex stood in the doorway as Sydney raised one finger and finished a complex string of code. She hadn't heard the door open and when she glanced up at her watch she saw it was now after one o'clock.

"No problem. I'm at a good stopping point anyway, so let's go." Sydney locked her computer, grabbed her purse and followed Alex out a back door to the employee parking lot. Zeke was leaning against a black Mercedes looking relaxed with his ankles and arms crossed. Sydney's first thought was *'My God he's hot,"* then she remembered she didn't mix business with pleasure and put her sunglasses on so she could stare at him without being caught. Sydney looked around as they got in the car and asked, "Annie isn't joining us?" and succeeded in keeping her voice neutral. Zeke swung around in his seat to look at her like she was crazy. Alex cleared his throat then answered.

"No. I didn't think it was a good idea to invite her along. Let's give her some time to get used to the fact that you're here. I'm sure once we show her what you've done she'll come around." Alex tried to sound positive but the hesitation in his voice made it clear he still had his doubts.

Zeke was much more succinct. "It'll be a hot day in Antarctica before that happens. Don't let her bother you, Sydney. Now that she knows you're staying, there's nothing she can do."

Sydney wasn't so sure. She had come across Annie's kind before and she didn't seem the type that would meekly roll over. Men were just butt-stupid when it came to women, and if Sydney knew anything, she was sure Annie was currently plotting Sydney's demise.

They drove a little out of town; Sydney had willingly taken the backseat so she could gawk at Zeke without drawing attention to herself, but was so struck by the beauty of the woods she forgot all about her plan of staring at him. Everything was so green, from the wild ferns that covered the forest floor to the canopy of leaves that filtered the sunlight. She counted six lakes in the ten minutes they had been driving. A couple of the lakes were probably called ponds, but even those were ringed by tall trees and dotted with a few houses.

As they pulled into a gravel parking lot, she was awestruck at the picturesque lake in front of her. It reminded her of one of those excruciatingly difficult puzzles where you don't know if the sky and trees are a reflection off the water or not. The lake was still and she couldn't see the end of it. She followed suit as the men exited the Benz.

"This is Ruby Lake. It's part of the biggest chain of lakes in the world. It's called Ruby Lake because of all the wild cranberries that used to float on top; they're all gone now but the name stuck. Pretty, isn't it?" Alex asked proudly.

"It's beautiful. I've honestly never seen anything like it." Sydney tore her gaze away, and followed the men inside.

They were seated at a table outside on the deck. Alex and Zeke answered a few work-related questions Sydney asked, but they spent the majority of the lunch amusing her with funny stories of growing up in Ruby Lake.

"One more then I'll quit making Alex look bad," Zeke said with a smile. He turned to Alex and asked, "Remember the time we tried to break into Old Man Jenkins cabin to steal all the liquor?" Alex turned red, while Sydney's eyes grew wide with disbelief. Zeke turned back to Sydney, "We were in high school, and he had this great idea that no one would be out there in February. So about six of us climbed in my truck, we had to use mine since I was the only one who had four-wheel drive, and drove out to Jenkins cabin. Old Man Jenkins was surly at best and a vicious drunk at worst, so picking his cabin was like a rite of manhood. Anyway, we all go out there and sure enough, no pickups, no lights on; he must not be home. So we all get out of the truck and just as we're about to let ourselves in, BLAM! A shotgun goes off from about six feet away. There we are, scrambling in the snow, falling on our asses while Old Man Jenkins is laughing hysterically and pointing the shotgun in the air."

"So, what happened? Did he call the cops? Were you all arrested? Did anyone get shot?" Sydney asked looking from one smiling brother to the other more embarrassed one.

"No one got shot, don't be ridiculous. And cops? Oh, hell no! He did worse, he called our parents. You have to remember, this is a town of seven thousand people and everyone pretty much knows everyone else. Things are handled a bit differently here," Zeke explained as he took a swig from his beer.

"I guess so! Sounds like you two were quite the trouble makers."

"Yes, well, that was a *very* long time ago, and now we're just boring law-abiding citizens," Alex said, waving at the waitress for the check.

Even though he was clearly embarrassed, Alex was much more relaxed and managed to leave his hair alone almost the entire lunch. It was nice to see the camaraderie, and it reminded her of the bantering she enjoyed doing with her sister, Jessica. Zeke was still cocky but not as obnoxious as he had been earlier.

During their lunch most of the other restaurant patrons stopped by to say a quick hello, and to be introduced to Sydney. She was a little taken aback at the directness of some of the questions. Why was she here? How long would she be staying? Where was she from? Her favorite question was from a woman whose sister lives in Sacramento: Do you know her? Sydney wasn't used to being grilled by strangers and if this was the norm, she realized how easy she had gotten off at the coffee shop. One man even invited her to dinner and offered to show her the town, but she was able to deflect the offer by saying she had to pick up her girlfriend from the airport. He then offered to take them both out after her friend arrived. Zeke stepped in and told the man to leave her be and if Sydney wanted to be shown around, he would do it.

If the men had been dogs, the other man would have backed away from Zeke with his head down and tail between his legs. The feminist side of Sydney was offended and she was ready to tell Zeke that although she appreciated his help, she really didn't need it. The feminine side of her won and told the other part to shut up for once and enjoy it.

After lunch, the three of them went back to work and to their separate domains. While Sydney was working she could hear the deep hum of the forklift and was unusually distracted. Normally, a war could be underway around her and she wouldn't have realized it. But today, she found herself gazing out the window fairly regularly. At one point when she got up to stretch, she noticed all the pictures on the wall behind her. There were almost as many as she had encountered in Alex's office. The dead elk bolted to the wall above the large desk had been so overwhelming when she first entered the office this morning she didn't notice anything else in there. Now, she took a few minutes to walk around the office and to peer inside this very interesting family's life.

One wall contained nothing but pictures of Alex, Zeke and an older man who she figured was their father, kneeling over dead animals. She was amused to see her boss, John, in one of the pictures, because he was wearing flannel and a pair of worn jeans. She had never seen him in anything less than a three-piece suit so she couldn't wait to show this one to Illana. There were only two pictures in the room of Annie. One was of her smiling broadly in graduation garb standing, perhaps a bit too rigidly, next to a pretty older woman, probably her mother. The other was a young Annie, maybe twelve or thirteen, dressed in a riding outfit and sitting tall on a horse.

As she leaned in to peer more closely at the picture, she noticed Annie was holding a huge blue ribbon.

"Annie won the Nationals that year. It was the only horse show Dad ever went to," Zeke said as he walked in the office. Sydney jumped at the sound of Zeke's voice, and felt embarrassed at being caught perusing the pictures. "It's six o'clock and everyone else has left for the day. Alex came up around four-thirty but he said you looked like you were in a trance and didn't want to bother you. How much longer are you planning on staying?" Zeke was casually leaning against the door jam with his arms and ankles crossed as he spoke.

"I must've lost track of time. Let me shut everything down, and I'll head out in a minute. I have to pick Illana up around seven, so it's a good thing you came in when you did. This'll just take me a minute." Sydney saved her work and as the computer shut down she stuffed some notes in the laptop bag. Zeke stood motionless, watching her like a wolf watches a deer, while she gathered her things. She was tempted to ask if he liked what he saw, but instead ignored him and waltzed out the door. He switched off the light and followed her down the stairs. She surged ahead of him and when she got downstairs, grabbed the door to go outside only to discover it was bolted shut.

"You could've told me it was locked," Sydney said, narrowing her eyes at him.

"Had you not rushed ahead of me, I would've opened it for you." Zeke pulled a key ring out of his pocket and unlocked the door. "Allow me." Opening the door, he stood back to allow her to lead the way.

"I can open my own doors," Sydney said as she stalked out of the building. Zeke was undeterred.

"So, you want to grab a bite to eat before you pick up your friend?" he asked, sticking his hands in his pockets.

"Thanks, but no. I need to get back to the hotel and make some calls before Illana gets here. Maybe some other time." *Why did I say that? Stupid hormones*, she thought while keeping a polite smile on her face.

"Sounds like a plan. See you tomorrow, Syd." As they walked to their vehicles, she was surprised that he drove a total beater. It was a large truck sporting multiple rust spots and it practically screamed, "Paint me!" Instead of remarking on it, as he seemed to be waiting for, she smiled brightly, waved goodbye, got in her car and drove away. He was still standing in the same spot by his truck and staring at her when she looked in her rearview mirror.

When she walked into the hotel, the first thing she noticed was all of her luggage sitting next to the registration booth. She marched over to the clerk, who had noted her arrival and was now busily rummaging through papers trying not to see her.

"Excuse me, why is my luggage down here?"

"Oh, Miss Myers, I'm terribly sorry but we're overbooked and because yours was the last reservation, we had to remove your things for the other customers. I personally packed everything, and folded it neatly, seeing as how you had everything hung up. Unfortunately, there are no other rooms. I'm so sorry." The clerk was clearly ready to cry so

Sydney tried to hide her irritation, but failed miserably as she felt her face turning hot.

"I want to talk to the manager. Now." The clerk scurried to the back room. Seconds later, a tall statuesque blonde walked out.

"May I help you?" the woman asked, a rude smirk plastered on her face.

"I was informed you have given my room to someone else and I'd like to get another."

"I'm sorry, but there are no other rooms," the woman said sweetly, in the fakest way possible. "In fact, its Cranberry Week so I doubt you will find a room at any other hotel either." The woman sounded triumphant, and not the least bit sorry. Normally, she would raise three different kinds of unholy hell, but after her promise to John about not making any more scenes, she gritted her teeth and accepted this time she was sunk.

"I see. Well, I guess I will have to find other accommodations. Can you call another hotel to see if there are any vacancies?" She was doing her best to sound pleasant, which is hard to do with clenched teeth.

"I would, but we are terribly busy," she said condescendingly, her gaze taking in the empty lobby. Sydney wanted to smack the smug look right off her face. "I hope you have enjoyed your stay, and do come back to visit us again." The last statement was laced with sarcasm as the woman turned and sauntered into the back room. Sydney had a nice visual of impaling the woman on the elk's horns in her new office, but decided that could be construed as a scene, so instead she elected to just gather her things and exit the building.

Sydney was willing to bet all her Microsoft stock that Annie was behind this. She had a little more than thirty minutes to find somewhere else for her and Illana to stay, but first she needed coffee.

She drove over to the coffee shop and was relieved to find it still open. Betty was sitting at the counter reading a book. She reluctantly tore her eyes away from it but smiled when she saw Sydney walk in.

"Welcome back. I didn't expect to see you so soon. How was the first day?" Betty's shiny brown hair swung around as she grabbed a mug from the wall behind her and filled it with coffee, a ton of sugar and just the right amount of cream. She was good.

"Interesting. I got to meet Attila the Bun and I believe she managed to get me kicked out of my hotel, but I have no way to prove it." Sydney sighed as she took a sip of coffee.

"Oh my God, did you call her that to her face?" Betty asked, clasping her hands in front of her like she was going to break out in prayer. Sydney shook her head no, but smiled. "Now why didn't any of us think of that? I take it you two didn't hit it off," Betty said with a trace of humor in her voice. "If you were staying at the Tamarack Hotel, her favorite minion is the manager there. Here's your coffee, it's on the house. Let's call around and see what we can find." They spent the next ten minutes calling various hotels and motels without any luck. Betty explained that Cranberry Week was one of their busiest times of the year, and it was just bad luck that there weren't any other rooms. Not all of it could be blamed on Annie.

"Let's call Alex and see what he has to say." Betty dialed Alex's number from memory and left a message on his machine. She dialed another number, and Sydney's stomach flipped as Betty said: "Hi Zeke. We have a bit of a problem here." Betty explained what had happened and after she listened to him for a couple minutes, said, "Thanks Zeke, see you in a few." Betty hung up, and turned to Sydney. "Zeke won't be here for a little bit to give you time to pick up your friend. I'll stay here until you get back."

"Betty, you don't have to do that. I can meet him outside just as easily. Have you been here all day?"

"Yep, the daycare called Suzanne because her little boy is sick. Poor thing has been sick a lot lately, so I had to pull a double. Being the owner is sometimes a drag." At Sydney's look of concern she said quickly, "It wasn't bad. After Amelia left for the hospital, she's a nurse, Lucy hung out with me for a little while. She was going to stay longer but felt guilty because she thinks she has to donate every second of her time at the food pantry." Betty reached across the counted and patted Sydney's arm. "Now, don't worry about a thing. I'll call my husband and tell him to fix his own supper, and you go get your friend. She might need a cup of coffee by now."

"Thanks, Betty, I really appreciate it. I'll be as fast as I can." Sydney downed the rest of her coffee, threw a dollar in the tip jar and headed towards the door.

"Take your time, there's no fire." Betty was already reabsorbed in her book, the newest Harry Potter.

"Hey, when did that come out?" Sydney asked standing just inside the open door.

"A couple of months ago. Where've you been? I'm reading it for the second time, but I'll loan it to you when I'm done," Betty said with a smile. With that, Sydney knew a new friendship was formed.

Sydney got to the airport just as Illana's plane was landing. Illana walked off in front of everyone else and stopped dead in her tracks as she took in the tiny airport. Sydney walked over to her laughing. "Close your mouth, you look like a tourist." The two women hugged and Illana found her voice.

"God, I thought I was going to *die* on that little plane! You're driving me to Minneapolis when I leave because I refuse to get back on the Wright Brother's plane. Is this what they call an airport? One turnstile? Who decorated this place, Mrs. Brady? I need a cup of java, pronto."

"You're in luck, and prepare to eat your words. The local coffee shop is staying open just for us and the coffee is excellent. As soon as your bags come up, we can go."

"No bags, just this. I'm a minimalist, remember?"

Sydney stared at the overstuffed, oversized carry-on, ginormous Louis Vuitton purse and matching laptop bag, but kept her thoughts behind her teeth for once. "Let's go get your coffee. There has been a slight change in plans." Once they were outside in the parking lot, Sydney quickly brought Illana up to speed. Illana exploded.

"Where the hell are we, on the set of *Deliverance*? How could she do that? Maybe we should go, we don't need this contract and I'm not about to put up with any shit from a prima donna."

"Oh no, I'm not leaving. No way am I letting her win. We'll be staying with Alex's brother until a room is available at another hotel. Did I mention Alex won four point two million dollars from the lottery?" Sydney tried to skim over the Zeke info, but her best friend's radar picked up a signal.

"Really? Wait. Rewind the tape sister. You didn't mention a brother before."

"Didn't I? He's really obnoxious and arrogant plus I didn't really talk to him very much. I'm sure we'll probably end up at Alex's, but since Betty couldn't get a hold of him Zeke offered up his house."

"Hmm. I sense there is more to it, but I'll drag it out of you later." They loaded her bag in the trunk, next to Sydney's stuff, and drove back to the coffee shop. While driving, Sydney relayed the conversation she had with the coffee ladies about Alex winning the lottery.

Sydney parked next to a Mercedes and wondered if Alex was inside. Craning her neck to see inside the shop, all she could see were cowboy boots propped up on a table. Not Alex then. Illana apparently had a better view.

"Whoa. Is that Zeke? Oh Lucy, you have some 'splaining to do." Illana said in her best Ricky Ricardo accent as she faced Sydney, while Sydney tried her best to appear confused. "Don't bother trying that look on me. If he isn't your type right down to the cowboy boots, then I'm Mother Theresa. No wonder you don't want to leave."

"Illana, you know I never get involved with customers."

"This one time I think you'll be making an exception." Illana flipped down the visor mirror to check her hair and apply a little more lipstick. After rubbing her lips together, she looked at Sydney and said with a smirk, "Let's go in so you can introduce me to the next lust of your life."

Chapter Three – We've Got 'Em Beat Kid

After following Zeke back to his place, he gave them the two minute tour, and led them to their rooms. Sydney closed her door, sat down on the bed and realized she hadn't called her dad yet. *Might as well get it over with.*

"Hi Dad. Did I catch you at a bad time?"

"No, not at all. I just finished doing the dishes. I was starting to wonder when you were going to call. How's it going so far? Are you done yet?"

"Not quite. I made some headway, but there were a few glitches." Sydney relayed the events of her day, with the exception of what she called Annie, and wrapped it up by letting him know where she and Illana were now and describing, in great detail, Zeke's house. Her dad asked for Zeke's Social Security number, which she didn't give him. She knew if he really wanted to, he would find another way to get it.

"Well, as long as you're safe with a roof over your head, I'm happy. I admit I feel better knowing Illana's there."

"You don't think I am capable of taking care of myself? What do you think I am, a walking victim waiting to happen?" Sydney felt her ire rise and stood up off the canopied bed.

"No, I didn't say that and I know you're perfectly capable of handling anything thrown at you. You're also my daughter and I worry about you." Sydney sat back down, knowing he wouldn't worry if Jessica was in this situation. "Now, what was the name of the manager at the Tamarack Hotel?"

"I've no idea. I was so mad at the time and I didn't think to check out her name-tag," Sydney replied, chewing on her lip and waiting for the lecture to start.

"For the daughter of a journalist you disappoint me sometimes. You definitely didn't get my observation genes. Instead, you got your mom's temper. So here's what I'm going to do. I have a few contacts I can call tomorrow morning, and as soon as I know anything, I'll call you back."

"What do you mean? Dad, I don't want you fighting my battles for me, I can handle this."

"I know, but I've nothing better to do. This is my idea of a good time, so you just concentrate on your job while I rattle some cages." Sydney could hear the excitement in his voice and knew he'd do it anyway. Trying to talk him out of it was useless.

"Alright Dad, but I don't want anyone fired over this, deal?" Sydney massaged her temple to quiet the headache that was threatening to start. "Promise me this won't be like my trip to Virginia."

"I don't know what you mean. I just did what any father would've done." It was his turn to sound affronted.

"Yeah, but not just any father can get the federal government involved at a moment's notice. Seriously, don't go crazy with this. It's not that big of a deal. Where I'm staying now is certainly an upgrade." Sydney walked over to the bay window with the window seat and pulled back the curtains to examine her view of the lake. "Did I mention the lake in the backyard? The logs used for the walls must be at least three feet thick. Oh, and did I mention the sunken living room or the granite counter tops in the kitchen?"

"No, but I'm very impressed." Graham sounded anything but. "You'd better go, and I'll talk to you tomorrow."

"I love you too, Dad," Sydney said to the sound of the dial tone.

After getting off the phone, she opened her suitcase for inspection to make sure everything was indeed there. She was shocked that all the contents had been folded neatly. After she hung her clothes up, again, she went in search of Illana. Walking down the few steps into the living room she saw her host and best friend on the deck being a little too chummy over a humungous grill.

"Can you *believe* this place?" Illana asked as Sydney walked out on the deck. "Talk about your luxury big house in the woods! It's way bigger inside than it looked from the driveway! This is so much more comfy than staying in a hotel. At least here we won't have to worry about Attila the Bun. Did you notice the kickin' sound system in the living room? What took you so long?" Illana asked, taking a seat on top of the wooden picnic table.

"I called my dad and unpacked. Thank you again Zeke for letting us stay here. My dad grilled me about the hotel manager and he was a little perturbed I didn't know her name. Oh, and he wanted Zeke's background check done."

"Michelle Stretlow is her name, and I'd be happy to give him my fingerprint card. I can understand him wanting to know about me, but why did he want the name of the manager?"

"I don't know," Sydney tried to act nonchalant and play the situation down. "He said he might call a couple of people he knows or something." Illana blew her cover by clapping her hands and jumping off the table excitedly.

"Woo hoo! That woman has no idea who she's messing with!" Illana did a little hip shimmy, her personal happy dance. "I can't *wait* for tomorrow. This is going to be so much fun. On second thought, I am very glad I'm here." Illana stopped dancing and narrowed her eyes at Sydney, "This isn't going to be like Virginia, is it?"

"No, I made him promise me it wouldn't be."

"What happened in Virginia?" Zeke asked, intrigued.

"Nothing," both women replied too quickly.

"Hmph. Since no one's talking, let's eat. Hope you ladies like steak." Zeke looked a little horrified as he asked, "Neither of you are vegetarians or vegans are you? I know Sydney isn't since she had a hamburger at lunch, but are you?" He directed the last question at Illana.

"Sooooo, you had lunch together?" Illana raised an inquisitive eyebrow at Sydney. "No, Zeke, I'm not. Well, not anymore. I had this phase were I was, but I really missed my leather shoes and jackets so I'm back to being a carnivore."

Zeke served up the three porterhouse steaks and they sat down at the table. They each helped themselves to salad from the thick wooden bowl that sat in the middle of the table and doctored their baked potatoes. Zeke's forehead creased as he took a bite of steak and with his mouth full, asked Sydney, "Just who is your father?" Sydney knew the question was coming, and hoped it wouldn't change anything after he knew. She swallowed a large portion of her wine to fortify herself, and then answered his question.

"You may not have heard of him, he's a retired journalist. His name is Graham Myers."

"*The* Graham Myers? The Graham Myers whose questions made all the politicians run for their spin doctors? Oh man, I used to love getting the Sunday *Washington Post* and reading his articles. They were the best. I've read all of his books, too. This is so cool!" Zeke said excitedly.

"Yes, that's the one, but I just call him Dad. I'll get you an autographed copy of one of his books if we can now change the subject. So, how long have you owned this place?" At Sydney's abrupt change of subject, and with a smile that wasn't reflected in her eyes, Zeke wisely pulled himself together, and then answered her.

"About seven years now. I'm sure you've already heard, since you met Betty and the coffee gang, Alex won the lottery and bought us each a house. In my case, he only bought me this land. I paid him back every penny, and not with the money I made working for his company. I was a carpenter until Alex hired me a couple years ago. I did some side work until I had enough money to pay him back and build this house."

"You built this yourself?" Sydney had a new appreciation for this man who she had thought was so shallow and arrogant. "That's amazing! How long did it take you? How did you set the logs? Did you do all the cabinetry too?"

"Hello? Remember me? I'm sitting here too," Illana said, waving her hands in the air. She rolled her eyes and said to Zeke, "Please don't start talking about building or, God forbid, woodworking with her, or she'll never shut up. On second thought, go ahead. I'm going to pack it in early. Syd, can you come in with me for just a minute though?"

"Sure. I should probably hit the sack a little early tonight myself." Sydney wasn't sure what the deal was with Illana, but she recognized the cue. She turned back at Zeke and said sincerely, the smile reaching her eyes this time, "Thanks again for having us over and the excellent meal. Are you all done?" she asked, pointing at his almost spotless plate.

"You two don't have to do the dishes, you're guests. If you insist, I'll let you do them tomorrow night."

"I'm sure we'll find somewhere else to stay by tomorrow, but if not, you've got yourself a deal," Sydney replied.

Illana practically dragged Sydney into the house and once Illana shut the bedroom door, she spun around to glare at Sydney.

"So, you hardly talked to him at all, huh? I suppose you just 'forgot' to tell me about having lunch with him." Illana was pacing and running her hand through her hair. "Do you realize he may be The One? I swear to God, if you screw this up, I will hurt you."

"Calm down, killer and back up the train. I don't think he may be "The One" and Alex was at lunch, too, so don't get yourself all in a frenzy. *This* is what you wanted to talk to me about? Listen, I have never, ever dated anyone who we have a contract with and I don't intend to start now. Plus, there's the fact he lives two thousand miles away from me. It would be pointless to start anything."

"Well, it seems to me you've put in an awful lot of thought into someone you 'really didn't talk very much to.'" Illana narrowed her eyes and placed both hands on her hips. "I've known you since the first day of high school and you have that 'I'm interested' body language whenever you lock eyes with him. I don't want to see you pass up what could be a good opportunity. I'm not saying to jump him, since I know you won't, but give him a chance. Get to know him. If nothing else, maybe you have found someone you can talk sanding or sawing or whatever with that won't want to stick sharp pencils in their ears to make you stop."

"I don't talk about it that much."

"Yes, you do. I'm going to bed, and not just to leave you two alone. I think I have jet lag or something."

"You can't have jet lag from a two hour time difference! God, you are such a princess sometimes. Sleep well, Snow White, I'll see you at six."

"Six? Six is four a.m. by my body clock. You'd better wake me up with coffee in your hand!" Illana yelled the last bit as the door closed. Sydney was sure she'd be out five minutes later. Sydney, coward that she was, snuck past Zeke, who was doing the dishes with his back to the living room, and went to bed. She didn't fall asleep for two hours.

Sydney woke up to the smell of coffee. As she sat up and rubbed the sleep out of her eyes, she spotted the still steaming cup on her nightstand. Taking a sip, she wondered briefly how Zeke had known how she liked it, because it was almost perfect. Lying next to the cup was an oversized bath towel, Egyptian cotton if she wasn't mistaken, and an unopened bar of Dove soap. She took another sip of coffee, grabbed the towel and soap and headed for the shower.

After getting dressed, and twisting a smaller towel on top of her head around her damp hair, Sydney went in search of more coffee. She didn't see Illana up and about, which didn't surprise her since she knew how much Illana liked to sleep. She poured Illana a cup of coffee and took it into her room. It was only six-fifteen, so she set the coffee cup on the desk across the room from her sleeping friend and went to find Zeke. He was just coming in from the deck. He saw her and smiling, said excitedly, "Come outside, there's something I want to show you. Leave your coffee on the counter, and be very quiet."

"Why, are we hunting wabbits?"

"No smartass, just come and see for yourself," Zeke stood by the slider and followed her outside. The sunlight was glinting off the lake and then she saw something she had never dreamt of seeing in real life. A couple of bear cubs and their mother were rooting around the wild blueberry bushes at the edge of the sandy shoreline. Sydney leaned against the railing, careful not to make a sound and stood in amazement at the sight before her. The cubs seemed more interested in wrestling than eating, and the mama bear was passively ignoring them while looking for food. It was the most peaceful scene Sydney had ever witnessed, and it filled her with a sense of awe. She could hear the miniature growls coming from the cubs and they rolled over each other. One was a little bit bigger, but the smaller one had his ear in its mouth. She stifled a laugh at the cute cubs as Zeke tapped her on the shoulder. He turned and she followed him back inside.

"They've been coming here for a couple of weeks now, ever since the blueberries fully ripened. One morning I went out on the deck with a cup of coffee in my hand. The mama bear must have smelled it, because she got spooked and they all took off into the woods." Zeke smiled widely at Sydney as he said, "I'll bet that's something you don't see every day in the city."

"That was the most amazing thing I have ever seen! No one will believe this back home. I have to get Illana, she'll be floored." Sydney raced off to Illana's room, but heard the shower running. She hoped the bears would still be out there by the time Illana got out, but she doubted it. Sydney thought about banging on the door to hurry her along, but it was never a good idea to rush Illana in the morning. Hopefully, Illana would try to curb her normal hatred of mornings in front of Zeke.

The bears were long gone by the time Illana made an appearance, with blue tipped hair today. After eating their fill of blueberry pancakes, the three of them each had one more cup of coffee on the deck. The view was spectacular. Sydney watched the lake ripple and felt the soft breeze play with her hair and saw an eagle swoop down and snag a good sized fish right out of the water with its talons and disappear into the trees.

"Was that an eagle? Did we really just see an eagle?" Illana had jumped up off the deck chair and was scanning the trees for the magnificent bird. "Remind me to buy a disposable camera before we come back here tonight."

"See the little island out there?" Zeke said, pointing to an island in the middle of the lake. "Maybe if you two are up for it tonight, we'll take the boat out and I'll show you the nest."

"Really? That would be awesome!" Illana's face lit up with the kind of delight typically reserved for children on Christmas day. Sydney thought she had better bring her down a notch.

"We might not be coming back here tonight because a couple of rooms might miraculously open up at the Tamarack Hotel today," Sydney said as Illana leaned over the railing trying to locate a nest on the far away island.

"You're both more than welcome to stay here for the rest of your trip," Zeke offered. "After the way you were treated, I'm not sure I could trust them to stay out of your rooms."

"Y'know Syd, he has a point. We could just stay here." Illana was practically daring Sydney to disagree.

"Let's see what today brings and decide later. You really don't mind having us stay here?"

"Not a bit. In fact, it's kind of nice getting to play host. I don't get to do this for two beautiful women very often. Maybe one, but I can't ever remember having two stay here at one time." Zeke's eyes twinkled with mischief at Sydney. She immediately started to turn red but before she could open her mouth, Zeke raised a hand to stop her. "I'm only teasing. I like having company, and besides you owe me dish duty." Zeke hopped up and drained his cup. "Well troops, ready to get going? Shall we all go in my car and make an entrance? You're Californians, carpooling should appeal to you." Knowing she would appear childish if she refused, she shrugged her shoulders at Illana and went inside to gather her things.

Annie swept past all of the women who were busy working the phones while typing up orders and came to an abrupt halt in front of Alex's office.

"I didn't see Shelly's car out front, did she decide to leave? I'll bet she didn't even call." Annie had been checking the office voice mail off and on since last night. She was a little surprised there hadn't been a S.O.S. call, because the girl did seem rather wimpy.

44

"Her name is Sydney and what makes you think she left? As a matter of fact, she and the web designer I hired, Illana Garet, rode in with Zeke this morning. There seems to have been a mix up at the hotel last night. You wouldn't know anything about that, would you?" Alex had heard the whole story from Zeke this morning after they had arrived. Zeke was furious with Annie, and Alex was having a hard time controlling his anger as well.

"What kind of problem? Why would I know anything about it?" Annie, her voice saccharin sweet, looked innocently at Alex, and then thoughtfully tapped her red fingernail on her mouth. "Oh, let me guess. The little twit thought she could stay for free with Zeke since it would be easier to pay in trade with our whore of a brother than pay a hotel bill? How, exactly, could she pin that on me?"

Alex stood up, yanked Annie inside his office and slammed the door. "How dare you talk about Sydney that way!" Alex raked his hand violently through his hair as he glared at his sister. He took a deep breath, sat on the edge of his desk while gripping it with both hands and spoke as calmly as he could. "I've done everything I could for you, Annie. From defending you to Dad, to putting up with your moods and trying to calm down our employees when you reduce them to tears. But I will absolutely *not* tolerate you turning your venom on consultants I hire. I still run this company, and you had best not forget it."

"Alex, are you trying to threaten me? What are you going to do, fire me?" Annie laughed, dismissing the idea. "Please, you know as well as I do this place would fall apart without me! You need me. Who's going to help you, Zeke? Oh, that's a good one. You mean the same Zeke that has consistently taken off on his Harley whenever it suits him without a word to anyone? I don't think so. After you threw all your money around and sunk it into this business, who, except for me, helped you? No one. *I* have been here from day one and *I* am the one that has pulled *your* company into the black. *You* had best not forget that." Annie brushed off her skirt, turned and opened the door, and said to Alex over her shoulder, "I'll leave the little tramp alone, but you tell her to stay away from me. Now, if you'll excuse me, I have business to attend to."

As Annie walked away, Alex hung his head and gripped the desk even harder. Once again Annie had the last word and left him feeling beaten.

Meanwhile, Sydney and Illana were busy at work when Sydney's cell phone rang. As soon as she saw it was her dad, she immediately answered it.

"Good morning Sydney!" he said happily. "I just wanted to let you know I tracked down the owner of the hotel, who was fishing on Lake Superior when I found him, and he said he would personally see to it that you and Illana would have rooms available today."

"How on earth were you able to do that so quickly?"

"Actually it was pretty easy, considering the owner is also an alumnus of Harvard. He was there a few years before me, but through my contact at the college, it was really quite simple. Anyway, I know you're working, but I wanted to tell you I did make him promise not to fire the woman, and he said he had something better planned for her."

"Thanks Dad, you're the best. I'll let Illana know. Are we supposed to call the hotel?" Sydney was looking at Illana, trying not to laugh at the open-mouthed expression on her best friends face.

"No, he said he would send someone over to talk to you. Have a great day honey and call me later tonight after you get settled. You just remember what I've always told you. A Myers against the world is even odds, but with the two of us, we've got 'em beat, kid."

Sydney quickly filled in Illana and they both sat there, shaking their heads, amazed at the speed Graham got things accomplished and wondered what was in store for the manager at the hotel.

Alex was helping one of the women design an "Under the Sea" party for a customer as his father walked in with Michelle Stretlow behind him. Annie was on her way back to her office from the copy room but stopped dead in her tracks when she saw them.

"Hi Dad," Alex said absently, then swiveled his head back to at his father, "Hey, what are you doing back home so early? You and Mom are supposed to be up at the cabin until next week. Hi Michelle, let me get Annie for you." As he turned around, he noticed Annie, who was as white as bone, rooted to the spot. "I didn't see you there," he said to Annie as he asked himself, *Why didn't people stay on vacation like they were supposed to?*

"Well, it's nice to see you too, son. Annie, you and I'll talk later, but for now, go get Sydney Myers and her friend. We'll all wait right here until you get back."

"I can go get them, Dad," Alex said as he looked between his sister and father.

"Oh no, I *really* want Annie to do it. Now." The command finally got Annie unstuck and after she regained her composure, she purposefully strode out to the warehouse. Zeke was just walking in as she walked out, and as he came around the corner he saw the visitors. He'd been on his way to get more coffee, but settled on leaning against the wall, grinned, and started laughing.

"What's so funny, Zeke?" demanded his father.

"Nothing Pop. I'm just glad I got here before the show started. Michelle, it's so nice to see you again. By the way, how does crow taste?" Michelle narrowed her eyes at him, but wisely kept her mouth shut. Annie followed Sydney and Illana in, her purposeful stride replaced by a gallows walk.

"Sydney, Illana, this is my father, Harry Greyson. I believe you've already met Michelle," Zeke said in the way of introduction. From the knowing smirk on his face, Sydney knew he was enjoying this.

"Yes, and I was hoping not to repeat the experience," Sydney said with disdain, as she looked at Michelle. Turning to Zeke's dad she said, "Mr. Greyson, it's very nice to meet you, sir. I'm sure you'll need your office back, so if you'll give me and Illana a few minutes, we'll find somewhere else to set up."

"You both can stay were you are, I'll only be here for a moment. Michelle, I believe you have something to say?"

"Yes, sir." Michelle's voice was devoid of any emotions as she turned to face Sydney and Illana. The smug, condescending expression that she had worn last night had been replaced with one of fear and contrition, and anger whenever she glanced at Annie. "I was mistaken that we were overbooked and I wanted to personally come here and apologize for the misunderstanding. If you'd like to come back, I can assure you there won't be any further problems." At a stern glare from Harry, she continued, "Both rooms will be free of charge to make up for any inconvenience last night's departure may have caused." The woman looked like she would rather be eating a cactus than standing there, and no one missed the daggers she was sending Annie.

"While I appreciate the offer, I don't think I would be able to sleep in your establishment, especially since we have found much better accommodation. Thanks for coming over and I accept your apology, but I have to get back to work now," Sydney said with a small grin.

"Why don't you tell everyone just where you are staying now?" Annie said triumphantly. Zeke pushed himself off the wall and spoke up immediately.

"With me, and if I hear of one person talking smack about either of these women, I will personally make them very, very sorry." Zeke's comment was directed at Annie, and Sydney decided she had better pipe up.

"You know what? On second thought, Illana and I'd love to come back to the hotel. We can share a room, as long as there are two beds." The last thing Sydney wanted was to start a big brou-ha-ha between her clients family members. Harry chose that moment to speak up

"I don't know exactly what's going on, but I will find out," he turned to Michelle whose face was turning an unbecoming shade of puce and said quietly, "You may go back to work now. However, if I ever hear of you treating another customer of mine like you did yesterday, you will be fired, and I promise you no hotel in the country would ever employ you again. Remember, no matter whose friend you are, I own that hotel." Michelle nodded while glaring one last time at Annie, and left the building. Harry turned back to face his grown, but apparently not grown up, children.

"You three, wait for me in Alex's office while I walk Sydney, and Illana is it? What an interesting name, back to my office." Sydney smiled at the gruff way Harry bossed everyone around. She saw a little of her own father in him, and it pleased her to see Zeke's father was similar to her own. As they entered the upstairs office, Harry walked behind his desk, sat down and waved his hands at the conference chairs, indicating they should sit.

"Now, will someone please explain what in the hell is going on around here? If I know my children, they'll all be pointing fingers at each other and I'd like it if I could, for once, get a straight-forward, honest answer." His tone brooked no option for argument, and Sydney told him what had happened starting with Alex's call to John and finished up with them being given an offer to stay with Zeke. "So you see, Mr. Greyson, it's all been one big misunderstanding. Illana and I'll be gone by Friday, and hopefully everyone will be happy with the results of our work."

"I'm sure they will be and please, call me Harry. Well, I guess I'd better get back downstairs before Zeke and Annie kill each other." Harry stood up, absently patted the dead elk on its neck, which almost made Sydney yack, and walked out of the room. He leaned back in the doorway and said to Sydney, "I'm glad you're here, we haven't had this much excitement around here since Alex won the lottery. Also, how else would I have ever gotten to speak with Graham Myers? I can't wait to go to the club and tell everyone." Harry's eyes shone with delight as he closed the door. Illana sighed deeply while staring up at the white ceiling.

"Good going, Syd. I hope this turns out better than Virginia."

Chapter Four - Hail, Hail the Gang's All Here!

The rest of the morning passed in relative quiet after all the excitement died down. Sydney and Illana managed to get enough done to warrant calling Alex to come up and take a look at his new web site, and get approval on the direction they were going. When Alex came in a few minutes later, Sydney was dying to ask what had happened with his dad, but showed some uncommon restraint and left it alone. The fact his hair was messier than normal gave her the indication it didn't go smoothly.

Illana showed him how customers could now purchase items on the web site and the stock would be automatically subtracted from the database. Sydney showed him a couple of dummy reports she had created and they spent a little time revising those with Alex's input. Alex had Sydney print the reports so he could show them to Annie and Zeke.

"While you are doing showing them our progress, Illana and I are going to get some lunch. Do you want us to bring you anything?" Sydney asked, as she stood up.

"No, you two go ahead. I'll see you when you get back." Alex left the office to round up his siblings, hoping they would share in his excitement.

"Um, Syd? How are we going to go anywhere? Our rental is at Zeke's, remember?"

Zeke stepped in the office at that moment, dangling his car keys in his hand. "I figured you might need these, Alex said you were going to lunch while I'll be stuck in a meeting. Thanks a lot." His smile belied the resentment in his voice.

"Thanks for letting us borrow your car. I offered to bring back something for Alex, do you want anything?" As soon as the words were out of Sydney's mouth, she regretted it.

"I do, but it isn't food." Zeke tossed the keys to Sydney and she caught them in mid-air. Shaking his head regrettably, he left the office.

"Nice catch and I'm not referring to the keys. Let's go before he comes back and makes good on the invitation you're trying to ignore," Illana said, slinging her purse strap onto her shoulder.

They drove downtown and ate salads at the Cranberry Café. Since they had only been gone thirty minutes, they decided to go across the street to the coffee shop. The same three women from yesterday were sitting and talking to Betty. As Sydney and Illana triggered the bell on the door, all talking stopped, but Betty recovered first.

"Hey! I was filling everyone in on the events of yesterday. Anything interesting happen today?" Betty asked as she grabbed a purple mug from the rack and made Sydney her coffee, then started on Illana's. Sydney told them about Michelle and Harry making their surprise visit; they all laughed at Zeke's 'crow' comment, and finished up by telling them of her and Illana's decision to return to the hotel.

"My, you two sure are stirring things up! I would have given just about anything to see the look on Annie's face when she saw Michelle walk in with her dad. I would've called Harry last night, but I knew he and Grace were up at their cabin. Plus, I thought the boys would take care of getting you two settled somewhere else." Betty put a ton of whipped cream on Illana's drink and handed her the mocha. "That'll be three-fifty, for both. By the way Sydney, how did Zeke do on your coffee this morning?"

"Huh?" Totally thrown by the question, Sydney couldn't manage a more intelligent reply as she handed Betty the money.

"He called here at a quarter to six to find out how you liked your coffee. Didn't he tell you he called me?" Illana cocked her head to the side and narrowed her eyes at Sydney, who forgot to mention her coffee in bed this morning.

"So *that's* how he knew! I wondered about that, and speaking of wondering about things, I was going to ask Lucy about her dog -"

"Hey Zeke, hi Alex, you boys want your usual?" Betty asked as Alex and Zeke walked in the shop. Sydney tried her best not to look flustered by their arrival, but was sure Zeke could see her heart beating out of her shirt like a love-struck cartoon character.

"You bet," Zeke said to Betty but never took his eyes off Sydney. "I thought we might find you here. Did you two get lunch?"

"Yeah, we had a couple of huge salads at the Cranberry Café. Is something wrong?" Sydney asked as she slung her purse strap over her head so it hung crosswise in front of her.

"Wrong? No I just wanted to make sure my car was okay. Women drivers and all that."

"Zeke, stop baiting her and take your coffee," Betty said as she flicked a dish towel at Zeke's arm. "Alex, yours will be done in a moment. You want yours in a to-go cup too?" Sydney was the only one, except the other members of the coffee klatch, to have a mug.

"Sure, thanks Betty." An uncomfortable tension filled the air and when Betty was done using the frothing wand it was dead silent. "Here you go." Alex paid Betty while Sydney was trying to think of something, anything to say. Illana rolled her eyes at Sydney, and then spoke up.

"So how did the meeting go? Did your sister give her okay?" Illana directed the question at Alex, who smiled at her as he replied.

"Actually, she did. We also showed a couple of the clerks what the new system will do and some of the staff volunteered to handle the data entry tomorrow night. Annie has always hated the card filing system, so she was actually happy about how the database and web site will work." All the women in the room exchanged a knowing look. Alex turned and asked Illana, "What? Did I miss something?"

Sydney replied before Illana could give her opinion, "No, I think it's great she has had this massive turnaround. Apparently the meeting with your dad this morning helped," Sydney said as she looked at Illana who was rolling her eyes again, but this time at Alex's naiveté. None of them could believe Alex actually fell for Annie's act. *Great, what was Attila planning now?* "Well, we should get back to work. It was nice seeing you all again." Sydney put her now empty cup on the counter and waved goodbye to the room at large. She and Illana left before Zeke could ask for his car keys.

As they walked into the main office, Sydney and Illana were given a standing ovation by all the clerks. Annie responded by slamming her door. Stella, the perky receptionist, came forward, grabbed Sydney's arm and said in a stage whisper, "Don't mind her, we're all thrilled by the system you created! You just have no idea how much of a time-saver this will be! If there is anything I, or any of us, can do, just give a holler." After patting her arm one more time and a little wave, Stella ran back to her desk.

Illana waited until they were walking up the stairs in the warehouse before she responded, "You'd think we had just created the wheel.

Well, I can no longer say I haven't had a standing ovation. Somehow, I don't think Attila is as happy as Alex thinks she is."

"What was your first clue?" Sydney asked sarcastically as she followed Illana in the office. They left the door open to let some air in and sat across from each other while they tied up loose ends. Simple things, like changing a font to make the web site easier to read and locking down parts of the database so none of the staff would accidentally (or purposefully) mess anything up. After working for a little over three hours, Sydney noticed Illana had stopped typing and looked over the top her laptop to see what the problem was.

Illana was staring off into space. She looked at Sydney and said, "Alex is just so cute, isn't he? The way he's constantly messing with his hair, and how those eyes of his just look right into the depths of my soul, and I do admire a tall man."

"Are you serious? Earth to Illana. We work for him, you can't be daydreaming about him." Sydney stood up to stretch and hoped looking down at Illana would be intimidating. Not.

"Really? What were you doing about twenty minutes ago? And don't tell me you were thinking, I know what your 'thinking' face is. Besides, we're leaving Saturday, and we're staying at the hotel until then so it's not like I'm going to get a chance at him anyway. I was just commenting on how cute he is." Illana folded her arms over her chest and stuck her chin out at Sydney. "At least I'm honest about it, unlike some people."

"What do you want me to say?" Sydney threw her arms up in frustration. "Yes, I think Zeke is hot, like burn-me-at-the-stake kind of hot. The man brought me a perfect cup of coffee while I was sleeping. Who does that? I almost spilled my coffee this afternoon when Betty told me he called her to find out how I like my coffee. So, yeah, I want him. How could I not? I mean, the only thing that would make him sexier is a gold-hoop earring! My heart does jumping jacks whenever he walks into the room," At Illana's wide-eyed look, Sydney said, "and he's standing right behind me, isn't he?"

"Yeah, but don't stop now, especially if you're going to do jumping jacks," Zeke said, leaning against the door jam and wearing a very satisfied grin.

"Were you a cat in your past life? How did you climb the stairs so quietly? Don't you ever knock?" Sydney furrowed her brow as she locked gazes with him.

"Illana saw me, so I figured I didn't have to knock," Zeke nodded his head towards Illana, but seeing how embarrassed Sydney was, he changed the subject. "I came up to tell you we're shutting down pretty soon, since so many people will be working late tomorrow. Will you two be ready to go in say, fifteen minutes?"

"Sure, we'll meet you outside." Sydney turned her back on him and hit some keys on the computer, hoping he would get the hint and leave. Because Illana was trying not to laugh Sydney guessed he was still leaning against the open door. She breathed a sigh of relief when she heard his boots, clomping extra loud, on the stairs.

Sydney and Illana walked outside to find Zeke leaning against his car talking to Alex. As the women approached, Alex stopped in mid-sentence, turned and smiled. After raking his hand through his hair, he cleared his throat and looking at Illana said, "Hey, thanks again for everything today. Zeke and I wanted to take you both out to dinner tonight. We could pick you up around six, if that would give you enough time to get settled back at the hotel." Before Sydney could offer up a polite refusal, Illana opened her big mouth.

"Sure we would! That should give us plenty of time, thanks for the offer. Do either of you play pool?" Sydney gritted her teeth behind her closed lips, ready to kill Illana.

"As a matter of fact, you are looking at the Ruby Lake pool league champions," Zeke responded, rising to the challenge. "There's a sports bar in town that has a few tables, so we could grab some hamburgers and a friendly little match at the same time. Don't worry, Alex and I will be on separate teams so you won't get slaughtered."

"That would be great if you could go easy on us. We really aren't very good, but I love to play," Sydney said smiling at Zeke, as Illana had narrowed her eyes at Sydney.

"Sounds like fun, and we'll just play a couple of friendly games after dinner. I just wanted to do something nice for the two of you after all the trouble you've had since getting here." Alex looked at his watch, then back at the women. "Since it's only four now, would five-thirty be okay?"

"Sure Alex that'll be fine. We appreciate the gesture, and we'll see you then," Illana replied as she climbed in the back of Zeke's car, leaving the front for Sydney. With a hint of the challenge to come reflected in his eyes, Zeke opened the front passenger door for Sydney. While Sydney would have rather taken a taxi, being a coward was not part of her makeup. She smiled innocently at Zeke and got in the car, but not without glaring at Illana first.

The ride to Zeke's was uneventful and after Sydney got over being highly uncomfortable, she and her car companions debated which 80's rock group was the best. Zeke contended it was Metallica since they were still around, but Sydney said hers would always be Mötley Crüe, which drew a withering glance from Illana.

"Hey, I like the Crüe, but as far as talent goes, you can't compare Kirk Hammett with Mick Mars, they're not even on the same playing field," Zeke replied.

"I don't know about that, and the Crüe are way more fun to listen to. They'll always be my favorite band, especially since I met them."

"No way! You met them? Cool! When did you get to meet them?"

"In Virginia," Illana said, sighing deeply.

"Is this the Virginia story? Spill it."

"Well, Illana and I had gone to Washington D.C. on our senior class trip, but we were staying at this hotel in Alexandria. We had just gotten back from a late dinner after visiting the Smithsonian, and the people above us were making a helluva racket, so we went up to check it out. It was them, the whole band, and so we stayed and partied with them." Sydney didn't feel she needed to include all the details, but Illana thought differently.

"Oh yeah, we stayed until your dad couldn't find us and demanded the hotel staff search for us. Then, after the manager found us, you didn't want to leave because you were too busy counting Tommy Lee's tattoos. About twenty minutes later, in marched the Secret Service to escort us to a more "appropriate" hotel. I've *never* been so embarrassed in my life!" Illana crossed her arms and stared out the window.

"So how many did he have?" Zeke asked gamely.

"How many what does who have?" Sydney asked.

"Tommy Lee – how many tattoos did he have?"

"Oh, well, I think I got to seventeen before we were, uh, interrupted." Zeke turned into his driveway and Sydney turned around and looked at Illana. "You're never going to get past this are you?"

"Maybe when we're ninety, but don't hold your breath." Illana opened her door before the car came to a complete stop. Sydney shook her head as she watched Illana waltz in the front door. She shut it so hard the long window next to it shook.

"Did you forget to lock your door? I hate when I do that. I have to go and check all the rooms and closets and still don't feel safe for a few days."

"I never lock my doors. I don't even know where the key to the front door is," Zeke said as he got out. Sydney jumped out and looked at him with her mouth open in amazement.

"Seriously? What if somebody gets in? Don't you worry about being robbed?"

"Not around here. The only places that have ever been robbed were the pharmacy and some of the summer cabins owned by non-locals. In both cases, the sheriff caught the teenagers responsible. I usually leave the keys in the car too. In winter there's a whole parking lot at the grocery store full of running cars." She followed him in the house and was completely dumbfounded by this new information. Sydney couldn't imagine living someplace where she would feel safe not locking her doors and she could never imagine leaving her car running while she was in a store.

"So, does that mean the doors weren't locked last night?" Sydney asked, her eyes wide with surprise.

"I guess so. I don't think I locked them, but I would've if I had known it would bother you. Of course, you went to bed without a word to me so I can't be blamed for not knowing." Sydney felt her ears turn pink and was glad she hadn't worn her hair up.

"I guess I was more tired than I thought. I hope it didn't bother you, and it was really nice of you to let us stay here last night. Thanks for the coffee this morning. That was really, um, sweet." They were standing on the brown tile in the entry way, and Illana was nowhere in sight. Sydney felt rooted to the spot, and although she had promised herself she wasn't going to ask about the coffee, the little romantic part of her had to know. "Did you really call Betty to ask her how I liked my coffee?"

Zeke took a step closer and tucked a wayward curl behind her ear. "Yeah I did, and there's a lot more I'd like to find out about you. Any chance I could convince you to stay here? In separate rooms of course. I just want to talk to you until the sun comes up, then have coffee and maybe see the bears again. I liked sharing that with you Syd." Sydney put her hand out as she took a step back to regain her personal space.

"Wow, okay, I - wow. Give me a second here to get my mind working again," Sydney put the heels of her hands in her eye sockets to keep her brain from exploding and then dropped her hands to look at

Zeke. "I can't deny I'm attracted to you, especially since you overheard that much already. But I have never gotten involved with someone I have a contract with. Ever. It's a line I haven't crossed and no matter how much I might want to, I won't. I'm sorry. The last time I crossed a line was the night my mom died, and even though I know logically the one had nothing to do with the other, emotionally I can't take the chance. Plus, I have some serious trust issues right now."

"What happened? With your mom first, then we'll come back to the other." Zeke asked as he leaned against the opposite wall.

"I got suckered in by a married man," Sydney quickly added, waving one hand in the air, "I didn't know he was married until after. Anyway, after we, uh, well you get the picture, he went to take a shower and his cell phone buzzed. It was two in the morning and me being nosy, I looked at the text message. It was his wife saying she missed him and his infant daughter had just woke her up, so she decided to brighten his day with an early message. As I was walking to the bathroom to confront him, my phone rang and it was my dad. My mom had just died of a cerebral hemorrhage. My dad said she woke up with a horrible headache and starting sweating so he called 911, but she died before they got there." A tear streaked down her face and she wiped it away. "So, I know it sounds stupid, but I can't take the chance of crossing another line. If there wasn't a contract, it would be totally different."

"I can respect that. I'll just get Alex to fire you and then you'll go out with me?" Zeke laughed at Sydney's horrified expression. "I'm only kidding. I'm really sorry about how you lost your mom, and thanks for trusting me enough to explain it. Forget I said anything and let's go out tonight and have a good time and we'll leave it at that, okay?" The mischievous look in his eyes betrayed his words, but she was willing to go along. What choice did she have? "So, does the married guy have to do with your trust issues?"

"Not really, but I do have a question for you. Have you ever heard of Manolo Blanik?"

Zeke blinked his eyes making him look like a star-struck owl. "Uh, is that the new margarine that won't block your arteries?"

Sydney let out a burst of laughter then said, "No, and it's a who, not a what!"

"In that case, no I haven't. Who is she?"

"It doesn't really matter, but it's a him not a her. Seriously, thanks for being so understanding about why I can't go out with you. I'll go pack my things and we'll get out of your hair." Sydney smiled and walked away and missed Zeke's comment about how it was already too late for that now.

Sydney didn't even bother to fold her clothes this time. She yanked clothes off their hangers and stuffed them into her suitcase. She couldn't remember ever being so conflicted. More than anything, she wanted to take Zeke up on his offer, but since she didn't have many rules that she lived by, she wouldn't allow herself to make an exception on this one. Even if he didn't have a clue who the couture shoemaker was. She was zipping up her suitcase as Illana strode in.

"Where are the keys to the Ford? I wanted to put my suitcase in. Are you ready to go?"

"All packed, let's find Zeke to thank him and then we'll go." Sydney handed her the keys and glanced around the room. She had to make sure she hadn't subconsciously forgotten something to leave her an excuse to come back. Not seeing anything of hers lying about, she pulled her roller suitcase into the entry way and went to find Zeke. He was sitting in a rocking chair on the deck, with his boots propped up on the railing. Sydney opened the door and poked her head outside.

"We're going to head over to the hotel. I just wanted to say thanks again. I really don't know where we would've gone last night had you not let us stay here. So, anyway, I guess we'll see you and Alex in about an hour?"

"Yeah, we'll be waiting in the lobby." Zeke didn't take his gaze off the lake as he took a sip from his beer bottle. Maybe he hadn't taken her refusal as well as she thought.

"See you later then," Sydney said as she shut the door. She took one last look at the living room and kitchen, grabbed her suitcase and joined Illana out by the car. Illana had retrieved their laptops from Zeke's car and was putting them in the backseat as Sydney's suitcase thudded over the stamped concrete. Sydney opened the back drivers-side door and lifted her suitcase to sit on the backseat, then slammed the door.

"What happened? Are you going to be bitchy all night or are you going to tell me what's going on?" Illana asked with her hands on her hips. Sydney took a deep breath and blew it out.

"I'll tell you on the way over. Let's go while I still can," Sydney said, wistfully looking at the house as she got in the car. Driving away, she told Illana what had transpired between her and Zeke, and how torn she was.

"Why must you complicate the crap out of everything constantly? That's so totally romantic and yet you turned him down. No wonder he wouldn't look at you, he's probably not heard the word 'no' very often." Illana strummed her hoop earring as she spoke. "You know what, this might actually be better. Please tell me you are playing hard to get." She expectantly looked at Sydney with a big smile, which faded quickly.

"Me? Have you lost your mind? I'm no good at playing games and you know it. No, I can't do this. God knows I want to, but I won't. I'm so glad that John got you on my flight on Saturday, it'll be easier for me having you here."

"What am I, a walking chastity belt? Why are you making this so hard? He's interested, you're interested, so explore it." Illana rolled her eyes at Sydney's determined look and flipped down the visor mirror to check her makeup. "Never mind, go ahead and screw this up, I don't care. You had better quit being so pious and lighten up since I'm planning on having fun tonight." Illana decided she'd fix her makeup at the hotel and flipped the visor back up.

"I'm not being pious! Don't worry about me, I won't get in the way of your fun." Sydney rolled her shoulders and exhaled loudly. "Listen, we have to kick their asses at pool tonight so there's no time for you and me to fight right now."

"Now you're talking! By the way, you might want to warn me when you're going to pull the 'I'm only a girl and I don't know how to play pool' gambit so I don't blow it. It's so fun to be underestimated." They pulled into the hotel parking lot and a wide grin lit up Illana's eyes as she said, "Speaking of being underestimated, let's go see how well we are received by the hotel. I hope Michelle is still working."

As they walked in the hotel, the same clerk who didn't want to look at Sydney the last time was behind the desk. As she saw Sydney, she smiled and went in the back. Michelle came out a moment later. The look of hatred was quickly masked by a professional smile. "Welcome back. You're already checked in and here are your card-keys. I upgraded your room to a two-bed suite. Please let me know if there's anything else I can do to make your stay more enjoyable." Michelle dropped the sleeve with the card-keys on the beige counter, showed her teeth in a fake smile and walked towards the back room.

Sydney tapped the bell on the counter which brought Michelle to a halt. Michelle turned around, barely veiling her hatred as Sydney smiled sweetly.

"I was wondering if you had one of those little sewing kits I could have. I seem to have ripped my sleeve earlier. Oh, I know how it happened," Sydney snapped her fingers as she looked at Illana, "It was while I was having my arm twisted to come back here."

Michelle yanked a drawer open and tossed the sewing kit next to the card-keys. "Well, at least some of us don't need our Daddy to fight our battles for us."

"I didn't need it, especially considering the living arrangement I had last night. And unlike some people, I don't let my friends jeopardize my job." Sydney swiped the kit off the counter as Michelle spun on her heel into the back room.

Illana picked the card-key sleeve up off the counter then said, "Well, that went well, don't you think?"

Sydney was hanging her clothes as Illana came out of the bathroom wrapped in a towel. Illana grabbed her clothes out of her open suitcase and shook her head as she walked past Sydney.

"What are you shaking your head for?" Sydney asked as Illana shut the door.

"Because you're anal retentive," Illana shouted through the bathroom door.

"No I'm not! I just like to wear clothes without wrinkles. How much longer are you going to be? It's five thirty!"

"Don't rush me, they can wait a few minutes." Illana opened the door and looked disparagingly at Sydney. "Please tell me you plan on doing something with your hair, or at least your makeup before we leave."

"Why, what's wrong with my hair and makeup?" Sydney quickly leaned to her right to look in the full size mirror.

"Nothing, if you want to attract a raccoon." Illana said as she looked back in the mirror and applied her lipstick.

"Thanks for telling me now." Sydney pulled her purple makeup bag out of her suitcase and went in the cramped bathroom to get at the sink. Michelle might be a bitch, but the housekeepers did a good job. There was no dust on any of the three clear light bulbs above the mirror, which was also spotless. After doing some quick clean up with

Q-tips and applying more eyeliner and mascara she considered herself done.

"Hair, you forgot to do your hair, and you aren't wearing any lipstick. Do you want to borrow one of mine?"

"My hair is fine, and you know I hate lipstick. Let's go before you decide I need a manicure, too."

They found the men sitting in the plush lobby chairs talking quietly while Michelle was trying to look busy at the counter. As Sydney and Illana walked into the lobby both men stood and Michelle shot the women a gelid stare.

"Ready to go?" Alex asked.

"Absolutely, I'm starving!" Illana said loud enough for Michelle to hear. Sydney glanced at Michelle and caught her looking at Zeke dejectedly. What was that about?

Alex held the door as the other three walked out. Zeke walked beside Sydney, and Illana found an imaginary pebble in her shoe and leaned on Alex to get it out. Talk about the oldest trick in the book, what was next? An eyelash in her eye?

"Just out of idle curiosity, what's the deal with you and Michelle? Were you two high school sweethearts?" Sydney asked before she could think about it.

"How'd you pick up on that?" Zeke asked, looking sideways at her. "We did go out for a while but it wasn't during high school, it was just last year."

"I take it you didn't part the best of friends?" Sydney knew she was being too obvious by fishing for more details, but her desire to know overrode her normal inclination to mind her own business.

"Not after she slept with my best friend, Tyler. To be fair, he had just gotten into town and didn't know we were an item. She believed a rumor that I had left the Crowded House, a local bar, with some skinny brunette and decided to get even. Michelle and I had been seeing each other for a little over a year, so after we broke up, I got on my Harley and rode around the States for a while with Tyler to get my head straight." His jaw tightened slightly and Sydney sensed some of the anger hadn't been ridden away. Illana finally had her shoe back on and was walking towards the car with Alex.

"What an idiot. Her, not you. Sorry I brought it up. I can be really nosy sometimes."

"I don't have any secrets. They tend to keep people sick." He jerked his chin at Alex and Illana as they walked over. "Looks like you aren't the only one who's doing jumping jacks."

"Who's doing jumping jacks?" Alex said as he turned to scan the parking lot.

"No one. Your brother is trying to be funny," Sydney replied dryly as she and Illana got in the backseat and the men climbed in front. Alex drove to the other end of town and parked in front of Buckethead's Sports Bar & Grill.

Four pool tables were visible through the window and it looked like more pool tables might be housed behind a half wall. They walked in and sat down in a booth that had a great view of three different TV's. The Olympics didn't start until next month, so all they had to watch was a baseball game and a rodeo. A busty redheaded waitress came over and handed out the menus. After saying the specials of the night (deep fried walleye and broasted chicken) she asked if they wanted anything from the bar.

"I'll take a Heineken, please," Sydney asked the waitress who was too busy writing to make eye contact.

"Make that two," said Zeke, smiling at Sydney.

"I'll have a Purple Hooter," Illana requested, not taking her eyes off the menu.

"A what? I don't think we make those here," replied the confused waitress.

"Just a Malibu and Pepsi then," Illana decided on her third choice, not wanting to push her luck by asking for a Sex on the Beach.

"I'll have an ice tea, thanks Shelia," Alex added. Sheila smiled at Alex and Zeke as she took down their drink orders, then sashayed back to bar. Illana was studying the menu like she was going to be tested on it, but Sydney flipped right to the burger section. Zeke and Alex laid down their menus and were patiently waiting for the two women to decide.

A few minutes later, Sheila came strutting back over, way over-exaggerating her hips Sydney thought, and set their drinks down.

"So are you ready to order?" Sheila asked, pen in hand.

"Do you broil or bake your fish?" asked Illana, looking at the waitress for the first time.

"We deep fry it," Sheila replied.

"Well then, you guys better go ahead and order and come back to me."

"I'll have the garlic bacon cheeseburger, cooked medium rare," Sydney said, and Illana whipped her menu down at stared at Sydney like she had lost her mind. For once, Sydney wasn't going to worry about her caloric intake.

"You want fries, cole slaw, garlic mashed or a baked potato with that?"

"Garlic mashed sounds great," Sydney said as she raised her eyebrow in challenge at Illana. Sydney could feel her arteries clogging in preparation, but decided one night of greasy food wouldn't kill her. Illana obviously did not agree.

"I'll have the same, all of it," Zeke added before Sheila was done writing Sydney's order.

"I'll have walleye, with fries," said Alex as he took a sip of his ice tea.

"Um, well I guess I'll have the Caesar salad with chicken. That's not deep fried is it?"

"Nope, we don't deep fry salads," Sheila replied with a straight face.

"I *meant* the chicken," Illana shot back.

"No, that's grilled. Anyone need another drink?" At everyone's negative shake of their heads, Sheila nodded, gathered up their menus and walked towards the back of the restaurant, pushing open the double doors to the kitchen. As soon as she was gone Sydney burst out laughing, and Zeke and Alex just barely contained themselves.

"I thought you were going to kill her when she said they didn't deep fry salads! Priceless, absolutely priceless," Sydney dabbed the corner of her eye for effect and Illana scowled at all of them.

"I didn't think it was very funny, it was a reasonable question." Illana unfolded her arms just long enough to take a long pull of her drink, and then resumed her pissed off stance.

"Get over it, it was funny. So gentlemen, are you both ready to play some pool?" Sydney asked sweetly.

"Actually, I was wondering if you wanted to start with a quick game of nine-ball, just you and me, and I thought I would throw in a friendly little wager," Zeke's Cheshire-cat grin kicked Sydney's adrenaline up a notch so she sat back and tried to look way more relaxed than she felt.

"Absolutely, but you'll have to tell me the rules again, it's been *ages* since I played. What's the wager?"

"Loser buys next round and racks for the rest of the night," Zeke's eyes twinkled with delight as the color blossomed on Sydney's cheeks.

Illana knew that meant she was getting mad, but Zeke took it as her getting flustered.

"I guess that would be acceptable." She stuck her right hand out and Zeke shook her hand, and then held it for just a moment too long. Okay, now the color *was* because she was flustered.

Their dinners arrived shortly thereafter, and the chatter died down while everyone ate. Everyone but Illana, who was certain Sheila had done something to her salad. She picked at it, turning over the lettuce, almost leaf by leaf, as if she was looking for a spider. After spending a couple minutes at this, she finally decided it was uncontaminated and started nibbling at it. Sydney, on the other hand, was scarfing down her burger, convinced it was the best burger ever. The garlic cheese sauce was seeping out of the burger and she licked it off her fingers while her eyes rolled to the back of her head due to the orgasm in her mouth. The men ate with their eyes glued to the baseball game on one of the big screens.

After the dishes were cleared away, Alex went up to the bar to pay the bill and get the pool balls. Zeke went out to the car and came back in with two very nice custom pool sticks. Illana and Sydney exchanged a secret smile and walked over to the wall where the bar pool sticks were. Alex came back to the table with the balls and told them another round of drinks was on the way.

After checking to make sure she had a straight stick, Sydney asked Zeke to explain the rules again and would he be so kind as to rack the balls since she would probably be stuck doing so the rest of the night. At that comment, Illana turned to look at the pool sticks on the wall again so her smile wouldn't give away the game.

After going over the rules twice, Zeke racked the balls and offered to let Sydney break. Sydney winked at Illana when Zeke had his back turned, and readily accepted. Sydney hopped off her barstool and strode over to the pool table, making sure to chalk her stick and powder her hands first. She put the cue ball a little to the right of center and on the break dropped the one and the seven balls. It took her a total of six minutes to clear the table. She was grinning as the nine ball fell in the back corner pocket and looked at Zeke, who was shaking his head. Alex chuckled as he said to Zeke, "Brother, I do believe we have been snookered."

"You should never underestimate your opponent," Sydney said as she chalked her stick. She then leaned on her pool cue, and stuck her hand on her hip. Smiling, she nodded toward the table and said to Zeke, "Rack 'em, toots."

The next few hours flew by in a blur, studded with insults and lots of laughter. The four of them found they were well matched, but Sydney and Illana ended up winning most of the games. Sydney won one game by bending over to fix her sandal strap as Zeke was aiming for the eight ball, and he ended up scratching the cue ball. He accused her of playing dirty pool and vowed not to be taken in again. After the first hour, Sydney tried to relieve Zeke of his racking duties, but he said a bet is a bet, and was good-natured about racking the rest of the evening.

Since the two men were the reigning pool champions, the four players drew quite a crowd. Alex and Zeke had, so far, only managed to win two out of the ten games they had played. There had been several comments from the regulars at the bar suggesting Zeke and Alex should give up their now undeserved trophies. The four of them decided to play one more game then hang it up for the night. Money was seen changing hands, as quite a few people were engaged in side bets, like who would drop the four ball or how many balls Sydney would drop in the left corner pocket.

After Zeke racked the balls, Illana broke and barely missed dropping the eight in, but succeeded in sinking the six ball. Some of the people watching groaned in disappointment, especially those who had placed a bet that she would, for the third time that night, drop the eight and end the game. Illana then dropped the one ball and followed up by banking the five in. Then she hit the two ball too hard, making it bounce against the back of the pocket then rolling a couple inches away from the hole. Alex was up next, and dropped four of their balls, but his fifth shot hit the corner of the pocket and rolled away. Sydney dropped two balls, and then scratched on her third shot. Zeke smirked when she dropped the cue ball in his hand and he quickly sunk the rest of their balls. By this time, you could have heard a fly land because everyone was watching so intently.

Zeke had to bank the eight into the side pocket since he had left himself behind one of Sydney's balls. He took the shot and barely missed the hole. Sydney uncrossed her fingers as Illana stepped up to the table and dropped the other two balls and had a straight shot at the eight. She called the corner pocket and bent over to aim when Zeke said to Alex, "Your shoe is untied." Alex stood up and bent over to tie it just as Illana took her shot. She missed the eight and sunk the cue ball instead. Zeke just smiled at Sydney, while the onlookers clapped Alex and Zeke on their backs. Illana looked at Sydney and shrugged her shoulders.

"Hey, eight out of eleven games ain't bad."

It was after ten when Illana and Sydney walked through the lobby with Alex and Zeke acting as escorts. After saying their goodnights with a round of handshakes, Sydney and Illana climbed up the open staircase. Zeke's eyes tracked Sydney's every step until she vanished out of sight. Michelle stood behind the desk, unnoticed, and watched him watching Sydney. She knew at that moment he was out of her reach. If looks could kill, the two women wouldn't have made it past the second stair.

By the time they got into their room Sydney was still fuming, so Illana ignored her and went into the bathroom. She came out while brushing her teeth, looked at Sydney, who was slumped in a chair and said with a mouthful of toothpaste, "Oh snap out of it. I guess you never missed a shot because you were too busy checking out a hot guy? Please." She walked back into the bathroom to rinse her mouth and called out, "So how long are you going to pout about this?"

"Until next year. We had them, totally and completely! If I didn't know you better, I'd think you did that on purpose." Sydney clicked on the TV and started watching "The Crocodile Hunter."

"Are you accusing me of throwing the game? Me?" Illana's eyes were wide with disbelief.

"No, I'm not," Sydney said, exhaling loudly. "I really wanted to win and wipe the sarcastic smirk off Zeke's face. We still won eight games, so I can't complain, and I can't fault you for getting distracted either." Sydney pushed herself out of the chair and went into the bathroom to perform her nightly rituals. As the door closed, Illana knew that was as close to being forgiven as she was going to get.

But it was so totally worth it.

Chapter Five - Attila Strikes Back

The next morning, the two women left the hotel and drove to the coffee shop. They could see Lucy holding court inside. She was standing in the middle of the room, arms flailing while the other women were rocking back and forth, laughing and wiping tears from their eyes. Illana got out and stared at the scene inside.

"Are these women here every morning? Don't they have jobs?"

"Well, Suzanne works for Betty in the afternoons, but stops by for a quick cup in the morning after dropping her son off at daycare. Lucy is a stay-at-home mom but donates most of her time to the local food pantry and Amelia is a nurse who works the graveyard shift and gets a cup of coffee before going home." Sydney shut her door and engaged the alarm as she caught Illana's open mouth stare. "What?"

"How do you know all of that?"

"I listen. Come on, I don't want to miss another of Lucy's stories, I still don't know what happened to her dog, oh – don't let me forget to ask her about that."

"Whoa. Why do you care?" Illana struck her usual pose, hand on her hip and a cocked eyebrow. "Unless it's about the latest gadget, your family, me or woodworking crap, you usually aren't interested. You tune out everything else, so I'm more than a little shocked you are concerned about some story regarding a dog. You don't even like dogs!"

"Yes I do, besides it sounded like a funny story and now I have to know what happened," Sydney said as she walked into the coffee shop, just as Lucy was sitting down. Betty's face lit up as they walked in.

"Hey, the new pool champions!" Betty exclaimed as she pulled two mugs off the pegboard. "We heard you two were the stars of the evening." Betty poured Sydney's coffee and added the cream and sugar then fired up the espresso machine to make Illana's mocha.

"How did you hear about that already?" Sydney asked as she pulled out her wallet.

"Honey, up here word travels fast. Gossip is like an Olympic sport and we all have gold medals. News of our reigning champs losing to two women from California was bound to spread like quack grass."

"What's quack grass?" Illana asked, taking the proffered mug from Betty.

"It's a weed that takes over your grass and, short of fire, there's no stopping it," Betty explained while putting the money in the register.

"Well, we would have won the last game too, if *someone* hadn't sunk the cue ball instead of the eight." Sydney said while stirring her coffee.

"For the last time, it was an accident! Like I told you last night, I got distracted for a minute when Alex bent over to tie his shoe," Illana saw the other women exchanging speculative glances over the rims of their cups and pointed at Betty, "I saw that look and I'm not about to apologize or be embarrassed for looking at a nice ass." Illana took a long drink of her mocha while staring at Betty and the others, practically daring them to say something.

Sydney dramatically whipped her wrist out and looked at her watch, "Would you look at the time? We'd better get going, big day today, can't afford to be late." After draining the rest of the coffee from the cup, she set it on the counter. "The coffee was great as usual, thanks Betty. We'll see you all tomorrow." Illana slowly drank the rest of her mocha, slurping it loudly through the straw, set the cup on the counter and sauntered back to the car.

They drove over to the office and parked in the back employee lot. Sydney noticed Zeke was back to driving his beater truck, and wondered why. Not that she cared, really, she was just curious. They walked in the back door and straight up to their current office to turn on their computers. While they were booting up, Sydney went to find Alex to see how many data entry volunteers they had for this evening.

Sydney walked in and saw a couple women openly crying and those that weren't were trying to comfort their distraught co-workers. Sydney wondered who died, and felt her heart skip a beat as she silently prayed it wasn't Zeke. Walking into Alex's office, she asked, "Alex is everyone okay? What's going on? Did someone get hurt?"

Alex turned from his computer to face her and his face was drawn, and his hair was messier than ever. "Let's go up to Dad's office and I'll tell you both at the same time, just let me grab Zeke first." The knot in her shoulder blades unraveled. *Thank God nothing had happened to Zeke.* Alex quietly talked to a few of his employees on the way out, assuring them everything would be ok. While he went to find Zeke, Sydney walked up to the office and filled in Illana on the funeral-like feeling emanating from the office staff.

Alex and Zeke walked in a moment later. The difference in the two brothers had never been so apparent. Alex looked tired and worn down, but Zeke looked like he was ready to kill someone. His face was red and his eyes were devoid of all emotion, his jaw was clenched and he kept balling his fists.

"Let's sit down, shall we?" Alex suggested, pointing to the other end of the table that was clear of computer paraphernalia. Alex sat at the head of the table with Zeke on his right and the women sat to his left.

"Alex, what happened?" Illana asked, her hand lightly touching his arm.

"It turns out our sister has been quite busy analyzing the new system and its potential for efficiency. She even made some charts showing how the work can now be streamlined. Which is great, and what I wanted," he assured Sydney, "but the downside is she gave almost half of the staff pink slips today. She informed them their services would no longer be needed after Friday."

"Isn't this your company? Override her! She is doing this out of spite and you know it." Illana pointed a finger at Alex to emphasize her last point.

"I realize that, but the problem is, well, she's right. I've looked over all the reports and tried to find a loophole, and I also thought maybe she was skewing the data to make her case. She's not, and on this one, she's absolutely right. I can't believe I missed it, I never saw this coming."

"This is bullshit and you know it Alex. Do you think it's a coincidence she gave pink slips to all the people who volunteered to help out tonight?" Zeke asked as he leaned back in his chair, arms crossed in front of his chest. "Tell me you are not going to stand by and let her do this to your employees, especially since most of them are family, too."

"There must be another way. What about starting a catalogue? That might spark more business and then you could justify the extra staff. Or you could open a retail outlet," Sydney suggested.

"Those are great ideas, but it would still take months to set up a catalogue, print them and send them out. The retail store is one I've been considering for a while now, and there some decent storefronts around town I could buy. Neither of those will help us today, but it's something to consider for the future though." Alex perked up a little, but only by a couple degrees.

"Who set up the web site to begin with?" Sydney asked

"Our cousin Gina did. She wanted to set it up so people could order straight from the web, but Annie talked me out of it. Gina is one of the employees who was given walking papers." Alex rubbed his forehead like he had a headache.

"Why not make her in charge of the new web site and database? We could train her and as long as you maintain a support contract with us, she can call or email us as many times as she wants. You might want to give her an assistant too, just in case of vacation or sick days." Sydney didn't normally make that kind of offer to clients, but made an exception considering the situation.

"This could work, good thinking Sydney," Alex said with a slight smile then turned to Zeke, "that's two employees, now we just need to save eight more."

"Hey, what about doing shifts? You could do two shifts, an early and late one, ten people on each, or eight on each with a supervisor for each team," Illana suggested.

"I thought of that too, but again the data points to not needing that many people." Alex said dejectedly.

"It might not be what the current data suggests. However, what your data may not be reflecting is the growth potential now that you have an actual online business. Did Annie incorporate any of those figures?" Sydney asked excitedly.

"Sure, she put in some minor growth, but not enough to need our current staffing level."

"There's your loophole Alex. You might need to hire more staff in a couple of months. Why not do a ninety day trial period and tell your staff you will reevaluate after that?" Sydney countered, relaxing for the first time since going downstairs.

"You know Alex, this may work. During that time period, we could pull together a catalogue and at least send it to our existing customers. After those go out we could get going on the retail store. I think you should do it," Zeke said, leaning on the table. Alex pushed his hand through his hair, and then nodded.

"We'll try it this way, thanks for all the input and great ideas. I think this just may work," said Alex as he stood up and looked at his brother. "You're right, this is my company and perhaps I need to make that point more clearly to Annie. C'mon Zeke, let's go tear up those pink slips."

After they left Illana looked at Sydney and said, "You do realize this is just going to piss off Annie more, right?"

"True, but then again, can you think of anything we could do to make her happy?"

"Short of dying, no. I'm not sure us leaving in two days is going to be enough make her happy now." Illana laughed as they heard someone marching up the stairs. Annie glared at the women as she walked into the room.

"I suppose you think this is funny. I don't know what you two are hoping to accomplish by driving my brother's business into the ground by having him keep all of the unneeded employees, but I can assure you no one in Ruby Lake will ever use your services again." Annie's voice quivered in anger as she went on. "What neither of you understand is Alex isn't stable. Before he won the lottery, he drank himself to sleep most nights and spent his days working at the hotel. He has never had any direction or ambition and if you think for a moment I'm going to stand idly by and watch you get his hopes up, you're dead wrong. You may think badly of me, but I don't care. Nothing is more important to me than my family and I resent you coming in here like you two are better than everyone else and taking over. This is your last warning." Annie pulled the door shut with a resounding slam and marched back downstairs.

"Great, I shudder to think what she'll do next. Do you think we should alert the fire department of an impending arsonist?" Sydney asked after hearing the warehouse door slam downstairs.

"Yeah, and maybe the bomb squad. I wouldn't put anything past her at this point. I'm curious about Alex's 'drinking problem,' somehow it seems a little over the top to me. She needs help. Or at the very least, she needs to get laid," Illana said as she focused again on the web site.

Around eleven-thirty, Zeke came up to get them for lunch. The three left out the back door to find Alex waiting for them by his car. To their surprise, Annie was waiting with him. The three women squeezed in the back seat, with Sydney in the middle, and Alex drove them downtown to the Cranberry Café. As they walked in, several people congratulated Sydney and Illana on their pool games and offered to buy them a drink. They thanked them with smiles and promised to take them up on the offer outside of business hours. After they were seated, Alex cleared his throat and looked around the table.

"Well, I thought it would be nice for Annie to come today and get to know you both better. I realize everyone got off to a bad start and I've only myself to blame." Luckily, Annie didn't see Illana roll her eyes, but Alex did, and directed the next comment at Annie. "No, I mean it. If I had just told you about my idea this whole misunderstanding would have been avoided." Zeke leaned back in his chair and crossed his arms while looking at Alex with a bemused grin. "So, with all that said, I see no reason why we can't all get along and start over." Alex smiled at everyone nervously, as he mussed his hair and picked up his menu. "Lunch is on me, by the way, so order whatever you want."

"Are you sure you're still hungry? After all the humble pie you just ate, I would think you'd be full," Zeke remarked dryly as he picked up his menu. Alex was saved from replying by the waitress showing up.

"I must say, it sure is nice to see you all out together. I can't remember the last time you three were here without your parents. Your mom would be just tickled to see this."

"It happens from time to time, don't worry Aggie, hell hasn't frozen over. At least I don't think it has. Did your realm freeze over sis?" Zeke asked while Annie glared at him over the top of her menu.

"You be nice Zeke, and quit picking on your sister. What would you ladies like to eat?" Aggie asked, after swatting Zeke on the shoulder.

"I'll have a French Dip with mushrooms, and a Pepsi please," Sydney said, handing over the menu.

"I'd like a club sandwich, dry, without bacon, and I'll have a glass of water with a slice of lemon." Illana gave the menu to Aggie and began rooting around in her purse to find her lipstick.

"Just the house salad with ranch and a regular glass of water for me, thanks Aggie," Annie said glancing at Illana, who was too busy with her lipstick to notice.

"Steak sandwich, all the trimmings and a bottle of Miller." Zeke winked at Aggie who then twittered.

"I'll have the Reuben and an ice tea. Thank you Aggie." Alex returned Aggie's smile as she took the last menu and hurried into the kitchen. Tension descended on the table like the fog in San Francisco Bay. Sydney checked her watch for the fifth time while Illana obliviously smudged her lipstick on a paper napkin. Zeke shook his head in Alex's direction while Annie rearranged her silverware, again. Sydney couldn't stand it anymore and spoke up.

"This is silly. Let's just put it all out on the table. Annie thinks, for some reason I'll never understand, that Illana and I are trying to run your business into the ground." Sydney turned and looked across Illana at Annie. "Care to explain why? Or are you afraid it will push Alex over the edge?"

"How dare you!" Annie looking imploringly at Alex, "See, this is what I mean. Every time I try to talk to her, she twists my words around! I never said that, I only said I thought it didn't make good business sense to keep all of those employees since we no longer needed them."

Aggie came over carrying the drinks and as she was putting them down, Zeke, seeing the situation spiraling out of control, said, "I guess hell is safe, but we aren't. Can you make our order to go?" After her affirmative nod and as she was walking away, Zeke turned to look at Annie. "I realize you can't stand that Alex has listened to someone other than you, but now you need to listen to me. I'm sick of your lies and of you stirring the pot. We'll go back to the office and air this out for once and all, then you need to drop it."

"Or what?"

"Or I will use my rights as a stockholder to see that your responsibilities are severely diminished, and I'll get Dad to back me." Zeke downed his beer and set it back on the table. "It was one thing when you ran the company and it was doing well. It's totally different when you start sabotaging its progress. Alex, I tried to tell you lunch was a bad idea, maybe next time we can order a pizza and do this in private."

To call the ride back to the office 'tense' was an understatement. Annie took the front seat so Zeke rode in the back and Sydney got stuck in the middle again. Zeke's leg was pressing against Sydney's but she was fairly certain he didn't notice. He and Illana both stared out of their windows looking like angry gargoyle bookends. Ironically, U2's "It's a Beautiful Day" was playing on the radio. Sydney didn't think her companions would appreciate the humor, so she kept her thoughts to herself.

When they pulled to a stop in the parking lot, the four doors opened like a synchronized CIA drill. Alex marched forward, yanked the warehouse door open, making Annie catch it, and led the way up to his dad's office. He sat down behind the desk as the rest of them sat down at the table. Zeke was to his right, Annie was on the left and Sydney and Illana sat next to Zeke. The alliance wasn't lost on Annie, who stiffened her spine as she brushed the wrinkles off her pink tweed skirt.

"I want to do this calmly, so no outbursts." Alex's polite demeanor cracked as he took control of the meeting. Sydney and Illana exchanged a glance at the new side of Alex. "Annie, never, ever give my employees walking papers without clearing it by me first."

"Don't you mean 'our' employees?"

"No, I mean mine. I've let you get away with far too much for way too long and it ends now." Alex started to rake his hair, but instead placed his hands on the table. "When I came up with the idea of this company, you're the one who made it happen and have kept us afloat the past couple of years. I don't deny the fact I want and need you on my team. But, I made a mistake by allowing you to think it was your team."

"Now Alex, calm down. There is no reason to blow things out of proportion." Annie smiled and waved her hand in the air. "I may have been hasty in letting go some of the employees, but you've never concerned yourself with it before. Fine, I won't do it again and I apologize to you if I upset you." Annie laid her hand on his arm, and Sydney couldn't take it anymore.

"God knows you wouldn't want to upset him, Annie. After all, you were the one who warned us he's unstable because of his prior drinking problem."

"You told them what? *I'm* unstable? I've never had a drinking problem!" Alex whipped his arm out of Annie's grasp and narrowed his eyes at her.

"I only told them that so they'd leave you alone. So what?" Annie sat back and rolled her eyes at Alex. "It's not like they're from here and could ruin your reputation."

"That's it, Annie, I've had it. As of right now you are officially on a two week vacation, and so help me if you open your mouth again, Annabelle Louise, it will be the end of your employment here." Alex rubbed his face with both hands, and shook his head slowly at Annie. "Why Annie? How could you do this? Don't answer now. Just go."

Annie grabbed her purse off the floor and quickly left the room, shooting Sydney a death glare as she went.

"Nice going Syd," Illana said quietly after Annie shut the door.

"No, it's okay Sydney. I'm glad you said what you did. I wanted everything out on the table, careful what you wish for I guess." Alex still looked stunned as he leaned back in the chair.

"I'll second that. You've needed to knock her off her high horse for a long time. She's all grown up and doesn't need our protection anymore, brother." Zeke stood up, "Well that was fun, but we should see if your employees are ready to start doing the data entry." Alex stood up as Zeke left, and as he walked past he patted Sydney on the shoulder.

"Alex, I must have left my purse in your car. Can I have the key so I can go get it?" Sydney asked.

"It's not locked so go ahead. We never lock the cars around here." Sydney shook her head the whole way down the stairs.

Sydney walked outside and immediately regretted it. Annie was sitting in her car, which was parked right next to Alex's, her head bent over her arms on the steering wheel clearly sobbing. Sydney froze and was about to go back inside when Annie looked up. She wiped her eyes, got out of the car and stood using the door like a shield.

"Did you come out here to gloat?" Annie asked accusingly.

"No, I forgot my purse in Alex's car, I had no idea you were out here." For the first time since meeting her, Sydney felt sorry for Annie.

"Well, I'm sure you and your snobby friend are thrilled to see me go. Don't think for one minute that this means anything. Alex will call me with an apology by tomorrow because he won't be able to run this place without me." Annie sniffed and lifted her chin up as Sydney got closer.

"What if he can? You don't give him enough credit and I sincerely hope he proves you wrong." *So much for feeling sorry for her*, Sydney thought as she walked to the car and got her purse. She turned around and walked back in without seeing the look of doubt on Annie's face.

Despite Annie's hasty departure, or maybe due to it, the rest of the afternoon sped by. The entire staff ended up staying to do the data entry. Zeke bought seven ginormous pizzas around dinner time, much to the delight of everyone present. After the staff had eaten their fill, he looked around for Sydney. He saw Alex and Illana in Alex's office huddled around the computer. Zeke grabbed two pieces of sausage pizza and a napkin then walked up to his dad's office. He stomped up the stairs and knocked on the door. Sydney raised a finger in his direction as she finished typing. Looking over at him, she smiled when she saw her favorite food.

"Pizza! You must have read my mind." She jumped up and took the plate, "I think you may have just saved humanity as we know it. Or maybe just me."

"I'd settle for just you. What are you doing up here? I thought you were all done?"

"I'm done with the database. Now I'm just running some reports to watch the progress," Sydney said as she inhaled half of her slice in one bite.

"My, what big teeth you have Grandma," Zeke said jokingly.

"Give me a break, this is brain food and I'm starving. Come sit and take a look," Sydney said as she turned her laptop so he could see it better. He sat down and watched as she scrolled though hundreds of customers.

"With this, you'll be able to send out mass emails to all your customers. Here, check this out, this is all the stock you have on hand." Another report popped up on the screen that listed all the stock with the price and what 'kits' they could go with. "Also, when orders are taken a report will be printed every hour for the needed stock, and the items on the report will be listed in the same order as it is on the shelves."

"That's awesome, I can't believe you set this up in three days."

"We just created it, the women downstairs are doing the hard part. I'm so glad my days of doing data entry are over, I really hated that part of it." Sydney wiped her mouth with a napkin after finishing off the second piece.

"Is that where you started?"

"Yes, I was a lower level clerk and when I got bored, I played with the database on my computer. After screwing it up a bunch of times, my boss sent me to training so I'd be less dangerous. It kind of went from there, turned out I have the aptitude for it and I love it. Guess that makes me a computer geek after all, with or without the cute glasses." Sydney admitted, sitting up a little straighter. Zeke winced as he remembered his comment upon meeting her.

"Hey, I'm sorry for the way I acted that day. I hope you know I really didn't mean any of it. Except for the fact you're hot. I meant that." Sydney laughed at Zeke's sheepish grin.

"No harm, no foul. So how long are you sticking around tonight?"

"As long as everyone else is here, I'll be here. I wish there was something I could do to be helpful though," Zeke said, a frown furrowing his brow.

"Well, I could think of a couple of things, but perhaps we'd better ask Alex if he has any thoughts on the subject."

Chapter Six – Locals Only

Due to everyone staying at the office until after eleven the previous evening, Alex told his staff not to come in until noon the next day. But Sydney, Illana, and Gina were meeting there about ten to give Gina a crash course in web and database administration. Sydney actually slept in until 8:00, which was nothing short of miraculous for her. Knowing she didn't have to be anywhere for a while, she took her time getting ready and decided to get her coffee. Illana would sleep through rampaging elephants, so Sydney didn't even bother to be quiet. After taking a leisurely shower and getting dressed, she shook Illana to wake her up to see if she wanted a mocha.

"What time is it?"

"It's a quarter to nine."

"Good Lord, Syd, go back to bed," Illana grumbled as she rolled away from Sydney.

"I'm awake and ready to go. Do you want me to bring you a coffee?"

"No, just leave the car keys and if you aren't back by the time I'm ready, I'll meet you over there. Now, shhh, you're ruining my beauty sleep, of which I have a half an hour more of." Illana snuggled back into the covers as Sydney set the keys by Illana's purse, and walked out.

Walking to the coffee shop gave Sydney a chance to look more closely at her surroundings. A pretty blue-green river rambled by behind the hotel, and on the deck attached to the hotel Sydney saw a couple sitting on the deck with mugs in their hands. On the other side of the street was a Wells Fargo bank housed in a gray brick building next to a liquor & bait shop. *I've never seen that combo*, Sydney thought as she walked by. Down the street there was a cute little boutique that looked promising, a floral shop, and a jewelry store. Driving by, none of these businesses had registered on her radar. She turned the corner and saw Betty sitting at an outdoor cafe table reading. As Sydney approached, Betty looked up with a smile.

"You're out late today, where's your friend?" Betty got up and held the door open.

"She's getting her beauty sleep. She'll be by in a while." Sydney waited at the counter as Betty prepared her coffee, and then sat on the wicker couch.

"I hear you all had lunch across the street and left in a hurry. What happened?" Sydney filled her in on the events of yesterday and finished with how smoothly everything went last night.

"Well, it's about time Alex woke up. I'm not surprised she lost it in the parking lot. She has always been the most sensitive of all of them. I will say she is loyal. Family has always come first to her, and they have all been so protective of her since she was small. So I imagine Alex insisting on a vacation was a huge blow. We'll wait and see if it has any lasting effects. Oh, I almost forgot," Betty jumped of her stool and went around the refrigerator to the back room. She came out holding the new Harry Potter book. "I meant to give this to you yesterday, but got sidetracked as usual. You can mail it back when you're done."

"I can buy a copy when I get home, you don't have to do this."

"How else am I going to hear from you again? No, take it, I trust you." Betty took a sip of her coffee as Sydney digested the fact that she had somehow earned this woman's trust.

"Thanks Betty, I'll return it as soon as I'm done." Sydney took the proffered book and set it gently by her purse. Amelia breezed in, digging through her purse as she walked. Betty fired up the espresso machine and Amelia looked up startled to see Sydney.

"Good morning! I didn't see you there, where's your car?"

"I left it at the hotel so Illana could drive over when she gets up. Am I in your spot?"

"Goodness no, stay right where you are," Amelia looked at Betty and asked, "Have you heard from Suzanne yet?"

"She called this morning to let me know Aaron, poor baby, is back in the hospital. I take it you saw him, is there anything you can tell me?" Betty furrowed her brow as she gave Amelia her coffee.

"Not much, other than we're running tests. Hopefully, it's just the flu, but the headache is worrying everyone. They did the spinal tap this morning and it's not meningitis so that's a relief. We may have to send him downstate depending on what the other test results have to say," she said as she handed Betty her money, "I think we should get a dinner schedule together, and rotate who visits when. I know she was at the hospital all night, and won't leave unless Aaron's with her. What do you think?" Amelia sat down as Betty took the calendar off the wall.

"I can visit tonight after I close, and I'll make a pan of tuna casserole to take to her house. I can also get a hold of everyone else and set up a schedule. What are you going to make?"

"I'll make lasagna, I know Aaron likes that. I'll be in and out of his room while I work, so leave me off of the visiting schedule. Gail from his daycare called Suzanne and the kids are making cards and Gail offered to bring those by the hospital this afternoon," Amelia looked over at Sydney and said, "Sorry to be such a downer this morning, how is everything going with Attila?"

"Oh no, don't apologize, I feel like I'm intruding. I don't have any problems, comparatively. Is there anything I can do? I don't have a kitchen to make something, but I'd be happy to donate some money if that'll help," Sydney said sincerely.

"It's nice of you to offer, but right now it's just food and time. If it gets to that point we'll let you know." Amelia patted Sydney's shoulder in a motherly way as Illana walked in. Betty must have seen her coming, because her mocha was sitting on the counter. Sydney didn't even notice the espresso machine running. Suddenly, all of her petty problems seemed to melt away, and she wanted to be a part of this. She wanted to help, and while no one said anything of the sort, it was clear she was an outsider.

"Thanks Betty. So Syd, are you ready to go?" Illana asked, oblivious to the tension in the room.

"I guess so," Sydney said as she stood up. Looking at Betty she said, "Please do let me know if there is anything I can do. I'd really like to help if I can."

"I will, you can count on it. Come by later and I'll let you know what we need." Betty's words and smile lifted the weight on Sydney's chest a little. When they got in the car, Sydney told Illana about Suzanne's little boy.

"Huh. I wonder what's wrong with him? I'm sure they'll figure it out, and we have a lot to do before we leave Saturday morning." Seeing the look of sadness on Sydney's face she said, "Why are you getting so upset about this? It's not like it's connected to you."

"I know. That's partially why I'm so sad."

Chapter Seven – The Devil is in the Details

Pulling into the parking lot they saw Alex's car parked in his usual spot. Figuring he wanted to oversee the training, they gathered their equipment and let themselves in the back door. They found Alex hunched over his monitor, his face about three inches from the screen.

"Alex? Is everything okay?" Illana asked.

"What? Oh hi, yeah everything's great! We've had over forty orders come in and I was just thinking I might have to order some more warehouse workers to help Zeke," he said as he turned off his computer and stood up.

"That's great! You'll have the justification for keeping all of your employees in no time," Illana said and then took a good look at Alex. He was still wearing the same clothes from yesterday. "Alex, you did go home last night, didn't you?"

"Actually, no. I shut everything down and meant to go home, but I wanted to see if any orders came in and how it worked. So I stayed. I was just about to head out when you two got here," Alex said giving them a boyish smile.

"You'd better go home and take a nap. Is Zeke coming in?" Sydney asked.

"I called him a bit ago, he should be here anytime." Alex looked at his watch. "I can't believe it's nine-forty already. Gina should be here soon, and you can call me at home if you need anything. I'll see you both later," Alex said as he closed the door to his office and left through the warehouse. Sydney and Illana went up to their temporary office to set up for the day. Zeke showed up a little while later and Gina came in right after him.

After spending a couple hours giving Gina the everything-you-need-to-know-about-databases-and-web-administration training, they all decided to take a break. Gina went outside to smoke, pretty overwhelmed by the amount of information that had been thrown at her, while Sydney and Illana went downstairs to make a fresh pot of coffee.

Zeke was busy pulling stock but seeing the two women enter the office, decided to join them.

"Hey, the new system is great! I can't tell you how easy it is to have the order sheets print out in the same order as what's on the shelves. Thanks again, this is an awesome improvement."

"We couldn't have done it without all of your help. The lists you gave us were the key. Do you want some coffee? It should be done in a couple more minutes." Sydney was trying to slyly stall him, except she had no talent at being sly. Illana rolled her eyes behind Zeke's back and walked back out to their office.

"Sure. So I guess you're leaving tomorrow?"

"No, we leave on an early flight on Saturday. John built in an extra night so we wouldn't have to take the red eye."

"Would you and Illana like to go to the Cranberry Festival tomorrow night? Friday night is when local bands come and play. It'd kinda suck if you missed our big annual event."

"Sure, if we can make it an early night, that sounds like fun," Sydney said as she realized she had run out of things to say. "Oh, did you hear about Suzanne's son?"

"Yeah, she called her mom, my dad's sister, last night from the hospital. I imagine the troops are mobilizing down at Stay A While."

"They were talking about dinners and visiting rotations. I told them I'd like to help, but there isn't a lot I can do."

"If I know Betty, she'll find something," Zeke said as he poured his coffee. "I'd better get back to work. Do you and Illana want to take an early lunch before everyone else gets here? I promise it'll be better than yesterday."

Sydney smiled and said, "Absolutely. Let me know when you're ready, and this time I'll pay." Zeke opened the door for Sydney and she went upstairs. It didn't occur to her a few days ago she snapped at him for doing the same thing. But Zeke noticed.

When the three returned from lunch, it was to find Alex and the rest of the staff in a panic. Alex exhaled with relief when he saw them.

"None of the printers are working, except for mine. I need to get ten new printers and Office Expo only has three of the same kind in stock."

"What do you mean they aren't working? They all worked fine last night before we left." Sydney said.

"I don't know what happened. All I do know is when you try to print off the order sheets, they come out garbled and the lines aren't where they are supposed to be, and you can't read a damn thing. Plus, the phones have been ringing constantly and I think Gina is going to have a heart attack."

"Sounds like a driver issue. Let me see some of the printed copies." Alex retrieved some crumpled papers from the trash and showed them to Sydney. It was definitely the drivers, which meant someone had erased them from all the computers. "You don't need new printers, all we have to do is reload the drivers and everything will be fine."

"Reload? Does that mean they were there before and somehow disappeared?" Alex asked, furrowing his brow.

"We should go into your office. I can reload all the drivers from the server and have it back to normal in no time." Sydney followed Zeke and Alex into his office, while Illana went to find Gina.

"I'm not saying someone did this on purpose, but it's a possibility. I'll be able to see the time the drivers were deleted, and that will give you some idea as to who did it. Keep in mind this could've been an accident. I'll let you both know when I'm done." Sydney walked over to the server room as Illana came in with a panic-stricken Gina.

"I didn't know what to do, I guess I'm not ready for this." Gina walked in with her eyes downturned, smelling like sweat and cigarette smoke.

"This is why you'll have a contact phone number so you can call us when there's a snag," Sydney said. "Did you see anyone in here earlier?"

"No, after you left for lunch, I ran across the street to grab a snack and have a smoke, but I didn't see anyone." Gina tucked her hands under her armpits, her eyes as big as quarters.

"Drivers do not disappear, so someone would've had to do something. Let's see who it is." Sydney logged in and pulled up the properties. Someone had done this last night around two in the morning. Remotely. Sydney showed Illana the evidence and briefly explained it to Gina. After disabling remote access and reloading the drivers, Sydney led the way back to Alex's office. There was just enough room for them all to squeeze in around the small oak table and sit down. Sydney repeated what she found to Alex and Zeke, and then asked who has remote access.

"No one that I know of," Alex answered. Zeke narrowed his eyes at Alex and tilted his head slightly to the left. "Oh, well I guess Annie would, so do Zeke and I, but how would she know how to do this?"

"She did go to Yale, so I imagine she could figure it out. I'll need to ramp up your firewall and I disabled all remote settings. The drivers should be loaded by now."

"You think Annie did this?" Gina asked. "Why? Is it because she is jealous of Sydney and Illana?" Sydney and Alex had dual looks of incredulity while Illana and Zeke smirked. The staff had been told that Annie decided to take her vacation after all, and none of the staff knew about the argument she and Alex had.

"No, I don't think she is jealous, and I don't want to know how you arrived at that conclusion." Alex waved his hand, dismissing the idea, and looked back at Sydney. "I think under the circumstances it might be wise for you to stay for another week."

Sydney secretly thought so too, but she didn't want to disappoint her dad who had already bought the tickets for the Music Circus for Thursday. "I can stay until Wednesday, but I have a prior commitment on Thursday I can't reschedule."

"That's fair. In fact, I talked to John last night and asked if you stay for another week. I thought Gina might feel more comfortable if she had another week of training." Alex and Zeke both smiled at Gina who slumped in her chair in relief.

"I'll call John and tell him I'll stay," Sydney said to Alex, then turned to look at Gina. "Stop worrying, you'll be just fine. Look at what you learned today, if this happens ever again, you'll know just what to do. After all, it's just computers, not brain surgery."

Chapter Eight – A Plane and Cranberry Candles

After calming Gina down and agreeing to meet her at the coffee shop Saturday morning, Sydney and Illana headed back to the hotel to get ready to go to the Cranberry Festival. Illana had talked John into rescheduling her flight to leave straight from Minneapolis so she didn't have to fly on another tiny plane. Sydney rolled her eyes as she listened to Illana whine about the long drive they would be doing later that night and finally couldn't take it anymore.

"You're the one who's scared of the itty bitty plane which would get you there in an hour, so don't bitch about having to drive. I'm so not looking forward to driving you there. I still don't understand why we can't leave in the morning."

"Hel-*lo*? Does 'The Mall of America' mean anything to you? Who knows if I'll ever get this close again? Besides, I thought you were going to stay with me and we could've gone shopping together," Illana said pouting while putting on more lipstick.

"Oh yeah, shopping in the largest mall in the Nation with you is my definition of a great day," Sydney said, and then sniffed the air, "Do you smell that? It's the smell of sarcasm."

"Very funny. I know you have girl tendencies in there somewhere; I was hoping a trip to the mall would bring them out." Illana was now applying mascara, eyes big and mouth open.

"Not in this lifetime. This is why I love online shopping. No crowds, no mirrors, no pushy salespeople, just me and my computer." Sydney turned around to check her reflection in the mirror, noting how big her butt looked in her short, jean skirt. "I think this mirror is defective. The fun house must not have wanted it anymore."

Illana glanced over to see Sydney twisting around to see her backside in the mirror. "Well, well, well. It's nice to see you're a girl after all. Don't worry, you'll look great once you do your hair and makeup."

"I did it already," Sydney said, furrowing her eyebrows at Illana.

Illana took a hard look at Sydney, and couldn't see even a hint of blush or the tell-tale sheen of hairspray. "If you say so," Illana said as she squirted a generous amount of gel in her hands then fingered it through her spiky black hair, purple tips tonight. Nodding at her reflection she turned to Sydney and asked, "Shall we go set the town on fire?"

Zeke and Alex were standing in the lobby when Sydney and Illana walked down the stairs. Zeke whistled quietly and said, "I do admire a woman with nice legs."

"Don't you think their shoes look uncomfortable?" Alex asked.

"You're looking at their shoes? Are you gay? Look higher," Zeke said, incapable of tearing his eyes away from Sydney's legs.

"Just because I look at their shoes doesn't make me gay, I look at other parts too," Alex said in an undertone as the two women approached them. Illana's sultry smile made Alex unable to formulate a sentence. Zeke looked sardonically at Alex and said to the women, "Ladies, your carriage awaits. Let's go drink some beer and listen to the blues."

The Cranberry Festival was being held on the county grounds on the other side of town. The two couples picked their way through the crowd and found some chairs just to the right of the stage. While a local band was setting up their gear, Alex excused himself to go get drinks for everyone. Fall had come early to the north woods, and the leaves were starting to change from green to gold, red, and orange. The crisp evening air blew gently on Sydney's skin making her glad she had brought a sweatshirt for later. Alex came back carrying the four drinks in a box and Zeke jumped up to help him pass them around. Everyone had beer, except for Illana who had a Malibu and Coke. Alex said he had tried to get her a Purple Hooter, but the bartenders here had no idea how to make it either.

The roadies were doing a sound test while people migrated to their seats. The stage sat at the end of a field surrounded by tall birch and poplar trees that swayed in the evening breeze. Brown metal chairs formed crescent rows in front of the stage, affording the crowd a better view of the bands. The aroma of cigarette and pot smoke were tempered by the scent of cranberries wafting from the assorted booths encircling the seating area. One could buy everything from cranberry cookies to cranberry wine.

Sydney lingered by the candle booth when they walked in. Slim tapers lay in weathered wooden boxes, while their squat counterparts stood in a row on low shelving just behind them. The candles she wanted were the braided beeswax tapers, sold by the pair in white boxes with clear plastic lids. Sydney had traced her finger along one of the boxes and was thinking about buying them when Zeke came back to get her. Later, she promised herself, she would come back and buy them.

The crowd roared to life as the members of the band streamed onstage. People all around them leapt to their feet to dance as the band hammered out a raunchy version of "Mustang Sally." Zeke stood up and asked Sydney if she wanted dance. Not trusting herself, especially with the seductive nature of the song, she said maybe later. Illana didn't have any inhibitions and pulled Sydney up to make her dance. Alex got up but what he was doing wouldn't be considered dancing, at least not in this country, or any other country Sydney had ever visited. Illana smiled and tried to show him some moves. He tried and failed with a self-effacing smile, and shrugged his shoulders. They ended up doing hip bumps while laughing and clapping along with the song. The band launched into some of their own work and after about thirty minutes, the singer was brought a guitar and a stool and the rest of the band left the stage.

"Thanks for coming out tonight, and it's great to be up here! You've no doubt noticed the rest of the band left. They refuse to be on stage for the next song. Something about it being too predictable, but I know several women out there who love it. I'm singing this for you, Annie." Sydney and Illana looked at each other and mouthed "NO WAY!" Zeke bent down to be heard above the crowd.

"That's Annie's ex-boyfriend. He plays this stupid song at every show."

The acoustic guitar sounded mournful and the singer had enough twang in his voice to make it sound like a sad country song:

You've been gone now
Since I don't know when
Just passing the time
'Til you come home again

The house is lonely
No smell of burnt toast
No jelly on the countertop
Don't know which I miss most

I hope you'll be home tomorrow
Along with the sun
I'll wander no more
To you I'll run.

Your side of the bed
Is unwrinkled and cold
Your pillow holding memories
And dreams untold

I hope you'll be home tomorrow
Along with the sun
I'll wander no more
To you I'll run.

The crowd clapped out of respect, except for a couple of enthusiastic fans who screamed and yelled. Sydney and Illana were stunned. For one, it had to be the cheesiest song they had ever heard and the fact it was written for Annie left them both pondering what the guy saw in her that they had missed.

After a couple songs, all of them much better than Annie's song, the band wrapped up and left the stage. During intermission, Sydney was going to go get the candles but got stopped by Stella, who wanted to introduce her family to Sydney. After talking to them for about ten minutes, she headed towards the concession stands when she was stopped by Gina and her boyfriend. The boyfriend, who wore his hair too long in front so he had to keep flipping the black bangs back and had on jeans that were two sizes too big so he was constantly hitching them up, went on and on about how much he knew about computers and how he would have handled this contract better, blah blah blah. Gina kept interrupting him and shooting apologetic looks at Sydney and finally managed to pull him back to their seats when the main attraction came out on stage. Sydney headed back to her chair determined to go back to the candle stand after the show.

The rest of the night was spent listening to great blues that spiraled from uplifting to abject sadness to happy and by the end of the show Sydney felt better than she had since her mom died. It was almost as if her mom had been there and told her it was time to live again. The guilt was gone and she laughed more in this one evening than she had in the past couple of months, and she liked it. As they left the arena area, Sydney let Zeke tuck her arm through his and hugged his arm close as they walked. Sydney noticed with a pang of regret the candle stall was closed. Maybe she would have time to come back tomorrow, but if not, there was always next year. For some reason, she was sure she would be here. Sydney looked up at the sky and whispered, "Thanks Mom."

A breeze caressed her cheek like a feathery kiss.

When they got to the car, Zeke snagged the backseat from Illana, forcing her to sit up front with Alex. This time, Sydney didn't care, and Illana was too caught up in a conversation with Alex to notice or care about Sydney's reaction. Alex was talking about where Illana should go in the Mall of America, and suddenly he said, "Hey, why don't I drive you? I know Sydney is meeting Gina in the morning, and I don't have anything going on tomorrow. This way I can show you around my old campus, if you really want to, and then we can have breakfast at the Mall."

"That would be great! I would love to get a tour of the college. I have to warn you, I can spend hours at a mall, so you'll have to let me know when you're ready to quit. My flight doesn't leave until six-thirty tomorrow night, are you sure you want to do this?" Illana asked. She half turned in her seat to face both Alex and Sydney, who was glaring at her, and tried to tamp down her excitement in case Alex backed out.

"Absolutely, I can't remember the last time I did something this spontaneous. I'll get a room by yours and you can wake me up as early as you want." Alex directed this comment at Sydney.

"Why don't we all go? I'll call Gina and reschedule for later in the day," Sydney suggested, looking pointedly at Illana.

"I really don't think it's necessary for all of us to go Syd. Besides, Gina is counting on you, and this way you won't have to pull an eight hour drive." Illana said through clenched teeth, her eyes narrowed and pinned on Sydney.

"Really, I don't mind and it will give me an excuse to get away for the weekend," Alex said, trying to reassure Sydney, who seemed a little perturbed. He looked at Zeke for help. Zeke was leaning back, arms crossed with a bemused smile on his face.

"Sydney's worried you're going to sleep with her best friend. She has a thing about mixing business and sex." At Zeke's comment, the people in car erupted.

"That's not what I said -"

"I would never take advantage that way -"

"Sydney is *not* my Jiminy Cricket or my mother -"

"Whoa, everyone calm down! Sydney, my brother is too responsible to do such a thing, and even if he wanted to, he won't now. Right?"

"It wouldn't have happened anyway, I was trying to be considerate and I'm a little offended you have such a low opinion of me," Alex said as his hands gripped the wheel tight enough to turn his knuckles white.

"Alex, I'm sorry, I really am. I didn't mean anything by it, honestly. Your brother thinks he knows everything and spoke out of turn," Sydney said, trying to placate Alex then whipped her head at Zeke. "You need to put the spoon down and quit stirring the pot!"

"I sit corrected. I was wrong. Has anyone ever told you that you look like a Viking warrioress when you're mad?"

Sydney closed her eyes and shook her head, then laughed. "No, I can't say anyone has. Thank you, I think. Illana, do you still want to leave tonight? You won't get there until two in the morning, even if you left right away."

"Yes, Miss Priss, I do. I'd rather drive tonight and not have to wake up at the crack of dawn. Alex told me earlier he's a night person, so as long as you don't mind driving tonight, I say we do it." Illana said looking at Alex, refusing to look back at Sydney as they pulled into the hotel parking lot.

"No, I don't mind at all. I'll wait out here while you get your stuff, then after we drop Zeke off, we'll be on our way," Alex smiled; relieved the tension was gone, almost.

"Sydney can take him home, right?" Illana asked as she got out of the car.

"Sure, it's the least I can do. Thanks for driving her, we'll be right back," Sydney said as she got out of the car. She had to practically run to catch up with Illana. Sydney caught the hotel door that Illana threw open and followed her in.

"Now Illana, I know you're mad -"

Illana raised her arm and flicked her hand at Sydney without turning around. Sydney knew this meant to wait until they were in private. This wasn't going to end well.

Neither of them noticed Michelle sitting in the darkened lobby, watching them.

Illana walked in the bathroom and slammed the door. Sydney knocked politely and said, "Will you please let me explain?"

"Leave me the fuck alone!" Illana shouted.

Sydney sat down and waited for the explosion. Illana opened the door, tears streaming down her face as Sydney jumped off the chair. Illana held her hand out to stop her.

"Don't say anything until I'm finished. We've known each other for almost twenty years, and you've never embarrassed me as much as you did tonight. For your information, I wasn't planning on having sex with him because you're right. I shouldn't act on my impulses with someone who hired us; it would make the company look bad. I'm hurt that you didn't trust me, and pissed at Zeke for calling it. You'd better handle that. I really like Alex and I'll never get to spend a day with him again, so yeah, I want to do this. Now, go ahead and grovel," Illana said waving one hand at Sydney while using the other to wipe away her tears.

"I'm really, really sorry. I'll kill Zeke later," Sydney said going for humor, but Illana wasn't ready to smile yet. "You're right, I should've trusted you and not said a word. I'll never make that mistake again." Sydney said as she hugged Illana. After about five seconds Illana hugged her back.

"I'm so mad at you, but I forgive you anyway. Besides, now with me gone, how are you going to stay away from Zeke?"

"I'm not shaving my legs, therefore, I can't sleep with him." Sydney said, looking at Illana as she opened the door. Zeke was standing there, hand raised about to knock on the door. Sydney hung her head, pinched the bridge of her nose and said, "Someone needs to put a cow bell on you."

"Go ahead, and by the way, leg hair has never bothered me when I, ahem, *sleep* with someone," Zeke said to the top of Sydney's head then looked at Illana. "I came up to see if you needed any help with your bags. Alex is using the restroom but he'll be outside in a minute. I also wanted to give Sydney this." He held out a small brown paper bag.

When she stood there staring at it he rolled his eyes and said impatiently, "Open it, it's a gift, not a snake."

Sydney took it and pulled out the very same candles she had admired at the Festival. Zeke cleared his voice at Sydney's shocked expression and said casually, "I saw you looking at them and then you got trapped by Stella and her crew, so I picked them up for you. And they are a gift so don't insult me by asking to pay for them."

Sydney looked at Illana, then back at Zeke. "Thank you. Normally I don't accept gifts from clients, but I'm going to make an exception in this case." She opened the white box and the sweet smell of cranberry filled the air.

"You're welcome," Zeke said as he picked up Illana's heavy suitcase like it was a pillow. He looked over his shoulder at Sydney and with a smile added, "And keep me posted on any other exceptions you're willing to make."

Chapter Nine – Codes and Worms

Sydney stretched lazily as the morning sun peeked in the room. Looking at the clock she saw she had a couple hours until she had to meet with Gina. Yawning, she got out of bed and went into the shower, thinking about last night. Zeke wanted her to stay, he even offered her the guest room Illana used which was the farthest from his bedroom, but she managed to say no. Of course, he did talk her into hanging out with him today to go fishing, since he was appalled she hadn't ever been fishing before. What does one wear to go fishing? Jeans? Boots? Maybe a hat; she made a mental note to stop and see if they had one in that cute little boutique she saw the other day when she walked to the coffee shop.

She stepped out of the shower and wished she would have asked Zeke for a couple of towels to borrow because, as usual, the hotel towels sucked. They were white, rough, and not long enough to wrap around your body and tuck in. Sydney made do, and after drying herself off, got dressed and wrapped her hair in the tiny towel. The phone was ringing as she walked out of the bathroom, and she bounced across the bed to answer it.

"Hello?"

"Good morning," her dad said, "I got your message late last night, I hope I didn't wake you up."

"Nope, I just got out of the shower. I called to let you know I won't be coming home until Wednesday evening. I need to train one of the employees here, so my contract got extended for a couple of days. I told them I had to be back because I had a prior engagement on Thursday."

"If you need to stay longer, do so. Work comes first, I understand that."

"No, family comes first. So don't give away my ticket. Can you pick me up Wednesday? My plane lands at 11:30 at night, if that's too late, Illana can do it."

"No, I'll come get you. How could Illana do it if she's there with you?"

"She left today, since her portion was done. Any word from Jessica?"

"I spoke with her two days ago. Everything is going good for her at Fort Knox, and she said to tell you the gold is still safe. She got a promotion and will be one of the trainers in the Armor School, so she's thrilled."

"Good for her! I wish she wasn't so far away, but I'm glad she's happy," Sydney said as she glanced at the clock. "I'd better get going Dad. I'll call you in a couple days and confirm my flight info with you."

"Sounds good, honey. Don't work too hard."

"I won't, I'm going fishing later today, but first I have to buy a hat."

"You are going fishing? Better get some sunscreen, I'd hate for you to get burned again like you did in San Diego." Graham chuckled at the memory. "Oh, and do have someone take a picture of you with a fishing rod in your hand. I'd love to see it."

"Ha ha, talk to you later." Sydney hung up the phone, smiling as she towel dried her hair.

Sydney got to the coffee shop about nine-thirty so she could chat with Betty before Gina got there. Amelia and Betty were talking as she walked in.

"Good morning! I was just thinking about you. Do you still want to help?" Betty asked as she made Sydney's coffee.

"Absolutely. Did the test results come back?"

"Yes, turns out little Aaron has leukemia. Suzanne will be off work for a while and luckily we have a good hospital here, so he won't be transferred downstate." Betty handed her the coffee in exchange for the proffered money.

"I'm so sorry to hear that. Suzanne must be a wreck. I'm glad he can stay up here. Is there anything I can do to help?" Sydney asked looking from Betty to Amelia.

"Well, since you seem to be an early riser, I was wondering if you would watch my shop for about an hour tomorrow from seven to eight? I'd like to sit with Aaron so Suzanne can go to church. I'll show you how to make the drinks, it's not hard, and on Sundays we don't have a lot of customers anyway, except for Doreen. She's our librarian and just gets black coffee, so she's easy. I'll be back before the after-church rush."

"Sure, I can do it. Do you want me to come a little early so you can show me the ropes?"

"Yeah, if you don't mind, come here about six-thirty and for the rest of your stay, drinks are on the house."

"Oh no, that's not necessary, just a cup of coffee tomorrow would suffice," Sydney said, waving her hand at Betty in dismissal. "What did the doctors say about his recovery?"

"They let him go home for the weekend and are going to start chemotherapy treatments immediately next week. We'll have to see how it goes. In the meantime, we wait and pray, and try to keep Suzanne's spirits up," Amelia said, taking a sip from her coffee as Gina walked in.

"Am I late?" Gina said as she looked at her watch.

"No, I'm early. Did you have fun at the concert last night?"

"No, and I'm so sorry about Kent. He was such a pompous ass to you last night! I don't know what got into him. Hey Betty, can I have a vanilla latte?" Betty nodded and Sydney got up to watch her make it. "I left before the end of the concert since Kent was being such a jerk. I felt bad about going anyway with everything my sister is going through. She told me to go. I ended up spending the night at her house last night so I could help with Aaron." Gina took the to-go cup from Betty who refused to accept payment for it.

"Gina, I'm sorry, I didn't realize Suzanne is your sister. Are you sure you want to do this today? It can wait until Monday. Really, I don't mind," Sydney said. She quietly pondered on what a tightly-knit community this was, and how everyone seemed to be related either by birth or circumstance.

"No, Suzanne told me to go and learn and that's what I plan to do." Gina took a sip of her drink and smiled slyly at Betty. "Plus, it'll really piss Annie off when she comes back from 'vacation'."

Sydney and Gina drove over to the office in Sydney's car, and they spent the morning reviewing some basic Access training from one of Sydney's Access Step-by-Step books. She gave Gina the book and decided to wrap it up for the day when Gina's eyes started glazing over from information overload. After helping Gina lock up, Sydney dropped Gina off at her car in front of the coffee shop. Sydney parked and walked over to the little boutique around the corner and found the cutest little purple fishing hat. It was floppy all the way around and had three little holes, like shoestring holes, in the top. She wore it out of the shop and walked next door to the liquor/bait shop and bought some worms in a little dish, then proudly walked back to the coffee shop. Betty looked up and cocked her head to the side.

"Y'know, not many people could pull off that hat, but I must say you can. Don't you think so, Lucy?"

"Yeah. Bitch. I really want that hat, but it would make me look like a pale Smurf," Lucy said, laughing.

"Thank you, I'll take it as a compliment. I'm so glad you're here. I've been meaning to ask you, what happened to your dog?"

"Which time?" Lucy asked with a snort.

"I think she means the story you were telling us the first day she came in," Betty said with smile.

"Oh, that stupid dog. I swear he will be the death of me. This is what happened. I took him for a leisurely walk in the woods, not that walking with a beagle is ever leisurely, and I bent down to tie my shoe. I tucked the leash under my foot, since I couldn't hold it and tie at the same time, the damn dog caught a whiff of something and tore off like he was on fire, which made me lose my balance and I ended up on my butt. I knew I could no more catch him than I could fly, so I headed home to wait for the stupid pooch to come back." Lucy slurped out of her mug and stood up. Sydney sat back for the show.

"By then, it was about nine in the morning. He will usually wander for a couple of hours and come home. I wasn't worried about him until it was dinner time and still no Buster. I had gone out periodically and called for him, but I know when he gets on the scent of something, he doesn't answer to any call except from the trail. Well, at nine that night I got a little worried so I told Al we had better go drive around on the fire roads and try to find him.

"We go outside on the deck and I was hit by the worst smell I had ever come across. Then I looked down, and there was Buster cowering on the deck, and I almost fell down laughing. Apparently the dumb dog chased a skunk that got him but good. Then, as best as I can figure, he must have bit into a porcupine, because his entire face was covered in quills. Al went and got the scissors and pliers so we could de-quill him while I grabbed some towels. There I am taking turns at cutting and pulling out quills," Lucy made snipping and pulling motions as she talked, her short blonde hair bobbing back and forth, "and puking over the rail from the skunk stench. After that happy job was done, we filled up the outside wash basin with tomato juice and gave him four baths in it, which of course, he wanted no part of. Buster would jump out and one of us would grab him," Lucy bent over acting like she was trying to grab the dog as it ran between her legs, "and then the poor thing would cry because we would've touched one of the quill punctures. Finally, after about two hours of this, we got him clean, although we didn't let him back in the house for a couple of days. Hell, I think I smelled like skunk for a week, but I have some nice quills for beadwork this year!" Sydney clapped her hands at the story, just as Zeke walked in.

"Thank you, I'll be here all week," Lucy said as she sat down.

"Oh, I thought the applause was for me. Nice hat," Zeke said, hooking his thumbs in his belt loops.

"Please, don't start getting a huge ego just because someone has a crush on you," Betty said, with a sideways glance at Sydney, who turned beet red. "And quit looking at her like that, you two are in public you know."

"Like what?" Zeke asked, trying to look innocent.

"You know like what, Zeke Abraham Greyson. Take your coffee and sit over there," Betty said, pointing to the other end of the room away from Sydney. Lucy looked at Sydney, winked and fanned her face.

"Hmmm, let me guess, a new fishing hat, Zeke's wearing tennis shoes and a cowboy hat, you two must be going fishing," Betty deduced.

"Right you are, but what else is new?" Zeke asked as he leaned the chair back on two legs. "So, are you ready to go?"

"Can I wear sandals to fish in?" Sydney asked, looking at her flat, strappy shoes.

"Sure, as long as they can get wet. You've really never gone fishing before?" Zeke asked.

"Nope, never in my life, this will be a first," Suddenly remembering what she got, she looked in her purse. "Oh, and I bought us some worms. The guy asked what we were fishing for, so I told him, duh – fish, and he sold me some big worms in a plastic dish," Sydney said, and then looked surprised when all the women started laughing.

Zeke merely chuckled and said, "He meant what type of fish are we fishing for. The answer is Muskie, so worms won't do us any good, unless they are at the bottom of a tequila bottle. On second thought, maybe we can try to catch some Perch too, so the worms don't go to waste."

"Oh, well, it didn't occur to me to think of the type of fish, guess I'd better stick with computer codes. Boy, do I have a lot to learn." Sydney was pink with embarrassment as she stood up, waved goodbye and walked towards the door.

"True, but you're damn funny in the meantime," Zeke said as she walked out. He waited for the door to close then turned to Betty and asked, "See why I want to keep her?"

As she laid her hand on his arm, Betty looked up at him and nodded. "Yes, and we all hope you get to."

Chapter Ten – Here Fishy, Fishy

They rode in his car and thankfully arrived at his house in one piece. It was touch and go on some of the turns since the music was cranked and Zeke was singing and driving like a madman. Sydney sung her heart out too, mainly because she thought it might be the last thing she ever did.

Zeke carried the cooler while Sydney carried her purse and the worms down to the boat tied to his covered dock. It was just a little aluminum fishing boat but it looked like it had a big motor. Zeke set the cooler in the back of the boat, and grabbed four fishing rods and a tackle box from the little boat house that was built over most of the dock. Sydney was standing there, worm dish in hand, and feeling totally out of place. Zeke must have sensed it, or seen her face go white, because he put the rods and tackle box in the boat and walked over to her.

"Quit worrying. It's just fishing, not brain surgery."

"Maybe we should just fish off the dock," Sydney said as she white-knuckled her purse.

"Haven't you ever been in a boat?"

"Not this small. I've taken the ferry to San Francisco, but that's the extent of it. Oh, and I went on a houseboat on Lake Shasta once. What do I do if it tips over? Do you have a life vest for me?" Sydney was backing away from the dock as she spoke, and Zeke finally grappled her hand off her purse, put it on a shelf, and pulled her towards the dock.

"Of course I have a life vest for you. Relax, I've been fishing since I was a kid and I've never tipped over a boat," Zeke said as they walked onto the dock. "But if you're too scared to do this, we can do something else. In fact, I can think of several other things we can do." Sydney, now flustered, grabbed her hand away before it started to sweat.

"I'm not scared, who said I was scared? It just looks tippy and I don't want to get my new hat wet."

"My mistake, I'm sorry. Here, let me help you in," Zeke said, trying not to laugh.

"I can get in all by myself," Sydney said as she handed him the worms and gingerly stepped in the boat. The boat gently rocked and Sydney quickly sat down. "See? No problem. Scared…ha." Her face was now going from white to red, and Zeke took it as a good sign.

"Again, I was wrong." Zeke stepped in and purposefully rocked the boat, while Sydney gripped the seat and tried to look nonchalant. He stepped over the middle seat and sat in the back by the motor. Using the oars to push away from the dock and after getting out of the weeds, he pulled the cord on the engine which roared to life and they sped off towards the island. Sydney was still facing him when he yelled over the roar of the motor, "I know I'll regret telling you this, because I really like the view, but your chair will turn around so you can face forward. Or, you can stay put and spend the day looking at me." She used her feet to spin slowly around, and then promptly forgot to be scared.

The trees were in full autumn regalia. Gold, red, orange, and yellow leaves danced on the breeze. An eagle, maybe the same one from the other day, glided above the lake in a circle riding the thermals. The lake was slightly choppy and the crest of the waves winked in the sun. The water looked blue-gray in the distance and as she looked down she was amazed at how clear it really was. They were almost in the middle of the lake by the island when Zeke cut the engine and the nose of the boat lowered to rest on the water.

"We'll row the rest of the way in," Zeke said as he climbed into the middle seat.

"So, we're sneaking up on the fish?" Sydney asked sarcastically in a stage whisper.

"No, smartass, we just won't be scaring them off with the sound of the boat." Zeke said, shaking his head and smiling at her. He rowed for a few minutes until they were close enough to see what look like an old fort on the island, and a huge nest high up in a dead tree. Setting the oars back in the boat, he grabbed two of the fishing rods and opened his tackle box. Sydney peered inside and saw pliers, scissors and was fascinated by the myriad of different lures. Some were rubber worms, while others were shiny, sparkly metal and some even had what looked like feathers. Feathers? Much to her surprise, those were the lures he picked along with a couple of wires that had a loop on one end and a metal ball on the other.

"This wire is called a leader, you put it on the end of your fishing line then attach the lure to it so the Muskie doesn't bite your line in half," Zeke said holding up the wire, then he held up the feather lure.

"These fish have teeth?" Sydney asked.

"Yes, and they're pretty sharp too," Zeke smiled, but swallowed his laughter. Holding up a lure he continued his instruction. "These are called Bucktails, and I prefer these over the Jerkbait lures my dad likes to use. He has caught more, but mine have all been bigger," Zeke said as put the leader and lures on both rods.

"I'll bet you never let him forget it either," she said with a smile.

"Nope. Now watch me cast and then you can try." Zeke pulled the rod back then swung it forward and released the line, flicking his wrist just before the line went into the water. "Try to do it just like that, but don't worry, no one is perfect their first day out."

Sydney assessed her rod, checked the release button on the reel and prayed she wouldn't embarrass herself.

"Pick a spot where you'd like the lure to drop and aim for it, but don't get too close to the shallows by the island or you'll snag your line. Oh, and try to drop it so our lines make a V in the water," Zeke said as he was slowing reeling his line in.

Sure, I'll just aim and it'll drop right there, no pressure, Sydney thought. Zeke wasn't watching her, just his line, so she pulled her arm back and swung it forward, forgetting to push the release. She quickly looked over at Zeke who was still intently staring in to the water. Taking a deep breath, she tried again and this time the line sailed about twenty or so feet out into the lake. "I did it! Did you see that? Oh, now that was pretty! You gotta admit that was pretty," Sydney said with a huge smile on her face.

"Yes, it was; much better than the first one."

"Oh, I didn't think you saw that," Sydney said, frowning and a little embarrassed but still proud.

"I didn't want to make you nervous. The last one was a nice cast though. Now, when you reel in the line, jerk the rod up a little after about every five turns on the reel. You want to make your Bucktail look like it's swimming, because fish don't usually swim in a straight line or at the same speed." Zeke demonstrated the technique and

Sydney copied as best as she could. Soon they were both casting again, and Sydney's line dropped just a little to the left of where she had been aiming. After doing this a couple of times, she became a little bit cocky and chided herself for being so nervous. This wasn't hard!

She decided to try to arc her arm to the right a little like Zeke was doing when he cast. It couldn't be much harder than the simple cast she had mastered. So, she left the line a little long, just like Zeke's was, and swung her arm out to the right behind her, raising her hand to shoulder level. As she followed through she hit the release button too soon and the lure went flying towards Zeke, who ducked, and the hook came back around in a circle when she jerked the rod, and landed in her hair along with the rest of the line. She didn't feel so cocky covered in wet fishing line as she did a couple moments ago. Zeke was trying his best not to laugh, and since she looked so pitiful, he bit his lower lip instead.

"Let me help you. You might want to stick with the cast I showed you until you've fished for a couple of hours." Zeke stood up and put his rod in the fishing rod holder attached to the gunwale of the boat and started untangling the fishing line that was draped over Sydney like ropes of mini-pearls. She stood, staring at her feet and feeling like a small child as he unwound the line from her hat, hair and shoulders.

"I feel like an idiot."

"Don't, we've all done it. Just not with as much style," Zeke said with a half-smile as he pulled the last of the line from her hair and dropped it onto the floor of the boat. She looked up at him with sad eyes and he cupped her chin with his hand. He widened his stance to steady the boat as he leaned in to kiss her. He wrapped his other arm around her waist to pull her close and picked her up off her toes. The tension that had been building all week broke and he hungrily kissed her, nibbling at her lips and burying his fingers in the hair of the base of her neck, tugging gently to move her head right where he wanted it. She was pressed tightly against him, her arms around his neck after sending the fishing rod clattering down in the boat and returned the kiss with equal fervor.

Suddenly, Zeke's line started making a zipping sound. Sydney heard it first and tried to break away and said, "It's getting away," while Zeke was kissing down her neck.

"I won't let us."

"Not us, the fish! There's fish on your line!" she said breathlessly. He stopped kissing her neck and turned his head to the side finally hearing his line going out.

"Holy shit, we have a live one!" He put her down and grabbed the rod.

"Wow, thanks. I've never gotten that reaction before," Sydney said, trying to get her pulse rate under control. Zeke yanked up on the rod and was rapidly reeling in the line. He looked at her, with bright eyes and lips that were slightly swollen and said, "Bad timing, sorry about that. Next time I kiss you, I'll make sure there won't be any interruptions. Grab the net, will you?" He asked nodding towards the front of the boat. Sydney's knees almost buckled as she turned around to get the net. As she turned back around, she heard a huge SPLASH as the largest fish she had ever seen flipped over backwards out of the water.

"Hurry, and put the net in the water halfway and I'll lead it into the net. When it gets all the way in the net, just lift it a little and I'll do the rest."

Heart pumping with adrenaline, she leaned over the side of boat on her knees gripping the net with both hands. With care, Zeke carefully led the muskie into the net. She barely began to lift the net when the fish realized it was trapped and started to thrash violently, rolling over and over, making it a struggle now between woman and fish. The muskie had to be about four feet long and seemed to weigh at least a hundred pounds. Zeke stepped over to help her, lifting the fish-filled net from the water with some effort and a smile as bright as any clear morning sunrise. In all the excitement, neither of them noticed the storm clouds rolling in until the rain poured down on top of them.

Zeke left the muskie in the net and set it on the floor of the boat, cut the line and started the engine. Sydney snatched her hat off her head and stuffed it under her shirt.

"Why did you do that?" Zeke asked yelling over the combined noise of the rain and boat.

"I told you, I don't want to get my new hat wet!"

"Why?"

"It'll ruin it!"

"What? No it won't!" He said incredulously.

"Maybe not, but I don't want to chance it. Hurry up, my shirt is getting soaked!"

"I'm going as fast as we can. Why in the hell would you buy a hat that can't get wet?"

"It's pretty! Does everything have to be useful?"

"Not everything, but fishing hats usually are!" Zeke yelled, nosing the boat towards his house. A few minutes later he cut the motor and it glided into the boat house. The rain was beating on the wooden roof, and several leaks allowed the rain to come streaming in. Sydney got out of the boat and stood where it was dry.

"Is there anything I can do to help?" Sydney asked, pulling her hat out and setting it on a dry pylon.

"Yeah, take these rods and lean them inside the doorway and set the tackle box next to them," Zeke said, handing her the aforementioned items. Turning, one of rods flicked the hat off the pylon and luckily Zeke caught it just before it landed in the water. Curious, he peered inside and looked at the tag and read out loud, "Hand wash in cold water, dry on low heat." Sydney, grateful to him for catching it, put the fishing gear away, walked back to him and held out her hand for the hat.

"Next time, I think you can leave your hat on, but your hair does look pretty when it's all curly and wet," Zeke said giving her the hat and hauling the net onto the dock. The fish was still twisting with the hook in its mouth so Zeke grabbed the pliers from the tackle box and asked her to hold the fish so he could get the hook out.

"You're kidding, right?"

"No I'm not kidding, how else am I going to get it out?" Zeke stopped and looked at her with a grin. "Don't tell me you're afraid of a fish?"

"A little, look at the size of its teeth. Plus it's all slimy and euww," she said, wrinkling her nose.

"All I need is for you to kneel down and hold it still while I pull the hook. Then, we have to get this baby over to the taxidermy shop."

"You're going to stuff the fish? You mean we aren't eating it?"

"Of course we'll eat it! My buddy, Fuzzy, is a taxidermist, so as soon as we bag this big guy up, we'll drive over there and drop him off."

"Fuzzy the taxidermist? You're making that up," Sydney said, putting a hand on her hip.

"No, really that's his name, not his real name of course, but that's what everyone calls him. Come to think of it, I don't even know his real name. Are you going to help me or not?" The fish was still flopping, but not as much.

"Can't you kill it first? That doesn't look very humane," Sydney said, furrowing her brow.

Zeke rolled his eyes and threw his hands up in the air and asked, "How exactly do you want me to kill it?"

"I don't know, you're the fisherman, don't you know how?"

"Yes, and I'm doing it. Now, come here and hold it and quit stalling."

Sydney put her hat on a dry part of dock and walked over to the fish. Squatting down, she put both hands on the fish while rearing her head away from it. It was slimy, just like she expected. The fish was also surprisingly compact, for some reason she thought it would feel squishy, but it didn't. Zeke ignored her and, using the pliers, quickly got the hook out.

"You stay here while I go get a garbage bag," Zeke said, jumping to his feet.

"Alone, with the dying fish?"

"Oh for God's sake, fine, go in the kitchen and grab a bag from under the sink. The heavy duty black ones."

"No, it's okay, I'll be fine, go ahead and get it. Stripey and I will be just fine."

"You can't name something we are going to eat and hang on my wall," Zeke said as he walked away.

"Sure I can, isn't that right Stripey? I'm sorry we caught you. Maybe I ought to put you back."

"Don't you dare put that fish back in the water! It's a trophy fish! I've got your hat as ransom," Zeke yelled from the deck.

Sure enough, her hat was gone. The fish wasn't flopping around anymore and Zeke was back before she could figure out a way to push it off and make it look accidental. She held the bag as he wrestled it inside and together they carried it to his truck and laid it in the back.

Ten minutes later they pulled onto a gravel driveway and parked in front of a rundown looking house that had "Fuzzy's Taxidermy" painted on it. As Sydney got out of the truck she shook her head, thinking if someone had told her two weeks ago she'd be driving down a gravel road to go see a guy named "Fuzzy" to taxidermy a trophy fish, she would've laughed her ass off at them. They got the fish out and by the time they got to the door a large man with a bushy beard and curly brown hair was holding the door open.

"What didja bring me this time?"

"We caught a good sized muskie, I'll need the meat sooner rather than later if you can," Zeke said as he and Sydney followed Fuzzy into the house. They set the bag up on the white counter that had a long ruler glued to the top of it.

"Let's see what you got," Fuzzy said as he and Zeke pulled the fish out of the bag. They laid it next to the ruler. "Pretty good, fifty inches even. Not the biggest one I ever seen but it ain't the smallest one neither."

"That's not the biggest one? It's huge!" Sydney exclaimed.

"Well now darlin' if you think that's huge you should see my -" Fuzzy said with a leer.

"Fish hanging in the other room, come look," Zeke said quickly to cut him off. He led her into another room where the walls were covered in dead things. She took a step back and tried to maintain control over her stomach. It was a close one.

Deer and moose heads and a wide assortment of fish covered two walls, but some of the dead animals were whole and standing around the room. There were raccoons, a wolf, a beaver and a fox. One week ago, she was freaked out by one dead thing on a wall, now standing in a menagerie of dead animals, all she noticed was the dust collecting on a muskrat's tail. Okay, her stomach was gurgling a little, but she was steady. Zeke walked over to one of the big fish and said, "This is a fifty-four inch muskie. Fuzzy caught this about seven years ago and still has the local title for catching the biggest one."

"Ours is prettier," she said.

"True, let's see if he'll take a picture of us with it."

"Why?"

"Because it'll be something to remember me by," Zeke said walking past her. She stood rooted to the spot. Until now, she hadn't really thought of the fact she probably wouldn't have any reason to come back here. Standing amongst the dead menagerie she prayed she would somehow find a way to come back. Sure, she missed her dad, but not much else.

"Sydney, are you coming? Fuzzy will take the picture but it would help if you're in it," Zeke said, calling to her from the other room. She walked back in and noticed a beige wall that was free of dead things that they could stand against. They picked up the muskie and stood in front of the wall while Fuzzy took a picture of them with a professional Nikon.

"Say, here, fishy, fishy!" Fuzzy said, and as Sydney and Zeke looked at each other and laughed, he snapped the picture.

Chapter Eleven – Never Judge a Woman by her Harley

A buzzing sound brought Sydney to consciousness, and she reached over and shut the annoying alarm off. It was a little after five in the morning and she decided she was too comfortable to get up just yet. She thought about yesterday and replayed in her mind the way Zeke kissed her. After they left Fuzzy's, they went out to a late lunch then for a walk around Fawn Lake. He didn't try to kiss her again, and she wondered why. After having pizza at Mama Mia's, he dropped her off at the hotel. He didn't get out of the car or invite her to his place. It made her wonder what he was up to now. Smiling at the thought, she flipped back the covers and started her day.

Sydney walked down the stairs into the hotel lobby and gave Michelle a Miss America smile and wave. It was answered by a death-ray glare. Sydney narrowed her eyes right back at her, while wearing a smarmy grin as she walked out in the brisk but glorious morning. The birds were chirping and the river meandered by the low lying tree branches on its banks. Sydney crossed her arms and picked up her pace in an effort to generate some warmth. Crossing the street she noticed how few cars were on the road at six in the morning, and thought about how busy the freeways back home would be by now, even on a Sunday morning. An elderly gentleman walking his wiener dog tipped his tweed hat and said, "Fine morning this morning!" as the pair walked by. There's another thing that doesn't happen very often in Sacramento, she thought. People tended to stay to themselves and not greet strangers in such an affable way. Some people would offer up a polite smile and perhaps nod their head at you, but that was about it. Oh, Sydney thought, I'm going to miss this!

Sydney rounded the corner and whistled at the most beautiful motorcycle she had ever seen. It was a purple Harley, with tons of chrome and saddle bags dripping in fringe. Looking at the bike, she thought about trading Zeke in if the owner of this bike was half as good looking as Zeke. It was parked right in front of the coffee shop, so she quickened her pace again and was surprised to see only Betty and a very pretty and well-dressed woman in her forties sitting in the shop.

The bell on the door jingled, announcing Sydney's arrival. Betty had her hands submerged in soapy water in the sink and half turned around to see who it was. Her eyes brightened with her easy smile as she greeted Sydney.

"Early as usual I see. Give me a minute and I'll show you how to make your drink first, then we'll move on to something a little more challenging – a cappuccino," Betty said while rinsing the soap off the mugs in the sink. "I usually do this at night, but yesterday was pretty hectic and I wanted to get home. I was hoping a shop elf would come in and do the dishes for me, but he must have stolen some socks from the shoe store next door."

"A house, or shop, elf wouldn't steal socks, they have to be presented. What kind of Harry Potter fan are you?"

"One who stayed up for the midnight sale and actually remembered there was a new book," she said, tossing the sarcasm gauntlet right back, while drying off her hands.

"Yeah, yeah, yeah, you win," Sydney conceded. "I'm ready to learn and need coffee, not necessarily in that order."

"By the time I'm done with you'll be ready for the national competition of barista's in Vegas. Here's an apron, prepare to get a little dirty."

The next thirty minutes Sydney learned the difference between a latte and brevé mocha. After Betty was convinced Sydney could be trusted not to blow up her machine, she made her an Americano and introduced her to the pretty woman who had been reading the paper.

"Hey Doreen, can I tear you away from the Times Book Review for a minute? This is Sydney, the girl from California I told you about. Sydney, meet our town librarian and proud owner of the Harley," Betty said with a triumphant grin at Sydney's shocked look.

"It's nice to meet you. Is that your bike out there?" Sydney asked as Doreen stretched to her full height of five-eleven and shook her hand.

"Yes. I bought it with some of my grandpa's iron mine money. It seemed fitting," Doreen looked her up and down and turning to Betty said, "She'll fit in nicely, just like you said. Betty, make me vanilla latte, will you?" Turning to Sydney she said, "Sometimes I have to have a little more taste in my coffee. Would you like to take a better look at my hog?"

The woman's words did not match her appearance. Doreen had short salt and pepper hair and was dressed in a very becoming blue pantsuit, with suede pumps the same color as the suit. She had a diamond bracelet on one arm, a gold wedding band with at least a two carat diamond, and on the other wrist there was a dainty gold watch. Her hazel eyes appeared wise and amused.

"I'd love to, but what do you mean about me fitting in nicely?"

"Never mind that now, here, after you," Doreen said holding the door open. Betty came out a few minutes later to say she had to leave soon. Sydney suddenly remembered why she was there and rushed back in the shop, leaving Doreen chuckling behind her. Betty grabbed her purse and said, "Don't break anything," and walked out the door.

Doreen took her freshly made latte off the counter, cocked her head to the side and asked Sydney, "So, you do like it here, don't you?"

"Yes, very much. Earlier I was thinking about how much I'm going to miss it. I know Alex can't extend my contract indefinitely, and I have to get back to my dad."

"What if you had a chance to come back permanently? Would you?"

"I don't know. I'd really have to think about it, but other than my dad and my friend Illana, I'm not really tied to Sacramento. Why do you ask?"

"Just curious. So tell me, what besides your friend and your father do you love about Sacramento?"

"Well, I really like the variety of cuisine. I could have Mexican one night, French the next, Italian another. Really, I could probably go a couple weeks without eating American food. I really wouldn't miss all the beige or dark beige houses, that's all there are anymore. Oh, and the traffic really sucks. But I would miss fences."

"Fences?"

"Yeah, it's one of the first things I noticed here, how no one has a fence. I wouldn't like the lack of privacy."

"Hmm, it's interesting you think you have more privacy there than you would here."

"I guess in Sacramento, I'm pretty autonomous. I've noticed everyone around here knows everyone else, or at least knows their business."

"True, but it keeps us honest, and there's hardly any crime to speak of, let alone traffic." Doreen said, putting down the now empty cup. "Well, thanks for taking the time to chat, but it's time for me to go to church, I'll see you after the service is over."

Alone in the shop, Sydney daydreamed about being able to stay in Ruby Lake. She could even revert back to the clerical field if necessary, and move in with Zeke, and...

What was she thinking? She couldn't leave her dad and Illana! Her dad needed her, didn't he? Illana had been her best friend for almost twenty years, and that type of friendship wasn't something that came along every day. No, she was being ridiculous. Wasn't she? She was saved from more contradictory musing by a couple who came in requesting dry cappuccinos. She needed all her attention on the task at hand, because those took some skill. And after her fourth try, she finally nailed it.

Betty sailed in just as the first church goers started to arrive. "Oh, I'm so sorry I'm late! We were all talking and making Aaron laugh and I lost track of time. Here, let me get that," she said as she tied her apron on.

"That's okay, I got this," Sydney said, making circles of whipped cream on the top of a mocha. She handed the man his drink, rang it up and put his money in the till. Betty took all the money out of the tip jar and shoved it in Sydney's back pocket.

"Here's some walking around money. Looks like you did a great job and I really appreciate you doing this for me. Want to give up your life in the city and come and work for me?" Betty said, only half-kidding.

"Don't tempt me," Sydney said wryly. "Actually, this has been really fun, but I think I'm more suited to codes than coffee. I'm here until Wednesday, so if you want me to cover for you any time before then, let me know," she said, taking off the apron and hanging it on the coat rack by the mugs.

"I'll keep you posted. Right now the concern is paying for his treatment. He'll get the treatment regardless of course, but Suzanne is starting to stress about the money."

"Where's Aaron's father? I hope I'm not being too nosy by asking."

"Honey, around here there is no such thing as too nosy. Aaron's dad, Billy, died in a car accident. He went out to get diapers late at night and was side-swiped by a drunk driver, who didn't get a scratch. Billy died instantly, it was terrible. Aaron was only three months old when it happened and now with this, well, my heart just goes out to Suzanne." Betty teared up and quickly turned around to grab a tissue.

"How awful! I can't imagine going through something like that. How did she manage?" Sydney asked as she sat on the couch.

"Her parents had her and the baby move in with them for a time, but Suzanne pulled herself together after a couple of months and decided Billy's legacy wasn't going to include her becoming weepy and depressed. She had his son to raise and she knows Billy's watching over them and wants to make him proud. Plus, she has us," Betty tried to smile, and then it became real as the next customer walked in. "You're up early. Don't tell me you actually went to church with your parents?"

"Yeah, I had nothing better to do, so I made my mom's day. They'll be along in a minute; you know how my mom is. She has to talk to everyone so as not to slight anyone," Zeke said as he sat down on Sydney's left and held her hand. Betty acted like it was an everyday occurrence, but unfortunately Sydney did not have a poker face. Instead, it went beet red and she was afraid she would start giggling like a little girl who was given her favorite toy. She gently tried to get her hand back, but Zeke held on a little tighter. Sydney was flummoxed by all the different emotions coursing through her. Before she could start identifying them, his parents walked in.

Sydney's first thought was to grab her hand away, but instead, she decided it felt right, and she was too content to make an issue out of it. Zeke stood up, pulling Sydney up with him.

"Mom, this is Sydney, Sydney this is my mom, Grace," Zeke said smiling at the petite, blonde woman who was wearing a beige pantsuit. Annie looked just like her, except Grace had a beautiful smile, and from the faint lines in her face, she wore it often.

"I've heard so much about you and it's a pleasure to finally meet you," Grace said as she shook Sydney's right hand in both of hers.

"It's nice to meet you as well. Hello, Mr. Greyson, nice to see you again."

"I told you last time, it's Harry. Betty, can you get me a cup of coffee and whatever the frothy thing is that Gracie likes?" At Betty's nod in the affirmative, he turned back to Sydney. "So, have you heard from you father recently? Did you tell him I handled the situation?"

"Harry, quit grilling her, she's not one of your employees," Grace said looking up at Harry. Turning her attention back to the woman who was holding her youngest sons' hand she said, "Now, every Sunday there's a command performance dinner at our house, and I would be delighted if you would come."

"Mom, not tonight, we have plans. Plus, I don't think it would be wise with the whole Annie deal going on right now," Zeke said.

"What Annie deal?" Harry asked, his voice booming causing everyone to look their way.

"I'll tell you in the car," Grace said between clenched teeth, and then turned back to Sydney. "You'll have to make it some other time then. Thank you Betty, you do make the best caps. Nice meeting you Sydney, I'm sure we'll see you again." Grace turned around and linking arms with Harry, dragged him out to their car.

Sydney watched them go and wished she could be as sure she would have the chance see them again.

"Betty, I'll have a triple mocha," Zeke said wiping his brow, but still holding on to Sydney.

"Sure thing, on the double," Betty replied, tickled by her joke. Unfortunately, the other people in the room didn't find it as amusing as she did. Zeke had to let go of Sydney's hand to pull out his wallet and pay for his drink. She sat back down and with a quizzical look asked him, "So, what are these plans we have tonight? Or was it just a cover to save me from your sister?"

"A surprise you'll have to wait and find out about and yes I was saving you from my sister. Are you busy tonight?" Zeke asked as he sat back down and hooked his boot under her ankles so her calves were resting on his shins.

"I was planning on getting my hair and toenails done, but I guess it can wait," Sydney said smiling as she took a sip of coffee.

"I hate to get in the way of personal grooming but I promise it'll be worth it. You might want to pack an overnight bag, this could take a while." At that statement, he drained his cup, set it on the little wicker table, grabbed her cup she was holding and set it down too. "Be ready by four," Zeke said as he laced his fingers through her hair, pulled her towards him and kissed her gently and chastely on the lips. "See you later."

Before Sydney could formulate a coherent sentence he was walking out just as Doreen walked in. Doreen looked at Sydney's stunned, flushed face and caught Betty's amused look. "You just missed Harry and Grace," Betty said to Doreen.

"I'm glad I didn't miss that declaration of territory. If I would have known I could've gotten coffee and a show, I would've skipped church!"

Chapter Twelve – Jumping to Conclusions

Sydney was ready. She had showered, done her hair, shaved her legs, painted her toenails and fingernails and even used an eyelash curler. Her curly hair actually responded correctly to a new product she tried and wasn't the least bit frizzy. Illana would be so proud. Unfortunately, it was only one-thirty. After straightening up her hotel room, she called to check on Illana.

Illana was laughing as she answered her phone, "Hey, do you have big news or are you bored?"

"Why does it have to be one or the other?"

"Because those are the only two reasons you have for making a phone call, hold on Syd," Illana said as she said, "Yeah, that's fine, I'll be right here. Okay, I'm back, Alex went to use the facilities. This has been such a fun day! We even rode the Merry-Go-Round and now we're eating at The Rainforest Café, and it's the coolest place ever! And before you ask, no, I didn't have sex with him."

"I wasn't going to ask, and I'm glad you're having a great time. Zeke planned a surprise evening out for me for tonight and won't give me any details except to pack an overnight bag,"

"We both know how much you like surprises," Illana said drolly. "Did you shave your legs?"

"Um,"

"Don't you dare! If I can't, you can't! Listen, I gotta go, Alex is headed back, the man is quick. I'll call you tomorrow."

The phone went dead in her hand and as she hung up, she looked around the room for something to do. Instead of packing her bag, she grabbed the Harry Potter book from the table and was instantly transported to an alternate world.

The knock on her door made her jump off the bed. She glanced at the clock and noticed it was three-fifty. Walking by the mirror, she noticed her hair was rumpled and her makeup was smudged. Great. "Just a minute!" she yelled as she fluffed her hair and ran a fingertip around her eyes to remove the wayward eyeliner. She turned and yanked the door open and was surprised to see Michelle. "Can I help you?"

"Why are you still here? I thought you were supposed to leave yesterday?" Michelle asked, taking a step inside the room

"It's really none of your business, and I believe my office called to extend my stay until Wednesday morning, which you very well know." Sydney folded her arms and blocked her from entering any further. Michelle's mouth was unusually devoid of lipstick and her fingernails were chewed down to the quick.

"Zeke is mine, and I won't let you waltz in here and steal him," Michelle said.

"I believe you lost him a year ago after sleeping with his best friend," Sydney said stepping closer to Michelle, who backed up slightly. Michelle was at least four inches taller but without any muscle. She had delicate features and Sydney knew she could snap Michelle in half, especially now the long, talon-like fingernails were gone. "This conversation is over. Zeke is not a possession, he is a kind, thoughtful, gorgeous and complex man and I'm so glad he saw you for the snake you are before it was too late. You didn't deserve him then, and you sure as hell don't deserve him now."

"And you do?"

"Yes, she does," Zeke said. Neither woman heard his approach and Michelle blanched at the sight of him. "Now, if you'll excuse us, we have a date. Sydney, don't forget your overnight bag."

Michelle spun away but Sydney saw the tears forming as she walked away. Zeke followed Sydney inside her room and firmly shut the door.

"You forgot to pack a bag?" Zeke asked as he looked around the tidy room.

"I started reading and completely lost track of time, sorry. It'll just take me a minute. What kind of clothes should I pack?"

"Duh, the kind you wear...sorry, couldn't resist," Zeke stifled a laugh as a deadly glance was thrown his way. "Warm clothes that will also be comfortable."

"Gee, you don't ask for much," Sydney mumbled as she looked in the closet. She picked an oversized sweater and a pair of worn jeans. *That should fit the bill*, she thought.

"Do you have a jacket? You'll want your boots and thick socks if you've got them."

"Just where are we going?" Sydney asked as she hung the coat over her arm, putting socks in her bag and grabbing her boots from the closet. Not really knowing what to expect, she had brought a little of everything, and most items had already been worn once. Well not all. The little black dress was definitely not going to be needed.

"It's a surprise. But before the main event, I thought I would cook for us at my house, unless you'd rather go out?"

"A home cooked meal sounds better right now. I'll take a rain check on the other," Sydney said as she swung her purse over her head and picked up the bag. "I'm ready whenever you are." Zeke smiled as he relieved her of the bag and opened the door.

"Allow me, after all, this is what thoughtful, complex, kind, and gorgeous men do." Zeke was rewarded with a glare and watched Sydney's face turn red. His slow smile told her just how pleased he was.

Zeke stopped off at the butcher to get brats and also picked up some steaks to have later that week. Sydney was sure she had gained five pounds during the past week, but she wasn't complaining, not out loud anyway. They drove over to the gas station and he got out to pump the gas. Sydney jumped out, thinking she could be helpful and washed the windows. There might be rust all over the truck, but at least the windows would be clean. He was headed in the station when she asked, "What are you getting now?"

"Nothing, I have to pay for the gas."

"You can pump it before paying for it? Really? Don't people steal it?"

"You think like a city girl. I've never heard of anyone stealing gas, someone would see them and around here there are only two degrees of separation. You'd have one of the sheriff deputies knocking at your door within twenty minutes. Do you want anything? Soda?"

"No, I'm good, thanks," Sydney replied, thinking what a different world this was from home. She couldn't imagine anyone being this blasé in Sacramento. Everyone she knew locked their car, just to go into the gas station to pay for gas, not to mention in their driveway. But here, everyone seemed very trusting and secure in their safety. She wasn't sure if she had ever felt that safe, until now. How much of that had to do with Zeke, well, she wasn't prepared to analyze that question just yet. She finished the windows and got back in the truck.

He came striding out the door, his jeans just tight enough to outline his muscular thighs and, as he passed her, a really nice ass. The view from the back was less confrontational and it had fueled many a daydream lately. The black T-shirt he had on showed off his broad shoulders and narrow hips, and the arms were stretched out and she could barely see a tattoo peeking out of the bottom. *Hmmm, I'll have to investigate that later*, she thought. She looked up, and knew she was busted.

"If you're done staring, we could go now." See? Confrontational. But the front was still pretty easy on the eyes.

Sydney stood on his deck and marveled at the view. The sunlight coming through the leaves created lace-like patterns on the grass below. Without a breeze, it was still a little chilly, but the slight bite of the autumn air didn't seem to affect Zeke any. Not a goose bump on him. He was intently grilling the brats and she was left still wondering what the surprise was.

"So, what's the plan for the rest of the evening?" she asked.

"Not telling. Nice try though. It's called a surprise for a reason," he said, not looking away from the grill.

"Just trying to make conversation, no need to get prickly about it," she replied, knowing full well it was she who was being prickly.

"Yeah right. I take it you aren't fond of surprises?" he asked, casting a side-long look at her, accompanied by a half-smile, half-smirk.

"Ok, no not really. They drive me crazy. I like to know things, surprises make me edgy."

"I'm sure you'll live, and I promise it'll be worth it. Can you grab the mustard and relish out of the 'fridge?"

"Sure," Sydney said as she went to fetch the needed condiments. As she rummaged for the mustard (why didn't he put it in the door like a normal person?), the phone rang. She considered answering it, but then yelled to get his attention. By then the answering machine kicked on.

"Hello Zeke, this is Mom. I'm a little unhappy you won't be present this evening, but I'll get over it. This Sydney seems to be a definite improvement from the floozies you've dated in the past, but only time will tell. Call me later this week and maybe we can meet for lunch." Zeke walked in during the 'floozies' comment, and put his hands on his hips and pinned his eyes on his ceiling fan.

"I'm sorry. Other than saying "sorry" three hundred more times, I've no idea what else to say to do damage control," Zeke said, throwing his hands up in embarrassment.

"There's no need, its fine. After seeing Michelle, I can sort of understand the comment." Sydney's chest felt tight and she was racking her brain trying to remember what she had said to his mom to give her the wrong impression. "I hope I didn't embarrass you today, did I say something wrong to her?"

"God no, Syd, please don't take it like that. It's not you. I wouldn't put it past her to think you might have heard her on the machine, only to put your guard up. She was there for me before I left on my cross country tour with Tyler and she's still a little over-protective," Zeke walked over and put his hands on her shoulders. "Please tell me this won't ruin our evening. If it will help, I'll call her right now and make her apologize."

"No, honestly, it's not necessary. I'll be fine." Sydney said. "I have just one question though."

"What?"

"Where in the hell did you put the mustard?"

They ate out on the deck and watched the sunset, each lost in their own thoughts. Zeke cleared his throat, looked at Sydney to say something then changed his mind and started collecting the dinner dishes instead. Sydney followed him inside to the kitchen and offered to do the dishes.

"No, I'll do them, you need to change. I don't think your thin sweater is going to cut it."

"I wish you'd tell me what we're doing. You're making me crazy!" she shouted as she walked down the hall to the guest room she had used before.

As the bedroom door closed Zeke replied quietly, "That makes two of us."

Zeke was drying the last of the dishes when Sydney came back. She was now in a snug pair of jeans, hiking boots, a purple tunic sweater, and her gray coat slung over her arm. Most women with red hair couldn't pull off wearing purple, but on Sydney it just looked cute.

"That should do. I'll get my boots on and we'll go."

"Now are you going to tell me where we're going?"

"You'll see when we get there. Can you take the cooler out to the truck? I'll be there in a sec," Zeke asked, pointing to the small blue and white cooler on the floor.

"If this is a clue, I still don't get it," Sydney said with one hand on her hip.

"It's not a clue, its beer and Pepsi," Zeke said, rolling his eyes as he walked away. Sydney picked up the cooler and went out to the truck. She noticed a folded up inflatable mattress in the back and set the cooler beside it. Zeke came out carrying two large quilts and two pillows. He set those in the truck behind the seat as Sydney got in. She was determined not to ask any more questions. That lasted for about one minute.

"So, I take it we're sleeping outside?"

"I wasn't planning on sleeping, but you can if you want. Nice night isn't it?" Zeke said, trying to get her to divert her one track line of questioning.

"You're enjoying this, aren't you?"

"The night? Yes I am. The moon is almost full, I'm with you and there's not a cloud in the sky. You only have about fifteen more minutes of wondering, why don't you relax and look at the scenery?" Zeke asked as he turned on the radio. "Nothing Else Matters" by Metallica was playing and she couldn't help but relate to the song. She liked that she could be herself with Zeke and felt closer to him in the short week she'd known him than she had felt with Sean. Of course, knowing the odds were in her favor that Zeke wouldn't turn out to be gay helped a lot. Also, it didn't seem to matter to him what she wore, and he never made her feel stupid for the things she said. Zeke rolled with whatever she threw at him and still came back for more.

She was jarred out of her silent musings when Zeke turned onto a gravel road that climbed up the side of a hill. When they reached the top, she saw a large clearing with nothing but grass and a pretty, panoramic view of the town below them.

"Where are we?" Sydney asked as Zeke cut the engine.

"My parents own this lot and plan on building a house here next year. They were going to do it this year, but it didn't get cleared in time." As Zeke got out of the truck, Sydney saw a shooting star.

"Did you see that? A shooting star, quick, make a wish!" she asked, jumping out and pointing at the sky.

"That wasn't a shooting star, it was a meteor. That's your surprise. Last night was the peak of the Perseids meteor shower, but tonight should be pretty good too." Zeke hooked up the foot pump to the air mattress and blew it up. Sydney put her coat on and stared at the night sky, touched by Zeke's thoughtfulness.

"Do you want to put the mattress in the back of the truck or on the ground?" Zeke asked.

"Let's put it on the ground over there," Sydney said, pointing towards the middle of the clearing. She got the blankets and pillows as he carried the mattress and cooler. She laid the blanket on top of the mattress and as she lay down Zeke shook the other blanket out and it landed perfectly over her. He climbed under the blanket and they both laid there stiffly staring at the sky, suddenly uncomfortable with each other. Sydney moved her leg so it was resting against his, just as he reached to hold her hand. They both laughed as the tension broke.

"I feel like a teenager," Sydney admitted.

"Me too. I don't like the tension any more now than I did back then," Zeke said as he let go of her hand and slid his arm under her shoulders and pulled her closer. "Much better." Two meteors shot across the sky, signaling their agreement.

"Let's play twenty questions, I'll start." Zeke said. "What's your favorite color?"

"Red."

"Favorite city?"

"I'm not sure anymore, pick a different question," Sydney replied, snuggling her head on his shoulder.

"Fair enough. Who was your best boss?"

"That's a toss-up. John White, who you know, has been the most fun to work for, but without Joe Munso I'd still be in the clerical pool. He was the one who gave me an opportunity to come work for him and arranged to have my I.T. training paid for by his company. Joe was great, I really miss him."

"Did he die?"

"Oh, no. I just never get a chance to see or talk to him anymore. John offered me a job so I haven't seen Joe in years. Is it my turn yet?"

"No, that was only three questions."

"Four actually, counting the 'did he die' one."

"Very funny. Favorite vacation spot?" Zeke asked, poking her in the ribs.

"Easy, Dillon Beach, it's a beach in Northern California, lots of people from Sacramento vacation there. My parents would rent a cabin there for a week every summer. My dad would bring some books and would stay the whole time. We'd climb the cliffs and the trees, go clamming, get up early and check out the tidal pools at low tide, then in the afternoon we'd go body surfing and dune diving."

"What's dune diving?"

"Jessica, that's my older sister, and I would climb to the top of the tallest sand dune and then we would run and dive off the drop-offs. Some were pretty deep, twenty feet or so, and it's amazing neither of us every got hurt. The sand was so soft we would just sink in. I still go camping there whenever I can get away. I'd love to show it to you, it's everything a beach should be, without any of the touristy crap to deal with. Do you like the ocean?"

"Yeah, I do. I spent some time down in Venice Beach in southern California and loved it, for a while. Then, all the people got to me. You see how many people I'm used to dealing with, and down there I felt completely out of place. Tyler stayed, but I came home. I wish you were going to be here longer, I'd take you up to Lake Superior. It looks like the ocean, but it doesn't smell like it. It sure is pretty though."

"What State did you like the best?"

"I thought it was still my turn?" Zeke asked. Sydney poked him in the ribs and he decided he'd answer. "Okay, okay. I have two actually. The first one is eastern Nevada in the morning, because of the stark beauty of the desert. It was so beautiful to ride there early in the morning when the dew was still on the sagebrush. When the sunlight hit it just right, the dew would throw these tiny prisms of light. I tried taking some pictures of it, but never really captured how striking it was. Iowa would be my second favorite, because after going through Nebraska I was thankful to see trees again." Meteors streaked across the sky, one after another. Sydney counted sixteen.

"Wow, that was so frickin' cool!"

"Yeah it was. I'm glad I get to share this with you," Zeke said, kissing the top of her head.

"Thanks for bringing me out here, and sorry I was such a pain in the ass about it."

"You're welcome. If you got this worked up over not knowing something for two days, I can't wait to see what you do at Christmas time."

"I go crazy. I have to shake the presents, and that's ended badly a couple of times. Now, my dad won't bring anything out until Christmas Eve, otherwise I drive him nuts," Sydney smiled sheepishly up at Zeke, then laid her head back down. "This will be the second Christmas without my mom. Last year, my dad and I tried to do all the things she did. We baked, made popcorn strings, hung the ornaments and put the Santa town out on the lawn. Maybe this year we can do a little less and start something new," sighing deeply she went on. "Starting new traditions would be a good way to begin the New Year, don't you think?"

Zeke tilted Sydney's chin towards him to look into her eyes. "I'm hoping to start something new this year myself, and I'll admit, I'm really looking forward to it."

Zeke must have dozed off at some point and as he looked down, Sydney was out cold, her hands tucked between her cheek and his chest, her red hair framing her face. Gazing at her lips he remembered how her tongue felt on his skin, how soft her lips felt on his neck. She looked so cute and peaceful he hated to wake her, but it was getting really cold, and he was getting hard. He gently rubbed her back and watched her face as she rose to consciousness.

"What time is it?" she asked, as she sat up and stretched.

"Late, we should be going. Do you want to just stay at my place tonight? You can sleep in the guest bedroom if you'd like."

Yawning, she said, "That would probably be best, I'm too tired to drive." Sydney got up and started folding the blankets and picked up the pillows, totally unaware of how aroused he was. Zeke dragged the mattress and tossed it, still inflated, into the bed of his truck. He dropped the cooler, which they never even opened, on top of it. Sydney climbed in the truck, stowing the bedding behind the seat and looked sleepily at Zeke.

"Do you think anyone would notice if we went to work late tomorrow?"

"Only the entire staff, but I'm game if you are," Zeke said, revving the engine.

Chapter Thirteen - Like a Bad Penny...

Early the next morning, Zeke dropped a still celibate Sydney off at her car and she followed him to work. They pulled in just as Alex was getting out of his car and all three of them looked at the matching Mercedes parked next to Alex's car.

"I'm pretty sure that's not Mom or Dad's car," Zeke surmised as he shut his door.

"Me too. This is really not how I wanted to start my day. Well, this'll be fun," Zeke added sarcastically.

"Do you want some backup?"

"No, thanks for the offer, but I got this," Alex said, straightening to his full height as he strode into the warehouse.

"I take it you think Annie is in there. Should we sell tickets?" Sydney asked.

"No, although we could make a few bucks. God, she's stubborn. Eventually she might come to understand we aren't ten and she'll actually give Alex the respect he deserves," Zeke said, shaking his head while looking at the building. "Had I known this was going to happen, we could've come in late and no one would have ever noticed."

Alex walked into Annie's office unannounced. She whipped around in her chair, her hand at her chest. "You scared me, why didn't you knock?"

"More to the point, why are you here? You are supposed to be off on vacation this week, or did you forget?" Alex asked, crossing his arms over his chest.

Annie rolled her eyes and laughed, "Are you still mad at me? I always forget, you're the sensitive one. I'm sorry I hurt your feelings or ego or whatever. I'm needed here, who else is going to do the payroll and billing? Really, Alex there's no reason to continue to have a tantrum. Now, if you'll excuse me, I have work to do." Annie turned back to her computer, presenting Alex with her back.

Alex walked around the desk and spun her chair around so Annie had to face him, "Don't you dare dismiss me, I'm your boss and until you realize that, there's the door," Alex said, pointing to the door. "If you think I sent you on vacation because I was having a 'tantrum' then our problem is bigger than I thought. I warned you if you came back you wouldn't like the results. You went too far. The fact you can rationalize me being upset by turning it into me having a 'tantrum' tells me you haven't learned a thing. As of right now, you are no longer the office manager. Your entire position is now in jeopardy. We aren't kids anymore Annie, and you need to realize that."

"Please, quit being so dramatic! For God's sake Alex, would you listen to yourself? Is one of your little consultants listening in? Fine, if it's so important to you to put me in my place and look like a man in front of your new lackeys, I'll leave. I'll call Mom and see if she wants to go up to the cabin. Call me when you've come to your senses." Annie got up and slung her small, white purse over her shoulder and walked out.

Alex stood there, stunned. He wondered what had happened to the sister he knew and respected. He knew she could be acerbic with some of the staff, but he had usually taken her side because it was easier. Reaching past the chair, he shut the computer down and remembered he hadn't asked her about deleting the printer drivers. He rushed through the open door of the warehouse and heard her talking to Sydney.

"-you'll see, he won't be able to run this place without me. You're a nobody around here, but I'm not. In two months he won't remember your name and he'll be counting on me again."

"Isn't that song getting a little tired? Maybe you aren't as indispensable as you think you are. Maybe now he sees you for what you are – oh, hey Alex! We were just talking about you," Sydney said as she caught sight of Alex.

"I heard, and just so you know, Annie, I have a contract with Sydney's company for at least three months. Also, you wouldn't know anything about the printer drivers being deleted off the system, would you?"

Annie blinked and looked confused. "What would I know about printer drivers? Why are you asking me this?"

"All of the drivers disappeared last week, and someone had to get in and delete them. Do you know anything about it?

"Oh, I see. It must be me. Of course. You know what Alex? Maybe I will look for somewhere else to work during this 'vacation' where they would appreciate a woman with my talents," Annie said, then turned her venomous look on Sydney. "I hope you're happy about the rift you've caused, and I'll be glad when I hear you're out of my state." Annie marched out and slammed the door.

"Don't take it to heart Sydney. You didn't cause the rift, she did. I did too, I guess. I let her get away with too much for too long. Don't let her take away what you've done for us, I think she might feel threatened by you for some reason."

Sydney wanted to say, *you think?* Instead she said, "Whatever the reason I'm still glad we came here and Annie aside, I'll be a little sad to leave. I'd better go find Gina so we can get started."

Alex watched her go in the office as Zeke came around the corner. "So did you give her the boot?"

"No, why would I fire Sydney?"

Zeke rolled his eyes at his brother, "Not her, idiot. I meant Annie."

"No, not yet, but it was a close thing. Let me ask you something. Has Annie always been this way, and if so, why haven't I seen it?"

"Yes and no. I think having Sydney and Illana here pissed her off because it's the first time since you started this company you made a move without asking her. As long as you let her run the show, she was great to you. I guess that's over now," Zeke said shrugging his shoulders. "I need Wednesday off, so can you reschedule the delivery for Thursday?"

"Sure, where are you going to be?"

"I have a few things I need to do that day that I've been putting off. Is it a problem?"

"No, you've just never asked for a day off before. But yeah, I'll reschedule and see you on Thursday."

"Great, thanks brother," Zeke said as Sydney walked out with Gina. He winked at Sydney as she walked up the stairs, and was rewarded by her cheeks going red. He was really going to miss that, but he hoped it wouldn't be for long.

Sydney spent the entire day and the next with Gina, only stopping briefly for Gina's smoke breaks and eating a quick lunch over the computers, consisting of sandwiches Zeke had brought to them from the deli in town. Gina was rapidly picking things up. Now, her biggest problem was her confidence level. *Not much I can do about that,* Sydney thought, tempted to crash the system, but she was afraid it would send Gina into heart failure. Instead, Sydney went over for the third time how to change query parameters and showed Gina some of the most common user errors and how to fix them. By Tuesday afternoon Gina seemed more at ease, and they decided tomorrow Sydney would just hang out and watch until it was time for her to leave.

Sydney got into her car with a heavy heart. She was not as excited about going home as she should be and felt guilty about it. She looked around for Zeke's truck and noticed he had gone home already, and hadn't stopped in to say good night. She was hoping he would invite her to dinner since she was leaving tomorrow. Granted, he had a life and probably had better things to do than entertain her. With that thought ricocheting around her head like a pinball, she drove over to the coffee shop. She noticed a man in front of his house burning a pile of leaves while leaning on a rake and opened her window to let the scent in. He lifted his hand casually to wave and she waved back, just a friendly exchange between strangers. The friendly gesture made between strangers caused her mood to plummet further, because she knew that simple exchange would never happen in Sacramento.

Pulling into a parking spot in front of the coffee shop, she noticed the gang was all here. She got out of her car with a smile on her face watching the women inside laughing. The bell dinged, and she was welcomed by nods and smiles as Lucy continued her story of trying to walk her dog who was more interested in chasing a squirrel. Betty got her coffee as Sydney listened and watched Lucy do the playback of the dog wrapping the leash around her legs, while she kept spinning around trying to undo the leash and ended up collapsing on a chair, explaining how she had to finally sit on the dog to get them untangled.

Sydney was laughing with the rest of them as Betty did the money-coffee exchange. Betty rang her up, then brought a red gift bag out with a huge white bow and handed it to Sydney. Amid demands from the women to "Open it!" she slowly pulled out the tissue wrapped gift and looked inside. There was a true fishing hat, decked with lures and fake worms, and a t-shirt that read "There is only One Great Lake" with a picture of Ruby Lake below it. She clutched them to her chest and looked at the others with tears in her eyes.

"Thank you all so much, for everything," she said, swiping at her eyes while holding up the shirt.

"No crying now, we just wanted to get you something to remember us by," Amelia said.

"I doubt I could forget any of you, and I love my gifts. I'm not sure when I'll get the chance to use the hat, but I'm sure this will become my new favorite shirt," Sydney said as she hugged the shirt to her.

"Well, you'll have to come and visit us this winter. You can stay with me and I'm sure *someone* will want to take you ice fishing," Betty said with a sly smile.

"I'd love to come back and visit, but I'm not so sure about ice fishing," Sydney said. "If you mean Zeke, I'm sure he'll have forgotten all about me by then."

"I wouldn't bank on it. Are you busy tonight?" Betty asked with a smile.

"I just have to pack, but that's the extent of my excitement for the evening."

"Great! We're all going to get dinner at Buckethead's, why don't you come with? It'll be on us."

"I'd love to, thanks for including me." Sydney's earlier melancholy melted away as she helped tidy the shop and left with her new friends.

Three hours later, stuffed with food and maybe one drink too many, Sydney thanked Betty for driving her car back to the hotel. She said goodbye to the other two women amid a round of hugs before they all left in Lucy's car. Throwing her purse strap over her head and carrying her gift bag, she walked into the lobby. She glanced at the counter and deflected Michelle's glare with a smile and wave and walked up the stairs. With each step, she was reminded this was her last night here. Turning the lights on dispelled the gloom in her room, but did nothing to erase her own. She screamed as the bathroom door opened and Zeke walked out.

"Jesus Christ! You scared the crap out of me! How did you get in here?"

"I wasn't always a law abiding citizen in my youth, and some things you never forget. Plus, I have an in with the owner of this establishment so I wouldn't be charged even if I were caught. Where were you?" Zeke asked, noting the gift bag.

"Betty, Lucy, and Amelia took me out to eat, and look what they got me!" She proudly put the hat on and held the shirt up under her chin.

"Well, I guess my gift will pale in comparison now, you probably won't even want it," he said, sticking his hands in his pockets.

"You got me something? You shouldn't have, you already got me the candles."

"This is a little more personal. It's in the envelope on the table."

Sydney set her purse, hat, shirt and the gift bag down on the bed and carefully opened the large padded envelope. It was the picture of her and Zeke holding up the fish. They were both laughing and she knew the moment had been captured perfectly. Every time she looked at it, she would be catapulted right back to that day. Tears threatened again, but this time she held them at bay. "I love it, I absolutely love it. I have the perfect frame for it at home, and I know just where I'll hang it. You know, you're making it really hard to leave."

Zeke walked over and cupped her cheek in his hand. "That's the point. I don't want this to be the end. Don't let it be," he said, leaning down to kiss her. He held her face in both his hands, pulling her closer while she wrapped her arms around his waist and clutched his back. The other kiss in the boat had been full of passion and unspoken desire. This slow kiss spoke of longing and tenderness. He broke off and rested his forehead against hers.

"Don't go."

"I don't want to leave. I feel like I finally belong somewhere, and it's not just you. It's everyone here," she said as she broke out of the embrace.

"I know, I can see it. You fit here," Zeke said as he kissed her on the forehead and walked to the door. "I'm leaving while I still can. Have a nice trip home. You'll hear from me soon."

"Won't you be at work tomorrow?"

"No, I have some personal things to attend to, that's why I came by tonight. You take care of yourself, Syd." Zeke took a long look at her, and walked to the door.

"Stay. I want you to stay tonight," Sydney said, a slight tremor in her voice.

Zeke stopped, his hand resting on the door knob and hung his head. Turning around he said, "Are you sure that's what you want?"

"Yes, more than anything," she said.

He walked over to her rubbed his thumb on her cheek, and pulled her close. He kissed her tentatively at first, nibbling on her lips, then as she leaned into him, kissed her harder. She snaked her arms around his neck, gripping his hair with both hands and traced his tongue with her own. He broke the kiss and tipping her head up, kissed down the length of her neck, sending chills down her arms.

He scooped her up, set her gently on the bed and laid down next to her. Leaning over her, his lips met hers as their hands were tentatively touching each other. Her hands felt along the muscles on his back, while his traveled down her side, his thumb barely skimming over one nipple, making them both hard with wanting. She pulled his shirt out of his pants and pulled it up so she could touch his skin. He leaned up and yanked it over his head and threw it across the room. Standing up, he pulled her to a sitting position, as he unbuttoned her shirt and slid it off her shoulders.

She reached behind her to undo her bra and dropped it to the floor as he watched. She was aching with need and while he was still standing, she hooked her fingers in his belt loops and pulled him to her. Not breaking eye contact, she used her teeth to unbutton his 501's, making him groan as he leaned her back on the bed and laid on top of her.

Gone was the gentleness of earlier, now they were fueled with desire. He bent down and sucked on her nipples, using his teeth to heighten her pleasure as she yanked on his jeans to get them off.

"Off, I want them off," she said, getting frustrated with her slow progress.

He shifted his body so he could pull his pants down with one hand while still squeezing her breast and licking and flicking her other nipple with his tongue. She used her foot to help him get his pants the rest of the way down, as he unbuttoned her pants with one hand and together they got them off.

Skin on skin they explored the unfamiliar terrain of each other's bodies until the tension built and Sydney was panting.

"I need you Zeke, quit teasing me!"

He leveraged himself up and grabbed his jeans off the floor.

"What are you doing?" she asked impatiently, feeling chilled now that his body wasn't covering her.

"Getting something, wait a second," he said as she heard a ripping sound of paper. He put the condom on quickly and rose up over her.

"You're mine now, and I mean to keep you," he said, plunging into her, filling her completely. An orgasm racked her body, making her even more wet as he slid in and out of her slowly while kissing and biting her neck. She wrapped her legs around his waist, moving her hips in a circle to keep pace with him.

He rolled them over, with her now on top he watched her ride him, both of them writhing in pleasure. Her hair fell in auburn ringlets over his face as she moaned and bit her lower lip. He grabbed her ass with both hands and guided her down, faster and faster until she screamed and his body went rigid as they both came almost simultaneously, her right after him. She fell on top of him and let the aftershocks go through her body. Not being in complete control, she squeezed him while he was still inside of her, making him growl deep in his throat.

"Stop that unless you want to go again," he warned, his eyes still shut.

"I can't help it, and no I can't go again just yet. I need a break. And water."

He lifted her off of him and pulling the covers back, laid her down and tucked the comforter around her. He got up and was back a few seconds later, a full glass of water in his hand. She drank greedily, not sharing a drop with him. He chuckled and walked back to the bathroom where she could hear the faucet running. She snuggled deeper into the blankets waiting for him to come back, feeling sore in all the right places. He walked back in, gloriously naked, and handed her another full glass of water.

"I had three, I figured you could use another one."

Struggling to sit up, her limbs still feeling as if the bones had been replaced with liquid, she sat up and tucked the blanket around her chest. "Thanks," she said, drinking the water a little slower this time.

Zeke climbed in beside her, scooting as close to her as he could get. She put the glass on the end table and lay on his chest, her hair tickling his nose. As he brushed it aside, he asked, "So are you still leaving tomorrow?"

"I have to Zeke, I don't want to, especially now, but I really have to go home. At least for a while," Sydney said with a sigh.

"We'll find a way to bring you back, no matter what happens, we'll find a way."

Chapter Fourteen – Leaving on a Jet Plane

After four hours of sleep and staying in bed for another hour, Sydney and Zeke finally decided it was time to get up and get going. She hadn't packed last night, so after her shower, she threw all of her clothes in the suitcase haphazardly, making sure the candles were well cushioned and slid the picture in her carry-on bag.

Zeke was dressed and sitting on the bed, watching her. "Just to remind you, I won't be at work today."

"Why?" she asked, putting her makeup case in her carry-on.

"I have an appointment I couldn't change, nothing's wrong by the way. But I'll come see you before you leave. What time is your flight?"

"Three-thirty. So you won't be there all day?" Sydney asked, her surprise clear in her voice.

"I'll try to be quick. Don't make anything out of this Sydney. If I could, I'd convince you to come home with me right now and never leave. Do you want me to ask Alex if he has a spot for you?" Zeke stood up and put his arms around her as he asked.

"No, not yet. Let me explore some options back in Sacramento first. If none of those pan out, then I'll ask him." Sydney pulled him close and inhaled his scent which was a cross between flannel, sweat and wood smoke. It was uniquely his, and had fast become her favorite smell. Smiling up at him, she was startled by the serious look on his face.

"Please come back to me Sydney. I'd hate to live in the city, but I will if I have to."

"You won't and I really do want to come back, and not just for you."

"Thanks a lot," he said with a laugh.

"That's not what I meant, and you know it. I mean for the town itself. And Betty, and Suzanne, and I really want to see a bunch of cars running in a parking lot in the middle of winter."

"Well, when you come back, you'll see all of that and more. I'd better go, be safe and I'll see you later." Zeke kissed her hard, picking her up in a tight hug as she clung to him.

"Do that again, and we'll both be late," she said as she slowly slid down his chest.

"It'd be worth it. Give me your keys and I'll put the bags in on my way out and start your car for you."

"Would you? Actually, if you wouldn't mind, could you take the big one for me, and I'll take the other? I just need to make a quick call to Illana, and then I'll be on my way." Sydney got the keys out of her purse and tossed them to him. "Have a good day, and at some point you'll have to tell me about your appointment today."

"At some point soon, I will." Zeke winked at her and picking her suitcase walked out the door.

Sydney quickly grabbed her cell phone and called Illana.

"What?" asked a very cranky Illana.

"Guess who stayed the night last night?"

"If you say Zeke, I swear I'm going to come through this phone and kill you." After a few moments of silence, Illana laughed. "No way! *You* slept with Zeke? After all the shit you said to me about Alex, you turned around and had sex with Zeke?"

"I know, totally unprofessional, and totally unfair to you. But yes. Oh my God yes."

"Well?"

"It was a 10 on my Richter scale. He wants me to move here and I want to too."

Illana was silent. After a few more seconds, Sydney couldn't stand it. "Are you still there? I thought that's what you wanted! You're the one who said to go for it, "explore it" you said."

"Well, yeah, but I only meant it might be nice for you to have quick fling, not a forever thing!"

"You know I'm not built that way, Illana. Can't you be happy for me? After all, you'll get to say 'I told you so' if he does turn out to be 'the one' like you said at his house."

"This is no time for humor. We'll talk when you get back home. Maybe some distance will bring you back to your senses. What time does your plane get in?"

"Eleven-thirty tonight, but my dad will pick me up."

"No he won't. I'll call him, I may be irritated because you woke me up and threatened to leave me forever, but I still want all the details. See you tonight."

Sydney smiled as the phone went dead, and shook her head. *Distance will only make me want him more,* Sydney thought as she stood in the doorway and took a last look around the room, and then shut it quietly behind her. It was still early enough for most of the other hotel residents to be sleeping soundly, so she was careful about not stomping down the stairs.

She walked over to the registration desk and was happy to see Michelle was absent this morning. She really didn't feel like trading barbs with the minion from Hades right now. She gave the clerk the key-card back and took the printed invoice, which came to a grand total of zero, and walked out to her car. When she caught sight of Annie and Michelle waiting for her by the car, she didn't so much as miss a step. Steeling herself, she pinned her gaze on the two women and walked forward.

"I believe you are leaning on my rental. How nice, a bon voyage committee. Did you bring coffee, or do I have to deal with both of you without the benefit of it?" Sydney asked as she walked to the driver's door and threw in her bag, making both women move.

"Don't flatter yourself, we just wanted to tell you not to come back here, you won't be welcomed a second time," Annie said.

"Funny, I don't remember either of you welcoming me the first time and that didn't stop me. Don't worry, when I do come back, I won't be staying here." She could see her breath as she spoke, and hoped this wasn't going to take too long. Her fingers were already starting to freeze.

"You stay away from my brothers! You have no idea the trouble your meddling has caused my family. It will take me *months* to undo the damage you caused." Annie's fists were balled up and she took a step forward and was almost nose-to-nose with Sydney. Well, nose to chest anyway.

"I take it you prefer to bathe in your perfume," Sydney said waving her hand in front of her face as she stepped back. "Look Attila, I'm not interested in your threats and if Alex was smart, he'd fire you. You were wrong, he doesn't need you, but for some reason he wants you there. Personally, I hope he gives you enough rope for you to hang yourself with, but whatever. As fun as this is, I really do need to go. I, unlike some, have a job to get to."

"Not before I've had my say," Michelle interjected.

"You've had more of my time than you're worth," Sydney said coldly as she got into her car and drove off, narrowly missing Michelle's foot. She smiled as she saw them raising their middle fingers, telling her she was number one. So far, her morning was pretty excellent.

She parked and grabbed the Harry Potter book along with her purse as she went into the coffee shop. She was glad to see Betty was alone this morning, of all the women she had met, she felt closest to her. Walking in, she was greeted by the smooth aroma of coffee and much to her surprise, her coffee cup was already sitting on the counter.

"How did you know when I would be here?"

"Hmm? Suzanne saw you telling off Annie and Michelle, so I figured it would be a matter of minutes before you came in to relay the newest drama in the ongoing Attila saga. Spill it. No charge on the coffee today," Betty said, waving away Sydney's money. Sydney put a dollar in the tip jar and told Betty about her confrontation with the two women.

"You really called her Attila? I do so love you! This will be all over town by lunch, and you'll be the new hero," Betty said smiling, then spied the book. "Are you done already?"

"No, but I'm really bad about mailing things, and I thought I'd better return it now. I'll pick up another copy at home. Thanks for the loan, these are the best escape books I've ever read." Sydney took a long drink of her coffee as the warmth of the coffee cup defrosted her hands.

"I agree, so keep it until your next visit. Besides, you'll want it for the plane."

"Did you really mean that? You want me to come visit you?"

"Of course I meant it, I said it didn't I?"

"Well, yeah, but people say a lot of things-"

"I don't, and yes I meant it. Here's my home number, and my email address. You can give me yours when you call." Betty slid the note across the counter as she spoke. "So you see, this isn't goodbye, it's only until next time. I don't do well with goodbyes."

"Me either. I'll give you a call next week and figure out when I can come back for a long weekend, and I'm giving some serious thought to staying for longer than that. Betty, I'm so glad I met you, I don't know what I would've done without you these last ten days."

"You would've been just fine, you don't seem the type to fall on your face. Now get out of here before I start leaking. I'll talk to you soon."

Sydney put down her empty cup and walked around the counter to give Betty a hug. After a moment, Betty returned it, holding on tightly, then patted Sydney's back. Both women had tears in their eyes now.

"See what you've done? I'll have to redo my makeup now." They both laughed since Betty didn't wear makeup.

"I'm a pain in the ass, I don't know why you want me to come back, but now you'll be stuck with me. Have a great day Betty, I'll bring the book back soon," Sydney said, walking out the door.

"I'll hold you to it," Betty retorted, absently wiping the already clean counter.

The rest of the day sped by. Gina handled all of the reports with ease and Sydney had her reboot the whole system as a final test. Gina was nervous, but did it without causing any problems. They went over a few more things with the web page and by the time they were done, it was lunchtime.

Alex bought pizza for everyone so the whole staff could have a chance to say goodbye to Sydney. Many of the women thanked her and shook her hand, but Stella cried dramatically.

"Honestly, you don't know how much good you've done here! You haven't just improved our business, but the lives of everyone working here. I hope you know how grateful we are!" Alex finally had to lead her away and back to her desk, giving her his handkerchief as they went.

Sydney gave Gina her work and home numbers and her email address, and told her to call anytime. She left the main office and went to gather her laptop and the other items that had been left in the warehouse office. Packing everything up, she was struck at how quiet the warehouse was without Zeke there driving the forklift. She was surprised in just one day the slight diesel smell she had come to associate with the warehouse had dissipated. What wasn't surprising was the fact her thoughts kept coming back to him. That had been happening all day.

At two o'clock, she walked into Alex's office to say goodbye. He turned around in his chair, offered her a seat, and got up to shut the door. Sitting down she said, "I hope we were worth all the trouble we caused you. I'm sorry about the problems with Annie."

"Don't worry about her, she'll either come around or she won't. I couldn't be more pleased with all the work you and Illana did. We already have a quarter more business than we had before you came here. At this rate, I'll have to hire even more staff! Thanks for everything you did, and I'm not just referring to the work. You and Illana being here opened my eyes in a way no one else has been able to. I know I have some changing to do, and taking the easy road all the time is a thing of the past. I'm sure we'll be in touch, and I have already sent John the check continuing the contract for three more months."

"I'm not sure Illana or I deserve that amount of credit, but you're welcome. As far as the contract goes, if you ever need me to be able to remote in, I can walk Gina through whatever problem she may be experiencing. I also gave her my contact information in case she needs it, but I really don't think she will. You made an excellent choice by putting her in charge of the I.T. department. I'm looking forward to seeing your business grow, and I'm grateful I got to come here and be a part of it, even for such a short time."

"Anytime you want to come back, just let me know. I'm sure I can find a spot for you. Oh, and I don't have any rules about employees dating each other, just so you know," Alex said, winking at Sydney.

Sydney's ears turned pink as she said, "I see. Well, I may take a rain check on your offer, and I'll keep you posted. I'd better get going, I know I don't have to be there an hour early, but being there any later makes me nervous." Sydney stood and Alex jumped out of his chair to open the door for her. They shook hands, said goodbye, and she left by the warehouse exit.

With her final goodbyes concluded, she drove to the airport. She thought about stopping again at the coffee shop, but drove on wanting to leave things as she had left them that morning. Checking in the car was a breeze, and since she was an hour early, there wasn't anyone else in line at the airline counter. She grabbed Betty's book out of the carry-on and was surprised when the airline personnel announced it was time to board. She stood up, stowing the book back in her bag and was the last person in line. As she stepped up to put her bag on the baggage conveyor belt, she was spun around by her shoulder by Zeke.

"You're really leaving?"

"I have to go home, we covered this already. I promise I'll find a way to be back soon."

"Not soon enough," Zeke picked her up with one arm, and anchored his other hand in her hair, kissing her hard and fast. As he set he back down he said, "I'm going to miss you, Syd. This isn't the end of this, it's just the beginning," then turned and walked outside.

Stunned, she turned back to the airline attendant, who smiled as Sydney put her bags on the belt. She was shaking as she walked through the metal detector and hoped they wouldn't think she was trying to smuggle something. Of course, they had all seen what had happened too, so no one questioned her trembling legs as she walked outside, up the stairs and onto the plane.

Finding her seat by the window, she stowed her bag under the seat in front of her and sat down. A kindly-looking older woman sat next to her and pulled a knitting project onto her lap.

"That's some young man you got there," she said, nodding out the window. Sydney followed the woman's gaze, and as the plane taxied down the runway, she saw Zeke leaning against his truck on the other side of the fence. As the plane sped by him, he blew her a kiss and raised his hand in farewell.

"Unfortunately, I'm not sure how it'll ever work, or if he really is mine," Sydney said, tears running down her face, her gaze still on Zeke as the plane climbed into the air.

"Sure looks as if he is from where I'm sitting. Love has a way of making the impossible possible," the older woman replied, nodding towards the window again. Sydney found she had nothing else to say, so sat back and let the rhythmic, clicking sound of the needles lull her to sleep.

Chapter Fifteen – A Change in Priorities

Back in her apartment the next morning, Sydney silently bemoaned the fact she'd never slept so badly in her life. Looking in the mirror, she leaned closer because she couldn't believe the dark circles under her eyes. She rummaged through her decades old makeup bag to find her old foundation. It was at the bottom of the bag, dried up and gross. She tossed it in the trash and decided it was a lost cause. Illana was right, she did need to buy new makeup. Glancing at the mirror again she shrugged, glad she wouldn't have to look at herself all day.

Driving to work, she realized she had never noticed what a pain in the ass it was to maneuver in traffic. Had people always been this rude? Why was everyone in such a big frickin hurry? Finally able to pull into her parking garage she let out a breath and appreciated the dark quiet of the lower level. She walked towards the stairs and opted for the elevator even though it was only one flight. You never knew if there was someone lurking in the stairwell. *Where did that come from?* Sydney thought as the elevator doors opened. Shaking off her unease, she pushed the button for the first floor and tried to switch gears and think about work.

By the time she had hung up her coat and logged into her computer, she felt a little more like her normal self. She answered a couple emails, shot off a note to John regarding the contract and was scanning her new project list when Illana came into the cubicle.

"Have you changed your mind yet?" Sydney turned around and Illana's smirk was replaced by surprise. "What the hell happened to you? What's with the dark circles?"

"I couldn't get to sleep last night, it was too noisy. I need to find a way to back to Ruby Lake, and soon."

"And so it starts. I knew this was going to happen. Give it a week and you'll be back to normal. Remember we have things like Starbucks and good Mexican food here. And sunshine all year long. Try to concentrate on the positives."

"It's not that, and you know it. I see you and I have a new project, have you started on it yet?"

"The Department of Motor Vehicles one? Yes, I did. I'll send you what I've got and maybe later we can go into the conference room and throw some ideas around. John wants it done in a couple of weeks so he can get the bid in. Do you want to grab some coffee in a little bit?"

"No, I need to catch up on some stuff. Let's go to Tres Hermana's for lunch though."

"Now you're talking!" Illana walked back to her desk but didn't let Sydney see the look of disappointment on her face. She was losing her friend and was afraid it was only a matter of time before she left for good.

Sydney was glad to be back at her apartment, the day had been brutal. Lunch with Illana was good, cheese enchiladas with green sauce always picked up her mood, but the rest of the day had dragged. She tried to throw herself into the new project, but her excitement level was definitely lacking. She tossed her purse and coat on the kitchen table and noticed her caller id was blinking. As she was scrolling through her calls (telemarketers were the bane of her existence), the phone rang. A blocked number. Great.

"Hello?" Sydney said impatiently.

"Hey Syd, what's the matter?" Zeke's baritone voice gave her goose bumps and her impatience turned into butterflies.

"Oh hi! Nothing, I thought you were a telemarketer. How was your day?"

"It sucked because you weren't here. Are you glad to be back in the city?"

"No. I had a hard time sleeping and the traffic sucked and I'm already sick of it. Illana keeps telling me it'll wear off, but I'm not so sure."

Zeke was quiet for a moment, and then said, "Well, hang in there. I'm working on a few things here, but I can't tell you about them yet. My day wasn't any better. It's totally different with you gone. Of course, Annie being gone is a plus, but, well, I miss you not being up in Dad's office. I turned the lights on in there today because it seemed too dark. I glanced up there at one point and was surprised you weren't there," he sighed, lowered his voice and said, "I meant what I said at the airport yesterday, and all day I've been afraid you'd get back home and change your mind. Did you?"

"No, in fact being here makes me even more determined to move. I want you and I want to move to Ruby Lake as soon as I can. That won't change. Are you sure you still want me to come back?"

"Yes. It's crazy and it has happened really fast, but I've never be more sure of anything. I can't believe how much I miss you. Hold on a minute Syd, I think Alex is here. I gotta go. Alex and I are going to play pool and try to regain our good name."

"Good luck with that. Have fun and I miss you too."

"I'll call you tomorrow, and I hope you sleep better. Try some earplugs tonight, that's what I had to do to sleep when I was out there."

"I'll try it, you'd better go, and tell Alex I said hi."

"I will, good night."

Sydney put the phone back on the charger and flopped down on the couch. Looking around, she picked up the remote and started channel surfing while thinking about everything, and everyone, she missed in Ruby Lake. When someone knocked at the door, she jumped, and looking out the peephole was surprised to see her dad on the other side. Flinging open the door she gave him a huge hug.

"I'm glad to see you too honey. Are you ready to go to the show?"

"What show?" She stood back and looked at him blankly.

"The Music Circus. Remember, I got tickets for *Annie Get Your Gun*? If you don't want to go, we don't have to."

"I can't believe I forgot! Give me just a sec, and I'll be ready to go." Sydney ran to the bathroom, chastising herself for not remembering why she had come back. She decided not to mention she was thinking about leaving to her dad yet. Within five minutes, she walked back out to her living room with a sincere smile on her face. "There, I'm ready. Do you think we can go to Leatherby's for a sundae after the show?"

"Don't we always? Let's go, I got us tickets for the second row." Graham helped Sydney with her coat and arm-in-arm they walked out into the night.

The next morning, Sydney stretched and opened her eyes to the sunlight streaming in her window. Pulling the earplugs out of her ears, she was horrified to see it was eight-thirty on her alarm clock. Yanking the phone off her nightstand she quickly dialed John's direct number.

"Hello?"

"John? I'm sorry. I overslept and I'll be there in twenty minutes."

"You overslept?" John asked, shock and confusion clear in his reply.

"Yes I did. I'll explain when I get there. Sorry!" Sydney hung up, tossed the phone on her bed as she frantically pulled her sweater over her head, stepped into her slacks as she hopped-ran into the bathroom. *No time for a shower today,* she thought as she put her hair in a ponytail and brushed her teeth. In less than ten minutes she was out the door and on her way to work.

She ran in and went directly into John's office. "I'm so sorry about being late," she said sitting down as he turned around in his chair. "I slept with earplugs in last night and didn't hear my alarm this morning. It won't happen again."

"Calm down, it's the first time in four years you've been late. I was starting to wonder if I should call the National Guard, but other than that everything is fine. I take it the earplugs are a new thing?" He asked, scratching his temple with his pen.

"Yeah, last night was a trial run. I guess I got used to sleeping without any noise in Ruby Lake and I had trouble getting to sleep the night before. I'll get accustomed to the white noise of the freeway again, and I won't use the earplugs. Clearly not a good idea for me."

"Apparently not. Don't worry, I'm not mad. By the way, I saw your write-up on Parties R Us and I've already sent the first invoice. You'll be on-call for the next three months and we'll go from there."

"Sounds good. Illana and I got started on the DMV specs and should have something to you early next week. Thanks for not being mad, it won't happen again," Sydney got up, and her hands finally stopped shaking.

"I'm sure it won't. Send me whatever you have so far so I can look it over."

"Will do, boss," Sydney replied with a salute and walked, leisurely now, to her desk to find Illana sitting on it with her arms crossed.

"Where the hell have you been? Do you realize I called your cell like twenty times this morning?"

"I turned off my cell last night and forgot to check it this morning," Sydney said as she pulled it out of her purse.

"Off? You turned it off? Why?"

"I didn't want to talk to anyone after I got home from the Music Circus last night. I overslept, okay? Let's not make a federal case out of it." Sydney's earlier panic was now turning into annoyance.

"You haven't overslept since the week we were in Cancun! You'd better snap out of this, I want my best friend back," Illana said with a hand on her hip.

"And I would like a little understanding from *my* best friend." Sydney was now mimicking Illana's posture and each glared at the other. Illana dropped her arm and gripped the desk with both hands.

"I get the fact you have to re-adjust, I just don't think babying you will help."

"Babying me? When have you ever done that?"

"When I picked you up from the airport and you had clearly been crying, I didn't mention how puffy your eyes were, did I?"

"That's it? That's all I get? Thanks a lot. Listen, I don't have time for this, I have work to do. John wants everything we have so far on the DMV project, so if you could send him your part I'd appreciate it." Sydney turned around in her chair and booted up her computer.

"I'll get right on it," Illana replied sarcastically as she walked over to her own desk. Again, Sydney didn't see the fear on her face. Nor did she see the tears well up in Illana's eyes.

Sydney spent the rest of the day buried in her work and avoiding Illana. That is, until John called both of them into his office. Sydney took a seat by the door and Illana sat on the other side of the room, both looked at John expectantly.

"Is there a problem?" John asked looking from one to the other.

"No," they both replied, without a sidewise glance.

"Hmm. If you say so. I wanted to tell you both to hold off on the DMV project. I need you to switch gears and start on something new." John spent the next twenty minutes explaining the new duties and dismissed them when his phone rang for the third time. Sydney walked out first and didn't stop until Illana said softly, "C'mon Syd, can't we talk about this?"

Sydney straightened her shoulders, inhaled deeply, closed her eyes to pull herself together, exhaled and turned around. She was surprised by Illana's tone, but more so by the defeated look in her eyes.

"I'm sorry I snapped at you this morning. Everything is happening so fast, and I miss Zeke like crazy. He called last night and really wants me to come out there, and I really want to go. Illana, I think I'm going to do it, but I'll wait until we complete this new bid. Please be happy for me."

"I'll try. I knew this was going to happen from the moment you stepped off the plane. It's hard to be happy for you when I know after you leave I'll be stuck here all by myself."

"I'll only be a phone call or a five-hour plane ride away. But for now, John needs us to work on this WAN project for the First Five Commission, so we'd better get to it. Sounds kinda fun doesn't it?" Sydney said with a smile and Illana heard the genuine excitement in her voice.

"Now there's the Sydney I know and love! Let's get started."

Chapter Sixteen – Busy Work

The next couple of days flew by and Sydney felt like she barely had enough time to come up for air before she dove once more into her project. Zeke's calls every night were the main reason she could convince herself to stop for the day and go home. He was trying to find time to come out and see her since there was no way she could even think of getting away, even for a three-day weekend. She really wanted to complete this bid for John before she left, she felt she owed him that much.

At some point each day she would think of something she had to talk to Zeke about and started writing notes to stick in her purse so she wouldn't forget. Feeling guilty about all the post-its she was stealing, she finally broke down and bought a notebook, just a small one, she could keep in her purse. Illana didn't believe she would really leave, but every time she saw Sydney writing yet another note, her heart sank a little more.

Sydney got to work a little before seven and turned on the lights as she walked to the break room to make coffee. Since this project started, she and Illana took turns buying ground coffee from Starbucks and making it at the office because neither of them had the time for coffee breaks. Luckily, there were a ton of places that could deliver lunch, so they spent most of their day in the baby blue conference room (which was now dubbed "Sydney & Illana's office") working and throwing ideas around. Some of the other guys came in from time to time, and John regularly stopped in a couple times a day to check on their progress.

The bid was for a major wide area network to go from a San Diego county office all the way to a sister office seven hundred miles north in Yreka. It was an enormous undertaking but if they got this contract it meant a raise for everyone, and they would also have to hire a few more people. This was one of those rare and coveted state contracts that would pay in the high six digits. Everyone who worked for John was involved in the process. John turned down small jobs so everyone could focus solely on this, so when he came in to tell Sydney she had a call, she immediately thought there must be family emergency and ran to her desk.

"This is Sydney,"

"Hey Sydney, it's Alex. We have a small problem with one of the database reports and need you to dial in or logon or whatever you do so you can look at it."

"Sure, just give me a sec and I'll ghost in. Where's Gina?"

"She's at the hospital today with Aaron. He started his treatment this week so Gina went there so Suzanne could get some rest."

"I'm sorry to hear that, I should call Betty tonight, thanks for the reminder. Okay, you should see a box pop up in a minute and just click on ok." Sydney walked him through letting her in, and within ten minutes fixed the problem.

"That should do it, but if you find anything else, give me a call. Hey Alex, is your offer of a job still good?"

"You bet! Are you thinking about moving back?"

"Yeah, I am. I have this bid I have to complete first, but I'm thinking about moving back there in a couple weeks."

"Consider yourself hired. I'd love to have you as a permanent member of my team. I'm sure there's someone else who will be thrilled by the news too."

Sydney felt herself blushing, but only said, "I think so too. Would you mind keeping this between the two of us for now? I'd like to be the one to tell Zeke if you don't mind."

"Not at all, my lips are sealed. Thanks again for your help Sydney. Call me later this week and we'll figure out dates and your salary. I gotta go, talk to you later."

Sydney got off the phone and sat looking out the window. She felt free now that she had finally made her decision. Thinking it was time to tell her dad, she called and left him a message asking him to dinner later that evening. Now all she had to do was tell John and Illana. She decided those conversations could wait until tomorrow.

Leaving work, Sydney checked her cell and saw her dad had called, twice. She called him while walking down the stairs to the lower level of the garage. Her heels clanged on the bumpy black metal steps and he answered as she pushed the flat silver bar on the door to enter the parking garage.

"Hey Dad, I was wondering if you had any plans tonight?" she asked while fishing for her keys.

"Not yet,"

"Great, can you meet me at Frank Fat's for dinner in about thirty minutes?"

"Sure, is everything ok?"

"Yeah, I just realized I hadn't spent any time with you since the start of this new contract and wanted to take you to dinner."

"I'd love to, I'll meet you there."

"Sound good, bye Dad," Sydney said as she folded her cell, flashed her key light in the backseat to make sure it was empty and slid into her car. It only took fifteen minutes to drive across downtown. Walking in, she scanned the crowd looking for her dad and seeing he hadn't arrived yet, sat at the bar to wait for him. Just as she ordered a rum and coke, Graham walked in. He saw her immediately and she stayed put knowing it would be a couple minutes before he could get to her. Sure enough, several people waiting for their tables stopped him to congratulate him on his newest book. About five minutes later, Sydney swung her legs around and picked up her drink and napkin so she could rescue him, just as she had seen her mother do so many times in the past.

"Hi Dad! Our table is ready if you are. I hope I'm not interrupting," she said smiling and trying to look innocently at the gentleman he had been talking to.

"Not at all honey," Graham said then turned to the man, "Perhaps we'll get to talk later, it was nice meeting you." He shook the man's hand and placing his other hand on the small of Sydney's back, they followed the waiter to the back of the restaurant. Graham usually sat in the very back so the likelihood of being interrupted at dinner was lessened. It rarely worked.

Graham ordered pepper steak, which he had been ordering for twenty years, while Sydney decided on a smaller rib eye, no peppers or onions on hers. They caught up as they waited for their food, and a couple of Graham's friends stopped to chat while Sydney finally answered her phone, it was third call in ten minutes. Not Illana again like the last two had been. This time it was Zeke.

"Hey, I tried you at home – you aren't still working are you?"

"Nope, I'm on a date with the most handsome man in the world, and we're about to have dinner."

"Tell your dad I say hello, and thank him for feeding you for me."

"You're no fun, and actually I'm buying him dinner for a change. Anyway, I'll call you when I get home. I have big news for you."

"I'll be waiting, have fun with your dad." Sydney hung up just as the food was brought. The couple had left and she had her dad all to herself again. "Sorry about the phone, I would turn it off but work might need me."

"I understand. It's a good thing there were no cell phones twenty years ago, or your mother might have left me."

"Ha, not likely. She might have broken it or thrown it out the window though." Sydney smiled as Graham shook his head and chuckled.

"You're probably right. Of course, I could have used one when you were little."

"Why?" Sydney asked.

"Well, the one time that stands out is when you had your tonsils out and I didn't find out about it until it was over. I thought you were never going to forgive me for that one. There I am in Baghdad interviewing Rumsfeld, and in rushes a staffer saying I have to get home right away because my daughter was in the hospital having surgery. Of course, I didn't know what kind of surgery, but I quickly excused myself and caught the first plane home. I tried calling your mother but she was at the hospital with you and for whatever reason your grandma didn't want to tell me what was going on. She kept telling me to pray for you and she had to get off the phone in case your mother called."

"Yeah, I remember you running into my room while I was eating ice cream. I thought you were going to cry."

"I did later. Natalie was so mad at your grandma! Turns out, her mom thought I knew what was going on. I learned how important leaving out one word was, and so did the operator who took your mom's call. That was the last time I went overseas. Rumsfeld never gave me another interview, but since he was such an asshole anyway, I couldn't have cared less," Graham said with a shrug as he sipped his beer.

"Dad! Someone might hear you!"

"I doubt anyone would care if they did. So tell me about this new project that has you so busy."

Sydney gave him an overview of the major points and finished by saying, "So now all we have to do is win the bid and we've got it."

"When is it due?"

"We have two more weeks to get everything ready, but we're already ahead of schedule so we should be ready in another couple of days," Sydney said as she sopped up her steak juice on a roll and ate it.

"Never underestimate the amount of red tape that comes with dealing with a bureaucracy. It still baffles me sometimes how anything at all gets accomplished."

"Too true. Of course, we'll be going up against the big outfits and we plan to bid really low since it will still mean raises for all of us," Sydney finished her roll, and plunged into the real reason she wanted to have dinner with him. "Dad, there's something I need to tell you."

"Is something wrong?" he asked, putting down his fork.

"No, not at all. I'm going to put in my two weeks' notice as soon as the bid is done and I've accepted a job in Ruby Lake."

"But I thought you said you were excited about this bid coming up? Tell me you aren't doing this for some guy out there." Graham sat back and crossed his arms.

"Not entirely, no. It's just, I feel like I fit back there. I don't know how else to explain it. I've felt so lost and out of place since Mom died, and while I was there I was truly happy. Life is so much simpler there. The fact that Zeke wants me to come is a huge part of it, and Dad, he really is perfect for me."

"This is ridiculous! You're basing this decision on how you felt for ten days? Have you lost your mind? Don't you realize what you'll be throwing away? This contract that's coming up could put you on a whole new playing field, and you are going to just walk away from it for a 'simple' life?" Graham waved the waiter over and asked for the check.

"What do I really have here? You and Illana, that's it. Sure I have a great job, but what if I want more? Don't I deserve more to be happy and finally fit somewhere?" Sydney asked just as her phone rang again. Illana's work number this time. "Hey Illana, what's up? You're still there?"

"No, I'm back, and we need you to be here too. How soon can you come back?"

"In about twenty minutes, what happened?"

"John had the date wrong. We have to have our bid in by noon tomorrow. I suggest you make here in ten." Sydney closed her phone and looked at her dad. He raised his hand and spoke before she could get any words out.

"I heard, and I know you have to go, so dinner's on me. I'll come by tomorrow night and we'll talk some more."

"You won't change my mind, it's made up. If you still want to come over tomorrow night, fine. Just don't do it if you think you'll be able to change my mind."

"I just don't want to see you make a huge mistake, I do love you." Graham said as Sydney stood up.

"I love you too, Dad. Thanks for dinner, and I'm sorry how it's ended, but I really have to go." She gave him a quick kiss on the cheek, and then ran out the door. She quickly called Zeke to let him know she was running back to work and left him a message on his machine. Curious, she wondered where he might be. Maybe he's sleeping, she thought. If so, he'd better be alone.

Sydney walked into chaos. John was in his office yelling in the phone. His secretary, Katie, had her nose to the computer monitor, eyes puffy, and fingers flying over the keyboard. Even the pink doilies all over her cubicle looked washed out. People were running around, grabbing paper from the printers and practically bumping into each other. Illana spotted her standing dumbly in the doorway.

"You're with me," Illana said, cocking her head towards the conference room. Sydney followed Illana in, and as the door shut she turned to face Illana.

"What the hell happened? Why did we all think we had two more weeks?"

"Katie got the date wrong, obviously. October fifth is when the contract will be awarded. I knew I should've gone to that stupid meeting!" Illana said, referring to the Q & A meeting held by the state office when they announced the request for proposals.

"We can't do everything, and there's no reason to make her feel any worse."

"Maybe if she paid as much attention to work as she does her upcoming wedding, we all wouldn't be here tonight. Oh, how I loathe her right now."

"C'mon, we've made tons of brain-dead moves so I think we can afford to be a little more understanding. Besides, it's not like we've never pulled an all-nighter," Sydney reminded her, logging on to the computer.

"Yeah, those occasions usually were a lot more fun than this will be," Illana said dryly.

By ten o'clock the next morning everyone resembled the walking dead, except for John. Not a hair out of place, his glasses clean and not a wrinkle to be seen in his shirt or pants. Sydney, Illana and the rest of the staff were waiting in the conference room for John to finish reviewing the demo in his office. They sat slouched in chairs or, like Illana, with their heads pillowed on their arms on the table. John finally walked in and closed the door.

"Looks good troops. I'll drive this over and get it signed in. Thanks for all of your hard work. Everyone is to go home and not come back until Monday." There was a murmur of "Thanks John," and "Thank God," from the staff as everyone got to their feet and shuffled out of the room. Sydney had to poke at Illana to get her to wake up.

"Let's go. We have today and tomorrow off. Do you want me to drive you home?" Sydney asked as Illana rubbed her face.

"Yeah. No. Can I just bunk with you today?"

"Sure, but first I have to talk to John before we go. Just stay here for a minute." Sydney said, patting Illana on the back.

Sydney walked over to John's office, and knocked softly on the door.

"Hey, good job Sydney, and thanks for working all night. What's up?"

"I need to talk to you for a minute. John, I've decided to take another job. One in Ruby Lake. I wanted to finish this bid for you first, and since that's done, I'd like to put in my two weeks' notice."

"Are you sure? Is it more money? If so, I can double whatever they're going to pay you. I'd hate to lose you now, Sydney. I need you for this contract."

"It's not more money John. This is just something I have to do. I'm sorry I'm leaving at such a bad time, but my mind is made up. Thanks for everything, and I promise I won't leave until you've found someone to replace me. I'll even train the newbie before I leave."

"Well, I hadn't planned on hiring anyone else, but if your mind is made up, I guess that's what I'll have to do. We'll miss you like hell, Sydney. Does Illana know?"

"Not yet, I'm going to tell her today. You'd better get the bid over there, and I need sleep. I'll see you on Monday." Sydney smiled and walked back to the conference room where Illana was sound asleep on the table again. Poking Illana in the ribs to wake her up, she said, "C'mon Sleeping Beauty, let's go home while I can still drive."

Sydney pulled the couch into a bed for Illana and then passed out on her own bed. She was woken up by the phone ringing five hours later.

"'ello?"

"Sydney? Were you sleeping?" asked Zeke.

"I was. We didn't get home until ten-thirty this morning. Illana's asleep in my living room."

"Do you need to go back to sleep?"

"No, then I'll just be up all night. Hey, thanks for the flowers, I love them."

"You're welcome, I wouldn't want you to forget me."

"Not likely to happen any time soon, but that doesn't mean I don't want more. What's going on there?" Sydney asked as she stretched under her down comforter.

"We're having a fundraiser for Aaron. The hospital bills are astronomical and Suzanne is stressed out enough with having to get him to his treatments. I was wondering if you could come back for it. It'll be at the end of this month."

"I can do better than that. I told Alex I'd like to take him up on his offer, and he hired me. I just put in my two-week notice today," Sydney said, and then had to hold the phone away from her ear when Zeke yelled, "YES!"

"You're really coming here? Please tell me you aren't messing with me."

"I swear to you I'm really coming there. Do you think I could stay with you until I find my own place?"

"No, but you can move in here. I guess if you really want your own place, you can. But I plan on doing everything I can to thwart that idea."

Sydney closed her eyes and smiled. "Well, let's just see how it goes. I told my dad last night, and he didn't take it very well. He's going to come over again tonight to talk."

"Would it help if I came out there and met him before you moved here?"

"Maybe. I'll have a better idea after I talk to him tonight. You're really willing to do that?"

"Absolutely. If it would make it go more smoothly for you, I'll be on the next plane. What did Illana say?"

"I haven't told her yet, I'm going to after she wakes up."

"Well, I hope it goes better with her than it did with your dad. Of all the people I don't want to hate me, your dad and Illana top the list."

"No one is going to hate you, don't be ridiculous. So tell me about the fundraiser for Aaron, we kinda skipped right over that."

"We're going to do a haunted house. Betty is in charge of it, you should call her."

"I will, today. Is there anything I can do? Do you need money for anything?"

"You'll have to ask Betty. Since you'll be here I'm sure she'll put you to work. It's a good thing you'll be here for it; I need you to protect me from the vampires and goblins."

"Sounds scary, but I'll do my best. I'll call Betty in a little bit but first I'd better go wake up the princess. Too bad you aren't here to make the coffee."

"Well, I see what I'm wanted for. I'd better go to the store today since I'm going to need a lot of sugar on hand from now on." Sydney laughed as they said their goodbyes and hung up the phone. Sydney sat up, laid the phone in her lap and looked out the window. The Sacramento River snaked by slowly, looking especially clear and peaceful today. Or maybe it was just she finally felt at peace.

"Was that Zeke?" Illana asked, yawning in the doorway.

"How could you tell?"

"Your voice always goes soft and gooey when you talk to him. Nice roses by the way," Illana said over her shoulder as she walked into the bathroom.

"Thanks. Are you going to be in there long?"

"Yes, I need to take a shower, make some coffee will you?" Illana shouted through the door.

"Yes, Your Majesty, I'll get right on it. Hurry up, there's something I want to talk to you about." Sydney said, throwing back her feather comforter and getting out of bed. She walked into the kitchen and called Betty as she made coffee.

Sydney had just hung up when Illana came out of the bathroom wrapped in a towel.

"Do you have something I can wear? I can go commando until I get home, but I'd rather have some clean outerwear to put on."

"Sure, I think I have a pair of jeans and couple of your shirts here, let me look," Sydney said as she walked to her room. She rummaged through her closet and found three of Illana's shirts and a two pairs of jeans she had left after the last time they went clubbing. Turning around, Illana was standing in the doorway, her eyebrows scrunched in confusion.

"Did you leave your window down in your car?" Illana asked, snagging the jeans and a fuchsia shirt from Sydney's bed.

"No, I never do. Why?" Sydney asked as she looked out the bedroom window. Sure enough, it looked like the window was down, except for the pool of glass lying beneath and around her car.

"Son of a bitch! Someone broke into my car!" Running out to the living room she grabbed her keys off the dining room table and threw open her door. She ran down the steps and strode to her car. The passenger window had been smashed and looking in, she saw her stereo and cd case were gone. She opened the driver's door and saw a screwdriver still wedged in the ignition. Illana came rushing out, wide eyed and shaking her head.

"Oh man, you'll have to have it towed now. There's no driving that. At least whoever did this didn't succeed in stealing it too."

"Great, thanks for pointing out the upside. Good thing we have tomorrow off, I guess I know what I'll be doing. Let's go upstairs so I can call my dad."

"Why are you calling your dad?"

"So he can give you a ride to your car, there's no reason for you to be stranded here too."

"Wait on that a while, I'll hang until you can get a tow truck," Illana said as they climbed the stairs. "In fact, why don't I get a hold of Brian from work? His brother owns a body shop over on Watt Avenue."

Going in her apartment, Sydney grabbed the phone book and looked up tow companies as Illana called Brian on her cell and got the number for the body shop. Brian said he would call and talk to his brother to make sure her car would get worked on first. Sydney shot

Illana a look of gratitude and mouthed 'thank you.' It really helped to know people in middle places.

While they sat on her couch and waited for the tow truck, Illana looked at Sydney and asked, "So what did you want to talk to me about?"

"What do you mean?"

"Before I got in the shower, you said you had something to tell me."

"Oh, I guess I got sidetracked. Alex offered me a job before I left, and I accepted it. I gave John my two weeks' notice today and told my dad last night."

"And you're just now telling me? Why the hell wasn't I first?"

"Because I wanted to finish this bid and then tell you. You're mad because I didn't tell you first?" Of all the reactions, this was the one Sydney didn't prepare for.

"Yes, no, hell I don't know!" Illana's eyes filled with tears as she asked, "So you're really leaving? You're sure?"

Sydney had a lump in her throat as she answered. "Yes, I'm sure. Please don't cry, Illana. I'm not leaving you, nothing will change. Any chance you want to come with me?" Sydney asked, wiping her own tears away.

"To a dead-shopping zone? Did it hurt when you bumped your head? I can't live in a place that doesn't have a mall! But I'll come visit, a lot. Did you tell Zeke?" Illana swiped her eyes with her sleeve as she asked.

Sydney nodded and said, "This morning. And I only told him before you because you were sleeping so don't get all pissed off about that too."

"I should, but I won't. When are you leaving?"

"As soon as John finds someone to replace me. I told him I wouldn't leave before I train someone new."

"How did your dad take it?" Illana asked, tucking one leg under the other as she faced Sydney.

"Well, we were in the middle of arguing about it when you called last night. He said he'd come over and talk to me about it tonight. I guess I'd better call him now and ask if he'll give you a ride." Sydney pushed off the couch to find the phone, which was on the counter.

"Is he mad?"

"Yeah, but he'll get past it. Besides, no matter how mad he is he'll still give you a ride." Sydney glanced out the window and saw the tow truck pulling in. "Great, can you call him and tell him what's going on? I'll stall the tow truck guy and be right back." Sydney tossed Illana the phone as she dashed out the door.

Sydney talked to the driver and ran back upstairs to find Illana on the phone.

"Sure thing, Sydney just walked in, I'll let you talk to her," Illana said, handing the phone to Sydney as she said, "It's your dad."

"I hear you've had an exciting morning," Graham said

"That's one way of putting it. Can you come over and take Illana to her car? The tow truck driver is here to take my car to the shop."

"I'll be over shortly to take Illana home, and then I'll pick you up from the body shop. Do you want to borrow your mom's car?" Graham asked hesitantly. Sydney was stunned for a moment. She knew the car was sitting in his garage, but the thought of driving her mom's Mustang made her uncomfortable. Graham sensed her indecision and added, "I just had it tuned up last month, and if she were here, she'd have you take it."

"True. I don't know Dad, I'd rather borrow yours."

"I'm sure you would, but you aren't driving my Jag. Nice try. Why don't you wait to decide until after I pick you up?"

"Good idea. Are you on your way?" Sydney asked, looking worriedly out the window.

"After last night I shouldn't be, but I'll leave right now," Graham said as he hung up.

Sydney was sitting in her dad's car and thinking how this would never happen in Ruby Lake. Zeke and Betty both told her they don't lock their houses, let alone their cars. She couldn't wait to get back there, but she wasn't about to say it out loud to her dad.

"So do you want your mom's car until yours is fixed?" Graham asked, pulling Sydney out of her reverie.

"Yeah I do. I was thinking about mom and if she were still here she would insist on it, so me saying no is kind of stupid. Besides, how many people get to drive a cherried out '68 Mustang?" Sydney asked with a grin.

"Oh, how she loved that car. I could have bought her any car on the market, but it was one of the few things she ever specifically wanted. I don't think I ever saw her as excited as she was the day I gave it to her. Well, except for when you and your sister were born."

"I imagine she was more excited about the Mustang, there was no pain involved in getting that," Sydney added.

"You may be right. Well, let's go home and get her car."

"Thanks Dad," Sydney said, squeezing his arm. Her phone rang, Illana this time.

"How did it go?"

"Fine, we're just leaving the shop now and headed to my dad's house to pick up my mom's Mustang."

"Wait. Are you planning on staying at your place?"

"Of course, why wouldn't I?"

"Hmm, let's see. Your car got broken into and almost stolen and you're going to park your *mom's* car in the same spot? Are you insane? The Mustang will definitely get stolen!"

"Good point, can I stay with you for a couple days?"

"Sure. Now I'll have time to talk you out of leaving. You can come with me to the spa tomorrow, my treat." Illana said smugly.

"Oh goody," Sydney said sarcastically. "I have to go; I'll call you from my dad's." Hanging up, she looked at her dad. "There, it's settled, at least for this weekend. The shop said my car should be ready on Saturday afternoon, and I'm getting an alarm installed as well. So I'll go home Saturday evening."

"What does Illana think of your leaving?"

"She's not happy, but she's my best friend so she's trying to be supportive."

"That's not what it sounded like to me. Let's not fight, we can have this conversation later once things calm down and you're back at your place." Graham gave her a sideways glance and looked uncomfortable. Sydney decided to let it go for now. She hoped in time they would both come around. She knew she couldn't make them, either of them, understand. In fact, in her more sane moments, like when she wasn't talking to Zeke, she wasn't sure she understood it herself.

Chapter Seventeen – A Root Canal Would Be Better

After picking up her mom's car, she stopped by her place to pack a bag and called Illana. "Hey, is there anything specific I need to bring?"

"Club clothes for Friday night and comfy clothes to wear to the spa. Oh, and wear open-toed slides since pedicures are on the list. So are Brazilians."

"Oh no, I'm not getting waxed...there. No way."

"Yes, you are. Don't be such a baby. This is coming from the same person who rocked a purple mohawk her entire freshman year? What Ever," Illana said, enunciating each word while rolling her eyes.

"I'll think about it. But if I do get one, you're paying for it."

"I already said the whole day is on me. Hurry up and get over here. I made spinach dip and rented the first three seasons of "*Sex in the City*" for us."

"I'll be there in twenty." Sydney hung up with her, and quickly dialed Zeke, who picked up on the first ring.

"So how did Illana take it?"

"Pretty well, she's paying for a spa day tomorrow. I wanted to let you know I'll be staying with her today and tomorrow."

"Girls weekend?" Zeke asked.

"Sort of. My car got broken into and I'm borrowing my mom's '68 Mustang and we thought it'd be safer in her gated apartment complex than here." Sydney spent the next several minutes convincing Zeke it wasn't necessary to come out and protect her, all the while staring out at her mom's car to make sure nothing happened to it. "So, anyway, she's talked me into this stupid spa day thing. She's been after me for years to do this. I've no idea why I said I'd do it."

"You don't need to do it for me, I like you just the way you are. So, what are you letting them do to you?" Zeke asked, and she could hear the smile in his voice.

"Don't you dare laugh at me. I'm just getting my hair cut-"

"Not short!" Zeke said, sounding like he was coming through the phone.

"No, don't be ridiculous, anyway, I'm getting my hair *trimmed*, a pedicure, a manicure, a facial and God only knows what else. I'll probably be there all damn day."

"You poor thing, it sounds awful. All that pampering, I just don't know how you'll deal with it," Zeke said sarcastically.

"You're no help, and quit patronizing me. Is my room ready yet?"

"Think you're going to use it?"

"Well, I have to have some place to hang my clothes," Sydney said with a smile while playing with her hair.

"I'm sure I have some room in my closet you can use. I'd better get going, Alex is coming over with his new girlfriend and we're all going out to eat."

"Alex has a new girlfriend? When did this happen?" Sydney had been sitting on the arm of the couch, but this news brought her to her feet.

"Gotcha, just kidding. You should tell Illana that and see what she says. It's pool night, and I need to go and win some more games before you come back and take my title again. He'll be here in about twenty minutes. Have fun tomorrow, and don't let her talk you into cutting your hair short."

"You have no idea. Have fun, I'll talk to you tomorrow."

Sydney double locked her door, tried the handle to check it then headed down the stairs. Pushing the button to disarm the alarm on the Mustang, she opened the driver's door and tossed her bag and purse onto the black leather passenger seat and started the engine. She couldn't help but rev it a little more than necessary. Man, she loved this car. Illana lived on the other side of Natomas, so she took the old river road where the cops rarely were so she could really blow the dust off the engine. With nothing but cottonwood trees and the river to see her, she pushed the accelerator to the floor, making the Mustang sound almost like a Harley. Her dad would disapprove greatly, but as she topped it out at 90 miles per hour, she could almost hear her mom laughing right along with her.

Illana shook Sydney awake the next morning saying, "Hurry up and take a shower, we've only got two hours before we have to go."

Sydney turned over to get away from the annoying hand shaking her shoulder. Yawning, she asked, "What time is it?"

"Six-thirty, and I've already taken a shower and made coffee so get up," Illana said standing over her like a stylish, but mean, house mother.

"Five more minutes. Why do I need to take a shower before getting a mud bath?" Sydney asked while pulling the down comforter over her head.

Illana flung the blanket off Sydney and stared at her grumpy best friend. "You just do, quit stalling and get up." Illana finished folding the blanket and Sydney could hear the closet cupboard shut after Illana stowed it in there. Rubbing the sleep from her eyes, she sat up to take in the mess of last night. Two bowls with the remnants of spinach dip sat on the coffee table among the bread crumbs that had come from the loaf of sourdough bread they had eaten. The wine glasses sat empty next to the two bottles that were in the same condition. Yawning again, Sydney grabbed the bottles and glasses to take into the kitchen since she was going in there for coffee anyway. She spied the pile of fashion magazines on the glass dining room table and briefly wondered why Illana had so many. After rinsing out the glasses in the sink, she put the bottles in the recycle bin and poured a cup of coffee.

"Shower, you need to take a shower and quit wasting time. We have a lot to do before we go," Illana said as she walked in the kitchen. "I'll clean up the living room, so don't worry about it. Then, we'll go through the magazines."

"Why?" Sydney asked taking her first sip of ambrosia.

"Because we need to update your 'do."

"There's nothing wrong with my hair, I was only going to get it trimmed."

"Nope, a new style is definitely needed. You've had the same one for two years now. Go take your shower! We're burning daylight here," Illana said as she grabbed Sydney's coffee cup and pushed Sydney towards the bathroom.

"Y'know, if I treated you like this in the morning, you'd be pissed and wouldn't speak to me for a week!"

"You're right, but that's beside the point. Quit frowning and go." Illana had already turned around and was organizing the fashion magazines into some Machiavellian system designed to torture Sydney as much as possible. Recognizing defeat, she went to do as she was told. But she took her coffee with her. And slammed the door.

Sydney came out, hair wrapped in a towel and wearing an old t-shirt and sweats.

"What are you wearing? You can't go in *that*!" Illana said, her eyes wide with horror.

"Good Lord, do you always have to be so dramatic? You said to wear comfy clothes, this is supposed to be relaxing isn't it?"

"I said comfy, not stay-at-home clothes. I'll find you something, just wait here. You'll be changing into a bathrobe when we get there."

"Then why does it matter?" Sydney asked as Illana went into her bedroom. She was back in two minutes with a pair of Nike exercise pants and a matching pull-over.

"Here, this is better." Illana said, depositing the clothes on the arm of the couch. Sydney swiped them and went to change in the bathroom. Walking out, with her now empty cup, she asked, "Happy now?"

"Extremely. Now, come over here and let's look at these magazines and see what might look good on you," Illana said, patting the chair next to her.

Sydney ignored her and made a beeline for the coffee pot. She was very sorry she agreed to this, and hoped Zeke would appreciate her great sacrifice.

Two hours later, Sydney was sitting in a waiting room with Illana, both of them naked under the thick, white terry-cloth robes. A Swedish-looking giant of a woman came in, her thin, blonde hair swinging with every step. She held a clipboard, and said in a thick German accent, "Sydney Myers? Ah, yes 'allo. I'm Callan, and I'll be your Beauty Therapist today. Come vith me." Sydney got up and her fight or flight instinct kicked in. She looked at her best friend for help, but Illana just narrowed her eyes and shooed Sydney with her hand.

Callan led Sydney to a bathtub filled with mud. "Gif me your robe, and step up then slide in. Very easy." Sydney stepped on the footstool and took off her robe. She stuck her foot in and involuntarily pulled it out.

"It's boiling! I can't sit in that!" Sydney exclaimed, looking at Callan as if she was insane.

"Don't be such a baby. Here, hold onto my arm and slide in, you vill be fine." Callan held out her arm, and Sydney grasped it as she tried again. She slid her foot in, gritting her teeth and was told to hold both sides of the tub and swing in slowly. Sydney managed to hold onto the tub, but had trouble "swinging." When Callan put her hand on Sydney's lower back to help her, Sydney slipped and plopped into the mud, splattering her face and Callan's shirt.

"Is okay, it happens. You stay there and try to float. I'll be back in a jiffy." As Callan walked out, Illana walked in and stepped up to the tub next to her. She untied her bathrobe and let it fall, and was caught by the thin, exotic black woman behind her. Illana then gracefully swung into the tub. She looked at the floor in between their tubs, which had mud all over it then laughed when she saw Sydney's face.

"You still have some mud on your eyebrow," Illana said, lying almost on top of the mud, while the helper scooped mud over her. Illana rested her head on the rim of the tub and closed her eyes.

"I hate you," Sydney said as she tried to pull her body off the bottom of the tub and lie on it like Illana.

"You won't by the end of the day. Do try to relax, this is supposed to be fun."

"I'd rather be getting a root canal," she said, finally lying towards the top of the mud. Callan came back to check on her progress.

"Very gut. I see your friend showed you how to lie properly. I vill be back in fifteen minutes and then you vill go to the showers and sauna. Such fun, no?"

"No," Sydney said, still not used to the hot temperature of the bath.

"Don't mind her, Callan. It's her first time," Illana said, not bothering to open her eyes.

"Ah very well. I understand. I'll go easy on you today," Callan said, patting Sydney on the head before she walked away.

"I swear on everything I hold holy, I will kill you before the day is out," Sydney said, glaring at Illana.

Illana just smiled in response and said, "I know the price of beauty is high, but you couldn't avoid doing this forever. Besides, we're only scheduled for this, the sauna, mineral baths, Swedish massages, facials, pedicures, manicures, a Brazilian and getting our hair styled. Most women would die to have a day like ours."

"Only if they are masochistic. How did I let you talk me into this?" Sydney asked, pulling her arms out of the mud, and resting them on top. She was finally used to the temperature, but wasn't about to concede that fact out loud.

Illana turned and saw Sydney still struggling to get comfortable. Sighing, she said impatiently, "Look, just lay there without moving. You need to sink down a little, the mud should be up to your neck and everything else should be submerged, even your arms. Quit being difficult."

Sydney waited until Illana's eyes were closed, then childishly stuck her tongue out and put her arms back under the mud. She vowed not to speak to Illana the rest of the day.

She was true to her word until they were laying on yet another table/bed, waiting to get their Brazilians.

"I can't do it, I already hurt from the massage and facial. I'll wait with you, but I'm not going through with it."

Illana sat up on her elbows and saw real fear on Sydney's face. "I can't make you, but I promise it's not as bad as you think. Really, it hardly hurts at all, and it's just for a second. Trust me, I get one every six weeks. C'mon Syd, you already have the numbing gel on, you can do this. Buck up, little soldier."

Callan and Kioni walked in and went to their charges. Callan rested her large hand on Sydney's shoulder, saying "Now this von't hurt a bit. You relax and trust me, ja?" Sydney nodded and stared at the white ceiling tiles, trying to find her happy place. Callan parted her bathrobe, and with a wooden tongue depressor scooped up some hot wax and began spreading it down below. The heat wasn't necessarily bad so Sydney relaxed as Callan put the muslin strips in place. Illana was further along in the process, and Sydney heard a huge ripping sound, then Illana screamed.

"Stop! If she screamed, there's no way I'm doing this! Wash it off or something."

"I can't, and the longer I vait the vorse it'll be, hold still here ve go," Callan said, holding Sydney's shoulder to pin her down with one hand, and with her other she ripped the muslin off. Sydney's body jerked up as she yelled "OW!" Callan quickly moved before Sydney's fist could connect with her body. "Sorry, I really didn't mean to take a swing at you. Holy Christ that hurts!" Illana screamed again, and then was done.

"See, I told you it wasn't that bad!" Illana said, breathing hard.

"You screamed! Twice! You told me it wouldn't hurt!" Sydney was trying to get up as Kioni walked over to help hold her down. Kioni stepped behind the bed and held Sydney in place so Callan could finish. Again with the hot wax and muslin strips, then without warning, a huge rip and it was done. Callan applied some sort of lotion which took the sting away immediately. A shocked Sydney smiled at Illana, "Hey, it doesn't hurt anymore!"

"I told you. So, you want to make another appointment?"

"Sure, schedule me for six weeks after I'm dead," Sydney said, hopping down from the table and tying her bathrobe tight.

The next day she picked up her car, which now had a brand new alarm system, and went home. Sydney was admiring her new haircut in the bathroom mirror. She had relented and allowed them to add some highlights and lowlights, but only let them trim her hair. By that time, she was done with new experiences. Walking out into her living room, she smiled at the picture of her and Zeke hanging on the wall in the living room and decided to call him. Okay, she was dying to call him just to hear his voice, not that she'd be admitting it to anyone. Ever. He answered on the second ring.

"Hey, how did it go yesterday? Will I still recognize you when you come out?"

"Yeah, the parts of me that are drastically changed will be covered up when I see you," Sydney replied as she sat on the couch.

"Huh?"

"Never mind. You'll be glad to know I didn't let them do any more than trim my hair and add some color to it. How was pool the other night?"

"It was fun, a couple people asked when you were coming back to claim my crown, and I told them not soon enough. I don't know if I can wait two more weeks."

"I feel the same way, but it'll go by fast, you'll see. Do I need to rent a car when I get there? It'll be another week before my car and stuff arrives."

"No, remember I have a truck and a car, so if you need a vehicle you have two to choose from. But I'd planned on driving you wherever you need to go, so unless you get mad and want to run off, I think we'll have it covered." Zeke said, and she could practically hear him smiling.

"I somehow don't see that happening. Other than the Haunted House, what's on our agenda for the first week?" Sydney asked, lying down on the couch, still staring at the picture.

"Well, my mom would really like it if you'd come to dinner," Zeke said in a rush.

A few seconds passed until Sydney could breathe again to say, "Oh. Uh, sure. Will Annie be there?"

"Probably, but she won't say anything bitchy to you with my mom sitting there. We don't have to go. I can make an excuse if you don't feel comfortable. But at some point, we'll have to. My mom is relentless."

"No, I'll be fine. Besides, I really like Alex and your dad seems nice. It'll be great," Sydney said with more confidence than she felt.

"Thanks Syd, and you don't lie worth shit, it'll be fine I promise. I'll call her later and tell her we'll be there your first Sunday night. So, tell me about your spa day."

Sydney spent the next half hour telling him about the various tortures of her day, leaving out the Brazilian. Some things had to be seen to be fully appreciated. When her phone beeped she said, "Listen Zeke, someone's on the other line, do you want to hold on while I get rid of them?"

"No, I've got some stuff to do. I was just headed out when you called. I'll call you later tonight."

"Okay, bye," Sydney said, wondering where he was off to, as she clicked over, "Hello?"

"Hey sis, what's up?"

"Jessica! It's so good to hear your voice! How are things at Fort Knox?"

"Safer than a baby in a bubble. I hear you have a new guy and you're moving to Wisconsin to be with him later this month. Have you lost your mind?"

Sydney rolled her eyes. "I see Dad called you. No, I haven't lost my mind and it's not just for Zeke I've decided to move," she explained about finally finding somewhere she fit, the coffee ladies, Aaron's benefit and ended by saying, "so, it's not just for 'some guy.' Give me a little more credit, will you?"

"Geez, don't get your back up! Even if was for 'some guy' it'd be fine. I'm just giving you a hard time, it's what I do for fun. I told Dad that I'll have some leave to use up at the end of the year and I plan on coming home for a couple weeks at Christmas. Will you be coming too?"

"I don't know, I haven't thought that far ahead. We'll have to see."

"I was planning on staying with you, but I guess Mandy and I'll have to stay at dad's."

"Jess, you know he doesn't care. It's not like he doesn't know what Mandy is to you."

"I know he knows, but I'm just not comfortable at his house. I guess we could stay in a hotel."

"Sure you could – not. Dad would be really hurt then. You'll just have to suck it up, solider," Sydney added with a laugh.

"Ha ha, very funny. Listen, I have to go, we'll talk more about this later. When do you move?"

"I gave my two-week notice on Thursday, but there are about a hundred details I need to plan."

"I'm sure you'll make a list and get it done. Call me if you need to talk, and at some point I want to hear more about this Zeke," Jessica said, sounding just like their father.

"Yes sir! I love you Jessica, say hello to Mandy for me."

"Will do. I love you too, little sis."

Chapter Eighteen – The Other Shoe Drops

Early the next morning, she yawned as she walked into her office. She and Zeke had been on the phone for hours last night. Two hours of sleep seemed adequate to the tasks of the day. Or so she thought before seeing a post-it stuck to her monitor from John, who wanted to see her right away.

Wondering what that was about, she bent down and turned on her computer so it would boot up while she was talking to John.

"Excuse me, I have an interview with John Anderson. Are you his secretary?"

Sydney spun around to face a well-dressed man with dark hair. Annoyance flashed in her eyes as she spoke. "No I'm not, and his secretary isn't in yet. I'll be happy to show you into his office. Follow me." Sydney walked past him and knocked softly on John's door. Opening it, she stuck her head in and said, "John there's a guy here for an interview. Do you want him to come in now or wait in the lobby?"

"Have him come in, thanks Sydney, oh and I need to speak to you when I'm done." She stepped back and with a sweep of her arm and saccharin smile waited for the intruder to enter, then shut the door. Slamming it would have felt better, but she didn't want to piss off John.

Illana breezed in about twenty minutes later, put her stuff down, waltzed into Sydney's cubicle and sat on her desk.

"So, are you speaking to me now?"

"Barely. I hurt in places I shouldn't and I won't mention all the red bumps I have."

"Oh, didn't I give you any of the cream? Hmm, I wonder how I forgot about that? It couldn't have been because you were being so surly or anything."

Sydney swung her chair around to face her, "If you have cream for this, I swear I'll never be mad at you again. Hand it over, sister." Sydney held her hand out as Illana dug around in her huge bag. Finally finding it, she slapped it in Sydney's palm.

"Twice a day for a couple of days should take care of it," Illana said as Sydney hid the small bottle in her purse.

"Is that the only reason you're so crabby this morning?" Illana asked.

"Don't start, I'm so not in the mood."

"Let me try again. Good morning Sydney, how are you today? There, is that better?"

Sydney gave her a half smile and said, "I overslept again, so I was late. Then I get here and I've a note on my monitor that John wants to see me, but before I can go find out what's up, some guy who's here for an interview asked me if I was John's secretary. So no, my morning hasn't started well."

Illana rolled her eyes, "If I had a nickel...anyway, since John's tied up at the moment, let's go get some coffee. We haven't gone for coffee in weeks. Oh, and by the way, you're buying mine today," Illana said as she stood up.

"Why, are you low on cash?"

"No, you owe me since I had to listen to you whine for six hours on Saturday."

Sydney was back at her desk, coffee almost gone, when John's door opened.

"Thanks for coming in. Let me introduce you to some of my staff," John said then knocked politely on the end cap of Sydney's blue cubicle wall.

"This is Sydney Myers. She's my database administrator, and who will be training you if you get the job. Sydney, this is Dan Turner." Dan's eyes went wide as he realized the gaffe he had made earlier.

"I apologize for my earlier assumption; it's nice to meet you."

"Likewise, and don't worry about it, it happens all the time." Sydney stood up to shake his hand and was glad to note he had a strong handshake.

"Brian and Jeff are over here, and then I'll introduce you to Illana Garet, our web developer."

Sydney turned back around just as a 'new email' box popped up. It was from Zeke. Grinning, she opened it immediately.

Good morning Syd. I have a laptop in the warehouse now so I can email you from work. I hope your day is going well. Betty said she talked you last night. Your room here is ready (but that doesn't mean you have to sleep there) and I bought 3 pounds of sugar so you should have enough for your coffee for at least the first couple of days. ☺ Just kidding. Aaron is doing okay, and Suzanne is holding up. Annie is back in full swing and next time we talk, ask me about the 'flags' she put on everyone's desk. I have a couple of new guys in the warehouse, and no, I'm not related to either of them. It appears we have run out of family members to hire. I have to go, a shipment just got here. I'll be waiting to hear from you – Zeke

Sydney reread the note twice, sat back in her chair and closed her eyes. She could almost smell the diesel fumes in the warehouse and longed to be there. She pushed the thought away and came back to the present, clicking back to the specs she was working on for the DMV contract. After ten minutes of staring at the same screen, she surrendered to her curiosity and emailed Zeke back.

Hey! Thanks for letting me know about Aaron and Suzanne. I really wish I was already there. Thanks for setting up my room, it'll be nice to have somewhere to store all my clothes. Oh, and since I use a pound of sugar a day, you may have to get more. I'm working on yet another boring spec and would much rather be there. I went to Starbucks earlier and hated the burnt smell of coffee, Betty's shop smells so much better. I'm dying to know what the flags are about, you'll have to type back and tell me! ~Sydney

She went back to her work and although she was concentrating on it, she kept waiting and hoping for the next incoming email.

John had two more people in to interview so Sydney still didn't know why he wanted to see her. At eleven o'clock John asked everyone to come into the conference room for a meeting. Sydney and Illana sat next to each other at John's right and waited for the rest of the staff to trickle in. Once everyone was seated, John stood up.

"As you may have noticed, I've been doing interviews today. In light of the new contract we may be awarded, we'll need more people. Also, as I'm sure some of you are aware, Sydney will be leaving us in two weeks." Sydney now guessed he was going to warn her, but didn't have time. She looked around and saw all the puzzled looks and tried to meet them with a smile. John raised his hand to ward off any questions and continued. "She's been offered a job from the people she had a contract with, and even though it's against policy, I've decided it's for the best." Turning to Sydney he said, "I and everyone else here will miss you, but I'm also happy you've found a place that suits you. Even as we'll be sad to see you go, this is also an exciting time, and I hope you will all share in that excitement with me. I've decided to hire one of the candidates, Dan Turner, who some of you met this morning. He's got a background in database administration and networking, so he'll be working with Sydney and Brian. I'll be letting him know today and since he said he could start next week, I expect he'll start on Monday. Also, I heard only six other outfits put in for the contract, which means we may hear sooner than two weeks. Sydney, I'll need you to bring Dan up to speed on the specs for that, and I want him to sit in with you and Illana on the DMV bid. Brian, I need you to prep him on the network end. Any questions?" John asked as he sat down.

"Where is Dan working now?" Brian asked.

"He's the LAN administrator for a State agency. If we continue to go after the government bids, he can be some help there too. No other questions?" John asked, looking around the quiet room. "Okay! As soon as I hear on the bid, I'll let all of you know. Sydney, stay for a moment, will you?" Everyone else picked up their notebooks and pens and shuffled out of the room. Illana raised an eyebrow at Sydney, shrugged her shoulders and walked out, closing the door behind her.

"Sorry I didn't warn you, but I needed to explain why I was hiring Dan before we knew about the contract."

"It's fine, I was a little surprised was all. I'm sure had I been on time, you would've told me this morning. Sorry about that."

"No problem. I'm sure you have a lot on your mind right now. I'm going to call Dan in a few minutes, and when he does start, I need to you stay for at least a week to get him up to speed on everything."

"Absolutely, I'll make sure he has everything he needs. I can make copies of all my files now to give to him when he starts." John nodded, and briskly walked out of the rom. Sydney left the room and was a little sad everything was happening so fast. She knew she wanted to leave, but hearing it announced to everyone so soon threw her off balance. Seeing how easily she was being replaced didn't give her warm fuzzies either.

"Well? What did he want to see you about?" Illana asked, sitting on Sydney's desk.

"John apologized for blurting out that I'm leaving and asked me to get things ready for the new guy."

Illana folded her arms as she looked at Sydney. "This is so unreal. Are you sure you really want to move to Ruby Lake?"

"I'd be stupid to say I'm positive, but after making my decision to go I feel more content than ever."

Illana looked at her best friend, rolled her eyes and said, "Well, I guess I'll just have to get used to little planes. Do you want me to come over tonight and help you pack?"

Sydney threw her arms around Illana and gave her a big hug, which Illana returned tightly. "I knew you'd come around! Yes, thank you and I'll buy us Chinese for dinner."

Illana broke the hug and said seriously, "I'll pick it up on my way over, my treat. You'd better enjoy it while you can, I don't think you'll be getting potstickers in Ruby Lake unless you make them yourself."

Sydney struggled to unlock her door and not lose her grip on the empty boxes she was carrying. After managing to open the door and fit herself and the trio of boxes through the door, she dropped them and looked hopefully at her caller ID, which was blinking. She scrolled through the messages: her dad, Zeke called twice (her lips twitched upwards at that), and Sean called three times. Puzzled, she called Sean first to get it out of the way.

"Hey, I saw you called. What's up?"

"Thanks for calling me back, I wasn't sure if you would and I really didn't want to leave this on your voice mail. Can I come over tonight?"

"No, I'm in the middle of packing, what do you want Sean?" Sydney was startled by how down he sounded, usually Sean was really upbeat.

"I really don't want to do this over the phone, it makes me feel like a coward."

"Just spit it out, Illana will be here soon so I don't have a lot of time."

"I'm so sorry, I'm not sure if you will be too, you might not, I mean there were only those two times-"

"What are you talking about? What two times?"

"When we didn't use a condom. What I'm trying to say is, I've tested positive, Sydney. I'm HIV positive."

Sydney's knees went weak and leaning against the wall, grabbing the counter, she slid to the floor. She opened her mouth but there were no words, no air, everything was sucked away.

"Sydney, are you there? Please, say something, yell at me! Something!" Sean pleaded in the phone.

"From who? The gardener?"

"No, my ex-girlfriend. The one before you. She called me last week and I just got my results today."

"I see. I don't know what to say, I have to go Sean. Thanks for letting me know. I have to, I have to go now," Sydney stuttered as she hung up the phone and let it fall to the floor as her head thunked against the wall. She could breathe again, but now all the ramifications were swirling around her head. How to tell Zeke? Or Illana? What about the move? Did any of it matter anymore?

The doorbell rang and she shot off the ground, thankful Illana would be on the other side of it. If ever she needed her best friend, it was now. She yanked open the door and saw her father on her doorstep.

"Hi Dad, come in. I didn't know you were planning on coming over tonight."

"I told you when you dropped the car off I'd be coming by once you got home. You must have forgotten. Now, have you completely lost your mind?"

Knowing he was referring to her moving she exhaled as she responded, "No, and I really don't want to get into this tonight. I have a much bigger issue to deal with right now-"

"How convenient. Of course you do. Whenever I've brought up something you don't want to talk about you run away. Just like this move. I know losing your mom was hard on you, almost as hard as it has been on me. But you can't run away from everything Sydney. Someday, you'll have to stand up and confront issues head on."

Sydney's nostrils flared as she looked up at her father. "I don't confront things? Are you sure you aren't talking about yourself? I wish just once, just one damn time you would see my side. I'm sick of my life here. It's the same day after day. Yes, I love you and Illana and I like my job fine, but I want more. In Ruby Lake, I think I might be able to have it, but I'm well aware there are no guarantees in life. It's not as if I'm going there without a job or a place to live. Give me some credit."

"Sydney, you were only there for ten days! This is just crazy! You're basing a life changing decision on a ten day visit. You've never lived in a small town, or even driven in snow for God's sake! You have no idea what you're getting yourself into. Once again, you are going forward without thinking this through." Graham walked over to the window and placed his hands behind his back while staring out into the darkened night.

"What do mean 'once again?' When have I ever made a decision like this?" Sydney was outraged, and walked over to make him face her. "Everything I've ever done in my entire life was to please you! Jessica was the one you looked at and admired, never me. She played soccer and you never missed a game. I only did ballet, and you came to one performance because Mom made you. Jessica joined the army and you were so proud for her making it in a man's world. But me, big deal, I just work with computers 'Monkeys could do that' you said. So I'm sick of it, why bother? I can't please you so I'm done trying. I'm never going to be who you want me to be, I'm just me. Maybe in Ruby Lake, it will be enough, because it sure as hell has never been enough for you. Oh and one more thing, I miss Mom just as much, if not more than you do. After all, I was around a lot more than you were," she said as she crossed her arms, glaring at hm.

"You watch your tone Sydney," Graham warned, pointing a finger at her as his face flushed with anger. "So, it finally comes out. This is to get back at me for never giving you enough attention. No one but your mother could ever give you that, and God knows I've tried since she's been gone. Fine, I wash my hands of you. Go, and don't come crying to me when this Zeke decides you aren't tough enough to make it in his world, because you aren't." Graham ignored the tears in her eyes as he stomped out and slammed the door. Seconds later Sydney, who was sobbing on the couch, heard him peel out of her parking lot.

Chapter Nineteen – Touch and Go

She was still sitting on the couch when her doorbell rang for the second time that evening. Slowing walking to the door, Sydney looked out the peep-hole and was relieved to see Illana on the other side.

Illana was looking in a plastic bag as Sydney opened the door. "I stopped at O'Mei's and got us two orders of potstickers, kung pow chicken, pork fried rice and moo shoo pork. There should be some fortune cookies in here too, ah, there they are." Illana had said all this while looking through the two bags as she walked in. Then she looked at Sydney. "Oh my God, what happened? Why were you crying?" Illana quickly set the bags on the table and wrapped Sydney in a hug, which made Sydney start crying again.

"Is it Zeke? Did he break up with you? Tell me what happened!" Illana ushered Sydney to the dining room table and got out plates for them while Sydney relayed the two events. At first, while she was dishing out the food, she just listened, but couldn't help throwing in certain comments like: "That son-of-a-bitch!" and "Your dad said what to you?" Finally Sydney sighed with tears welling up in her eyes as Illana sat down.

"I can't believe your dad, well, okay I can. But still, I think you should've told him about the call from Sean. I think the conversation would've gone way differently," Illana said as she plopped a whole potsticker in her mouth.

"Maybe, I don't know Illana. How am I supposed to tell Zeke this? I have to tell him, I can't keep this to myself. As far as my dad goes, I'll have Jessica talk to him about the move and she'll make him see my side. Or at least calm him down." Sydney continued to push the food around on her plate, not really seeing it as she spoke.

"I hope so. Tomorrow, we can call and find out how long you have to wait before being tested for HIV. I think you should call Sean back and find out a little more info too."

"Like what? I really don't ever want to speak to him again. I feel gross just thinking about it."

"You shouldn't. You should find out more about his past partners before you get tested. I saw a documentary on AIDS that followed how it started, anyway – my point is when you get tested you might be asked some embarrassing questions and you need to have the answers."

"You're probably right. At least it can't get any worse, right? Unless the test comes back positive."

"Never tempt the Fates by saying that, they'll only prove you wrong. Now eat, everything will seem better on a full stomach."

Sydney stabbed her moo shoo pork and took a swig of her beer. They had opted for beer as the drink of choice for the evening. Wine was to celebrate, beer was to console. They had made it halfway through their meal when the phone rang. The caller ID read: Unknown caller. Thinking it might be Zeke calling from a bar since it was pool night, Sydney answered it with a smile on the second ring,.

"Hello?"

"May I speak to Sydney Myers?" asked an authoritative male voice.

"This is." Sydney raised an eyebrow and shook her head at Illana, not knowing who was calling.

"I'm Doctor LaSage from UCD Trauma Center. I'm afraid I have some bad news. Your father has been in a car accident. I would've called sooner, but it took my staff a while to find you. I needed to get him stabilized first. I'm preparing to take your father to emergent surgery."

"What, how – what happened? Stabilized? Emergent? Is he okay? Where did you say you were calling from?" Sydney looked wide-eyed at Illana, and mouthed across the table, "My dad was in a car accident." Illana got up immediately, gathered the dinner dishes and started putting the food away.

"He's resting in the ER right now. He's in the trauma section at the UC Davis Med Center. Do you have someone that can drive you here? Do you know how to get here?"

"Yes, I have a friend over who will drive me. She knows the way. What happened?"

"The paramedics said your father ran a red light at a busy intersection, Fair Oaks and Howe. A UPS truck hit him on the driver's side door. Medics had to tourniquet his left leg. He has an open fracture of his femur with a lacerated femoral artery-"

"I'm sorry, is that a broken leg?"

"Yes, but the torn artery is a serious problem. He has lost a lot of blood. We're controlling the bleeding, but we need to get him to surgery soon if we want to save his leg – possibly his life. He broke multiple ribs, has a flail chest and collapsed lung. The medics had to needle his chest to relieve the pressure. They put a tube in his windpipe en route to the hospital. When he got here we did a CAT scan and found a ruptured spleen. I must tell you, it was touch and go for a while. We have to get him stabilized before surgery, which is why he is in the ER now. He arrived in shock and needed blood transfusions and IV fluids. He's on a ventilator right now to assist his respirations. A vascular surgeon is on her way and will be repairing his femoral artery. Oh, and I may have to remove his spleen."

"Oh please, is he, do you think, what are his chances?"

"Very good, but let me finish. An orthopedic surgeon will assist me in repairing his broken leg. It looks like his foot is broken as well. He'll be in surgery before you get here. Look for him in surgery recovery. I'm afraid I need to get back to him right now. There is no need to rush here, it's going to take a couple hours so take your time. Ask for me when you arrive." Dr. LaSage hung up and Sydney turned to Illana.

"I have to call Jessica, can you drive me? He's at UCD Trauma Center."

"Of course, let's go." Illana was standing at the door holding out Sydney's purse and keys to her.

"It's all my fault, if I hadn't argued with him, oh Illana I said horrible things to him, what if he doesn't make it?" Sydney was sobbing again, feeling like an earthquake had zigzagged through her life and no part remained untouched. Illana put her arm around her best friend, her sister in all but blood, and walked her out, locked the apartment and helped her down the stairs. Illana drove just over the speed limit while Sydney called her sister.

"Jess? Oh God, Jessica, Dad's been in a bad car accident."

"What happened? Is he okay?"

"The doctor just called, Illana is driving me to the UCD Trauma Center right now."

"Jesus, Mary and Joseph. It has to be bad to ship him there. I'll get a flight tonight. What the hell happened?"

Sydney tried to breathe but the tears wouldn't stop now, "We got into a fight, a bad one. He and I said things we shouldn't have, didn't mean, at least I didn't – I was fi-fighting back-" Sydney was inconsolable now.

"It's okay Sydney, I'm here. I'm not going to be mad at you, take a deep breath now, honey. The accident, what happened? Do you know?"

Sydney took several deep breaths, but it didn't help. "Y-yes, he ran the light at Fair Oaks and Howe and was broadsided by a UPS truck."

"What are his injuries, here hold on a sec-" Jessica covered the phone to talk to her partner, Mandy, asking her to go to their captain to say they needed an emergency flight tonight. "Okay, now tell me what his injuries are."

"The doctor said something about a broken leg and severed artery he had to fix, and I think a collapsed lung – I'm not sure, it was all doctor speak, I don't know the rest, I will once I get there. I'll call you as soon as I do. I should've asked more questions." Sydney said, gripping her forehead in her hand.

"Don't worry, we all know you fall apart first, but you regain yourself faster than you used to. Call me as soon as you know anything, and I'll make arrangements to get there. I love you little sis."

Sydney placed the phone back in her purse, closed her eyes and let the breath she didn't know she was holding explode out of her lungs in a whoosh.

"We'll be there in fifteen minutes, just hold on Syd," Illana said, lacing her fingers though Sydney's. Sydney didn't let go until they pulled in the parking lot.

Chapter Twenty – Doctor's Orders

Sydney walked quickly to Surgery recovery and said, "I'm here for Graham Myers, I'm his daughter, I was told to ask for Dr. LaSage."

"He's in surgery with your father right now, I'll page him so he knows you're here. Please have a seat in the waiting room, he'll find you when he's done," said the brown-haired nurse with a quiet smile.

Sydney and Illana sat down to wait. Sydney was worrying her purse strap as Illana tried to focus on the wall-mounted television. The hours stretched in front of them, and Sydney was numb, leaning on Illana's arm, doing nothing but watching the ticker tape on the bottom of the screen listing who was winning medals in the Olympics when a doctor walked in the room.

"Sydney Myers? I'm Dr. LaSage. Let's go in here so we can talk." After the introductions were completed, the doctor led them into a smaller waiting room behind the registration desk, a sign over the door ominously read, "Family Consultation," and closed the door. After everyone was seated around the circular wooden table, Dr. LaSage steepled his hands and looked at Sydney.

"Your father was in a near fatal accident, and he's not out of the woods yet. Had the paramedics not gotten to him as quickly as they did, he probably wouldn't be here. Like I told you on the phone, his femoral artery was torn by his femur which snapped in the accident. We've managed to repair the artery. If all goes well, his leg will survive. The orthopedist is repairing his femoral fracture with a steel plate right now. Since I spoke to you, we also discovered a Lisfranc fracture of his foot. That's a serious complex of dislocations and fractures of the mid foot. The orthopedist had to spend considerable time repairing it as well, and it will require one more surgery, but he lost a lot of blood. He's already had a couple transfusions. He may need more. Fortunately I did not have to remove his spleen."

"That's good, right?"

"Yes, even though we still don't know what the spleen does, we're all in agreement it's there for a reason, and it's no longer common practice to remove it. I also found a pelvic fracture on the CAT scan as well. The good news is it's stable and won't require surgery. Pelvic fractures can be a problem because they bleed like a leaky water hose."

"So you won't have to do surgery on that?"

"No, like I said, it's stable. He also has a fractured scapula, and multiple broken ribs. It takes a lot of kinetic energy to fracture the scapula. It must have been one hell of a blow to his body! His left lung deflated and was pushed to the side of his chest. Before he went to surgery, I put a suction tube in his left chest - to drain the blood and keep the lung inflated. His lung was bruised-"

"I didn't know you could bruise your lung." Sydney looked at Illana, who shrugged in agreement.

"Yes, you can actually bruise a lung. Because his left lung is bruised, it can't do its job very well, and it's adding to his respiratory problems. We'll have to leave the endotracheal tube in his windpipe for a few more days. The tube goes between his vocal cords, so he won't be able to talk until we remove the tube. Exactly when, depends on how his lungs recover. Bottom line? Your father will be in the Surgical ICU for five to seven days. He won't be able to leave the ICU until he is extubated. I'm sorry that means we remove the tube from his trachea. If all goes well, he'll spend a couple of weeks in the hospital. A broken bone takes six weeks to mend. It will take months of physical therapy before he walks normally."

"I get most of it, but can you explain some of the unfamiliar terms? I apologize for my ignorance, but I really don't know what a scapula or a list something fracture is." Sydney said, looking at Illana who raised her eyebrows and shook her head in response.

"Certainly. A fractured scapula means his "angel bone" is broken. The Lisfranc fracture means he has a fracture and dislocation of the joints mid-foot. He won't be able to bear any weight on it until the cast comes off, usually in about six weeks. Your family needs to start planning now for his discharge. He will require significant care when he leaves the hospital. He's going to need at least six months of physical therapy if not more. He'll also need to be moved, once he's stabilized, into a care facility where he can receive physical therapy for at least the first six weeks. After that, he'll need someone to stay with him. I wanted you to know the extent of his injuries before you saw him. I also want you to know his chances are good. The biggest worry right now is making sure his breathing is stabilized. I'm going to see what I can do so we can repair the Lisfranc fracture tonight, just as soon as an OR opens up." Dr. LaSage stood up, and turning his steely gaze on Sydney asked, "Would you like to see him now?"

"Yes, absolutely." Sydney stood up while digging in her purse and looked at Illana. "Here's my cell phone in case Jessica calls. Can you tell her-"

"Sure, don't worry about it. I'll be in the waiting room if you need anything." Illana took the cell phone and squeezed Sydney's hand. They followed the doctor out of the room, Illana turning into the waiting room while Sydney continued to follow the doctor down the hallway. The antiseptic smell was stronger here, mixed with other more unpleasant stenches Sydney didn't want to think about. They passed a room where a woman was moaning loudly in her sleep, but the doctor kept going at his clipped pace seeming not to hear her.

He abruptly stopped at a door and turned so quickly his white coat whooshed around him. "He's heavily sedated, so he probably won't wake up, but you can sit with him for a little while if you'd like to. Try not to be disturbed by all the tubes you see. Remember he won't be able to talk, and he has a tube in his chest, which is plugged into a bubbling suction machine. Expect to see some blood in the chest tube. Try not to be overly emotional, it's important he stays calm."

Yeah, thanks Iron Heart, I'll get right on that, Sydney thought as she offered a half smile to the doctor and let herself into her father's room.

She let the door close soundlessly behind her as she took in the scene in front of her. Her father laid helplessly on the bed hooked up to a myriad of tubes and wires that led back to blinking and beeping machines. Multiple bruises darkened his face and arms, looking black against the backdrop of the white sheets. Still rooted to the spot, she hastily wiped her tears away knowing now was not the time. She walked forward, her sandals loud on the gray tile floor and turned the black, cushioned chair around so she could face her father. Looking between his face and arms, she carefully enfolded one of his hands in hers. Leaning forward, using her other hand, she brushed a lock of hair off of his forehead, just as her mother had done so many times before.

She rubbed her dad's hand lightly with her thumb, and sat back in her chair.

"I'm here Dad, and I'm so sorry. I won't be moving now, I'll stay as long as you need me. Don't worry about a thing, I'll take care of you."

She sat like that for a long time, and when she wiped her tears away this time, she wasn't sure if they were for her father, or herself.

The door opened about an hour later and Sydney sat up, looking behind her as the doctor walked in. "Your father appears to have stabilized, so we're going to get him in the OR in about thirty minutes. I'm afraid you'll have to go out into the waiting room while we prep him. I'll come and find you when we're done."

"Thank you. Can I have one more minute?" Sydney stood up, still holding her dad's hand.

"Sure, I'll be back shortly. Can you find your way out?"

"Yes, I remember the way, thank you Doctor LaSage." The doctor nodded and walked out closing the door quietly behind him while Sydney looked down at her father.

"Well Dad, you always said a Myers against the world was even odds, so with Jessica and I both here with you, I know you'll be just fine. I love you and we'll be waiting for you when you wake up." Letting go of his hand, she smoothed his hair off his forehead then kissed him on the cheek. She walked to the door, and turned around to take one more look at her dad, knowing nothing was certain at this point, and he still had to pull through the next couple of days. She raised her chin as she walked out, determined to have only positive thoughts. As she went into the waiting room, she found Illana still sitting by herself, leafing through a magazine. As soon as Illana saw her, she stood up and asked, "Well, how is he?"

"The doctor just told me Dad's stable enough for surgery on his foot. Did you hear back from Jessica?"

"Yeah, she and Mandy will be flying into Mather Air Force Base around midnight. Zeke called too, and all I told him was your father had been in an accident and you were with him. He asked me to give you a hug, and to call him whenever you can." Illana leaned over and gave Sydney a hug, and the two women clung to each other. Sydney started crying and shaking. "Hey, sit down, he's going to pull through and your sister will be here soon. You're going to be fine, take a deep breath. Do you want a soda? Chips?"

"No, Illana this is all my fault! Why did I say those things to him? What if those are the last words I ever get to say to him? He's in there all alone, hooked up to god-knows-what kinds of machines, with bruises and cuts all over his body, and I put him there. I'll never be able to forgive myself, never." Sydney covered her face with her hands and starting sobbing soundlessly, bent forward until her forehead was almost touching her knees.

"Hey, c'mon Syd, you know that's not true, don't do this to yourself. You did not put him there, it was an accident, plain and simple." Illana's eyebrows furrowed in concern as she used her right hand to rub her best friend's back, using her other hand to locate the tissues she had in purse. Pulling a couple out, she handed them to Sydney. "Here, let's take a walk, we'll just go right outside and I'll tell the nurse where we're going so they can find us. I'll be right back."

Illana walked over to the nurse's station as Sydney wiped the tears away with one of the tissues, sticking the others in her coat pocket. Illana came back over and linked arms with Sydney as they walked out into the night.

Chapter Twenty-One – Long Row to Hoe

Hours later, Sydney was gazing at the television not hearing the newscaster when she heard two pairs of boots on the white tile floor. Standing up, she walked out of the waiting room towards the nurses' desk and found her sister and Mandy talking quietly to the nurse.

"Hey sis."

"Sydney! How are you holding up?" Jessica pulled her little sister into a hug and held on as Sydney patted her back.

"I'll be all right. Dad's in surgery for his foot, I thought he'd be out by now but we're still waiting for the doctor to come talk to us."

"Here, let's sit down, hey Illana," Jessica nodded in Illana's direction as they walked in and took their places along the wall in the bucket chairs.

"How was your flight?"

"Fine, long and we're kinda tired. Depending on how long we're going to be here, I may have Mandy go back to your place to crash."

"Jess, we've talked about that, I'm staying as long as need be." Mandy patted Jessica on the back gently, and then came around to give Sydney a hug. "Long time no see. I'm sorry for the circumstance. What did the doctor say about what comes next?"

"He didn't really, only that he would need pretty extensive physical therapy and someone to stay with him for a few months. I guess I'm not moving now, I'll have to talk to John next week about keeping my job."

"We'll wait and see Syd. Dad is a fighter, and I'll bet whatever you were told time-wise for his recovery, Dad will cut it in half."

"Ms. Myers?" Doctor LaSage asked.

"Yes, and this is my sister Jessica. How is he?"

"Why don't you both come with me and we can sit down for a few minutes."

"Is he okay?" Sydney demanded, rooted to the spot.

"Yes, yes, but we have a few things to go over, he's in recovery right now, as soon as he's moved into ICU you can see him."

The four women let out a breath and Sydney and Jessica followed the doctor back into his office. He sat down behind his desk, waving a hand at the seats in front. Once they were seated, he steepled his hands and looked over them at the sisters.

"He came through just fine, no problems during the surgery. However, we're going to keep him here for five to seven days, like I told you before, and then we'll need to talk about where to send him. I can recommend two very good physical therapy facilities, one in Vacaville and another in Roseville."

"Probably Roseville, since that'll be closer to home," Sydney replied looking at her sister who nodded.

"I'll have the nurses get the paperwork to you so we can start on that. Remember, he won't be able to talk for a couple of days. He might be frustrated when he first wakes up, what with not being able to talk and all the tubes. I cannot stress enough how important it is for him to stay calm and for everyone around him to do the same."

Sydney leaned forward to respond, but Jessica put her hand on Sydney's arm to stop her. "Trust me, neither one of us is the hysterical type, so don't worry about that. Will he be able to write? I was thinking of bringing in a pen and notepad so he could communicate with us that way. It might relieve some of his frustration."

"He'll be hooked up to an IV, but he should be functional enough to write." Standing up, the doctor indicated it was time for them to leave. "I'll get word to you when we have him moved so you can see him. The anesthesia should be wearing off fairly soon, and I'm sure it'll be good for him to see you both."

"Thank you, we'll be in the waiting room, thanks for your time." Sydney said, reaching across the oak desk to shake his hand, Jessica following suit. They walked out, Jessica closing the door behind her and side by side, went back into the waiting room. Mandy stood up, hugging Jessica, whispering, "He'll be okay, trust that."

Sydney collapsed into the hard chair, bent over and let her head fall into her hands, her elbows propped on her legs so she could stare at the floor, and the tears that were collecting at her feet. Her breath came out in a rush as she sat up straight and pulled her cell out of her pocket. "I'll be back in a minute. I have to make a call."

Once outside, her heart heavy, she pushed the "1" and waited as Zeke's phone rang.

"Syd – are you okay? I can get a flight out in the morning if you want me, need me, whichever."

"Yes, no, oh Zeke, I'm not going to be able to move to Ruby Lake any time soon. My dad's in bad shape and if he makes it through the next couple of days they're saying he'll need at least six months of physical therapy." Tears she was trying to hold in broke through, her breath hitching up on her exhale. She spotted a cement bench next to a potted plant and sat down.

"Jesus. Don't cry baby. On second thought – yeah, go ahead, do it if you need to, I'm right here." Zeke's voice was like honey on a raw throat.

"Zeke, I have to tell you something, and I don't want to, not right now, I need you, but I have to and it's going to kill us," Sydney said, tears flowing unchecked down her cheeks.

"Whatever it is, we'll deal. You just talk, I'll listen."

Sniffing and taking a deep breath, she said, "Well, right before I came to Ruby Lake, I found my then current boyfriend, Sean, in my bed with someone, a man – my landscaper actually. Shit, I'm screwing this up, that's not the important part. Christ, okay – he called me earlier tonight, please don't hate me-"

"Sydney, no matter what, I'll never hate you, shh, calm down, we don't have to do this right now."

"Yes, I do, because I can't have this hanging over me, us. I have to know if there's going to be any 'us' so I have to do this. Okay, he called tonight to tell me he's HIV positive, and I might be too since he got it from an ex-girlfriend before me. Zeke, I might have it, there was an accident one night. Breakage, if you get my meaning, and then another night of drunken irresponsibility where we didn't use anything. I have to be tested, but I had to tell you." Syd listened intently to the pause before Zeke spoke. It seemed longer than it probably was. When she heard him take a breath she felt her heart breaking.

"You thought I'd hate you? Seriously? Good Lord, woman you just scared ten years off my life for something that is totally not your fault! Get the test, hell, I'll be there tomorrow and take you. I'm in this Syd, I'm with you. Get used to it, I'm not going anywhere. I love you Sydney."

Sydney choked on a sob, which turned into a laugh-hiccup. "That wasn't a reaction I saw coming, I love you too, thank you. I wish you were here, I really do."

"That's good, since I just bought a ticket for six a.m. and I'll be there at eleven-thirty tomorrow morning. Gotta love the internet. If you can't come get me, I can rent a car-"

"I'll be there, no matter what, I'll be there waiting for you. Seriously, I'm not sure what I did to deserve you, but I'm glad I did it, whatever it is. I'm not making any sense, but you get it, don't you?"

"Oh yeah, I do. Listen, we'll talk tomorrow and you can tell me everything. I'll wear layers so if you need to cry, I'll have a few shirts you can use up, okay?" Sydney could almost see the sexy as hell half-smile on his face.

"Good, but by tomorrow, I hope I'll be pulled together a little tighter. I gotta get back in, Jessica's here with her partner and the doctor said we'll be able to see him in a little bit. And Zeke?"

"Yeah?"

"Thanks for being the best part of this fucked up day."

"No problem and you don't need to thank me. You're not alone anymore, there's the two of us now. I'll see you tomorrow."

Sydney walked back in the hospital with a lighter heart. She sat down by Illana and smiled. "It's going to be okay, Zeke's flying in tomorrow at 11:30, and I told him about the Sean thing, and he's still coming."

"What's the Sean thing?" Jessica asked.

"He called me earlier, before Dad came over-"

"Miss Myers?" Doctor LaSage stood in the doorway of the waiting room, hands in the pockets of his white coat. "Your father is still groggy and on morphine for the pain, but the anesthesia just wore off and he's awake so you both can come back and see him."

"Oh, that's wonderful! Thank you so much Dr. LaSage, for everything."

"You're welcome, right this way."

Jessica and Sydney followed the doctor through the double doors of the ICU. Graham was in a different room than before. There was only one bed in this one. Two chairs sat side by side along the wall and Jessica took the one closest to him, after kissing him on the cheek. Graham still had a tube in this throat and an IV was attached to his right hand. Sydney carried the other chair to the opposite side of his bed and sat down.

"You know, next time you can just invite me Dad. No need to almost kill yourself to get me to come home," Jessica said with a smile, taking his left hand in hers.

Graham smiled weakly, and shrugged his shoulders. With his right hand he made writing motions, so Sydney opened her purse and pulled out the notebook she used to write notes to Zeke in. Flipping to the middle to find a blank page, she handed it to her dad as she rummaged for a pen. After locating it in the bottom of her purse and wiping off the lint, she uncapped it and gave that to him also. She and Jessica leaned toward him to see what he was writing.

"Jess – I need a moment with Sydney." Looking up at her to gauge her reaction, he quickly wrote. "I love you both, glad to see you – just need a moment."

Jessica couldn't hide the surprise, but smiled gamely and said, "No problem Dad. I'll be right outside." She kissed him again on the forehead then walked out, shutting the door behind her quietly.

"Dad, I'm so sorry for the things I said! I'm not moving, I'm going to stay-"

Graham raised a hand and mouthed, *My Fault not yours*. He put the notebook in his lap and wrote: "Had a dream about your mom tonight. She's pissed, at me. Told me I was an ass and wouldn't let me stay with her. Said I had to fix this first. Natalie said to let you go and to tell you she likes your Zeke and for me to be nice when I meet him tomorrow."

Sydney's eyes filled with tears as she whipped her head to look up at her father. "Dad, I love you too. But how did you know Zeke was coming here tomorrow?"

"I didn't – she did. It was her and I wanted to stay, came back for you and your sister. It was entirely my fault. I pulled a U-Turn to go back and tell you I was sorry – didn't see the UPS truck. Not your fault – OK?" Graham looked up at Sydney with tears in his eyes. Sydney got up and gingerly wrapped her arms around her father, laying her head gently on his shoulder while he hugged her best he could. Sitting back down, she took the pen and wrote back to him, not trusting the words to come out of her mouth right, and also, to make it permanent.

"Our fault, we're too stubborn. I love you and will be here as long as you need me. If Mom comes back, tell her I miss her every single day. Tell her I'm staying to take care of you because I love you, not because she'd want me to."

Handing the notebook to Graham, she watched as his eyes tracked her words. When he finished, he looked up at her, smiled and mouthed, "Okay," and wrote, "better go get Jess now, give us a few minutes, have things to say to her too."

"I'll send her in. I love you, Dad." Sydney walked into the hall to find her sister leaning against the wall, head back and her eyes closed. "Hey Jess. He wants to see you now. Everything is good between him and me."

"I'm glad but, oh man Sydney, he looks terrible. I don't know if I can be in there by myself for long. He's always been so strong, I can't stand seeing him look so helpless!"

Sydney pulled her into a hug and pressed her cheek against Jess's. "You'll be fine and so will he. Go on, he's waiting." Letting go, she smiled at Jess who straightened up to her full height, chest out, chin up, looking once again like the soldier she had become. As the door clicked shut, Sydney slid down the wall to sit on the floor, wrapped her arms around her knees, closed her eyes and said, "We're all going to be okay Mom, and thank you for sending him back to us."

Chapter Twenty-Two – Oh, How I Hate Thee, Let Me Count The Ways

Early Monday morning, Sydney dropped her purse and coat on her desk and seeing the light on in John's office, knocked quietly on the door.

"Come in."

"Hi John, do you have a few minutes?"

"I do if it means you changed your mind and have decided to stay," he said, turning around to face her. Seeing the puffy eyes and look of concern, he asked, "Is everything okay?"

"No, my dad was in a really bad car accident last night and is stable, but will be in ICU for at least a week. He's at UCD right now. I know Dan is starting today, so I came in, but I really need to leave in a couple hours, and I'm not sure how the rest of the week is going to go."

"No problem, here sit down. Is there anything I can do? What happened?" John leaned forward in his chair, resting his arms on his desk.

Sydney brought John up to speed, and finished by saying, "So, I won't be moving anytime soon, he's going to need help for a least a couple of months. I was wondering if I can keep my job and also if I could work from home part time."

"Absolutely, whatever you need. Of course you can keep your job. I'm sorry for the circumstances, but I'm personally glad you'll be staying on. You can log in from home or anywhere."

"Great, thanks John."

"Sydney, why don't you just take this week off? We're not going to hear about the contract for at least a couple of weeks, and family comes first."

"I will, I'll just meet with Dan first, then I'll take off. If you need anything, you can reach me on my cell, and I'll be checking my email and my voice mail-"

"You just worry about your dad, I'll handle everything here."

Taking a deep breath, she smiled at John and tried to blink the tears away.

"Really if you don't feel up to meeting with Dan today, it can wait until next week."

"No, I'll be fine, besides it shouldn't take long and I'll leave right after." Sydney nodded and walked out, straight back to her desk to put away her coat and purse. She booted up her computer, and gathered her files to give to Dan. His cubicle being next to hers was a bonus and would make training him easier. She walked into his very empty space, and put the files down to the left of his monitor.

Back at her desk, she logged onto the network and realized there were a couple more reports she needed to give Dan and printed them off. Sydney was bent over Dan's desk adding one more report to the contract file and was startled when she turned around and ran right into him.

"Good morning! Well, this is a pleasant way to start my day. Do I get to look forward to having you run into me every morning?" Dan asked with a leer as he set his briefcase on the floor and loosened his tie.

"No, but welcome aboard. I made you some files to review, so let me know when you're done and we can get started. If you drink coffee, you can use one of the courtesy cups above the sink in the kitchen, its fifty cents a cup." Sydney said, as she squeezed by him and into the hallway. He made her uncomfortable, and she tried to cover it up by being overly chatty. "I hope you'll like it here, and just so you know, we don't have a lot of time to get you up to speed today. I'm going to be leaving in about an hour, so if we can I'd like to meet with you before I go. I'll be at my desk if you have questions on anything and let me know when you're ready to meet. "

"I'll do that. Thanks," Dan said, his eyes straying to her chest and back at her face.

Sydney caught the glance, and decided to ignore it – for now. She merely nodded at him and went to her desk. Illana came in a few minutes later.

"What the hell are you doing here?"

"I work here, and will be since John is letting me keep my job."

Rolling her eyes she leaned on Sydney's desk. "We all knew he would. I figured you'd still be at the hospital. How's your dad?"

"Sleeping, I left there about an hour ago to take Mandy to my place so she could get some sleep. Jess is still with him, I'll only be here for about an hour. I knew Dan was starting today and wanted to touch bases with him. I'll be off the rest of the week."

"Good. Let me know if there's anything I can do." Illana leaned down to hug Sydney just as Dan walked in.

"My day just gets better and better. Good morning, Illana right?"

Illana exchanged a glance with Sydney and said, "Right. Morning Dan, Sydney come see me before you leave," Illana said, pulling herself up to her full height of five feet ten inches to look him in the eye.

"Sure, sure I understand. Sorry to interrupt your girl time, but Sydney, I was wondering if you could explain why you chose to go the way you did on a few things. Whenever you have time is fine." Dan said, shrugging his shoulders nonchalantly. Illana rolled her eyes at her best friend and walked away as Sydney stood up.

"Now's good. Let's use the conference room, no reason to be cramped in a cubicle."

"Whatever you think is best," Dan replied as Sydney walked past. She couldn't be sure, but she thought he was staring at her ass from the look on Brian's face, which went from friendly to stony in two seconds flat as they walked past him.

Illana rescued her an hour later and, after collecting Sydney's things they practically ran down to the parking garage.

"That male chauvinist son of a bitch! 'Girl time?' Did you see the way he looked at us? By the way, he royally pissed off Brian this morning."

"I noticed, I figured Dan was staring at my ass and Brian saw him."

"That and the fact he made some comment about showing you how a real database is built. I say we go to John now."

"Not yet. Let's give him a couple days. Besides, I really need to be off this week, and who knows how long I'll be working from home so I can take care of my dad. If John gets rid of him, I won't be able to."

Illana stopped walking and grabbed Sydney's arm. "You mean to tell me you're willing to put up with Dan's shit even when you know he's going to be an asshole to work with?"

"Yes, that's exactly what I'm saying. C'mon Illana, we've dealt with his type before, it's not like I don't know how to shut him down. One more comment and I will. He's argumentative, and not as knowledgeable as John said he was, but other than those flaws he'll be okay." They reached Sydney's car and Illana shook her head.

"If you say so. But I don't trust him. I have a bad feeling about this guy."

"Here we go again. He's harmless, hell Annie was way worse than this guy! Lighten up, you're just pissed because he looked down at you."

"Maybe, we'll see. Call me later tonight and let me know how your dad is, okay?"

"I will. Try not to kill Dan while I'm gone. I gotta go, Zeke's plane is going to land in an hour, and I want to go home first."

"I'd forgotten he was coming. Go, and I promise I won't kill Dan. At least, not today," Illana said with a mischievous grin as she walked away.

Chapter Twenty-Three – Fast Cars and Impatient Patients

Traffic was fairly light, for once, on the way to the airport. Of course, finding a parking space was a nightmare, but Sydney finally found one in the general vicinity of where she wanted to be. She wrote down the marker she parked next to because with all the things on her mind, she didn't trust her memory. Not wanting to make a spectacle of herself, she walked as fast as she could without running.

Walking in the doors which led her to the Northwest ticketing counter, she glanced up at the clock on the wall. *Whew, I still have ten minutes before his plane lands.*

"Looking for someone?"

Sydney spun around and found Zeke smiling at her. "You're early!" she said as he picked her up in a bear hug. Sydney wrapped her arms tightly around his neck, and kissed his cheek. He set her back down, took her face in his hands and in front of all the other travelers, kissed her silly. Had she not been standing on them, her toes would've curled.

"I missed you Syd. How's your dad?" Zeke asked, his arms still locked around her waist.

"Probably giving the nurses hell. I called Jess on my way here and he had written a note stating he was ready to leave."

"So he's not talking yet?"

"Not yet. He has a tube in his throat so he can't. The doctor said they might be taking it out tomorrow. Knowing Dad, it'll be today. How long have you been waiting?"

"Only about five minutes, I'm still waiting for my bag to come out."

He tugged her closer, and she laid her head against his chest, feeling safe and content for the first time since...well, the first time ever. It was crazy she felt this way about someone she had known less than a month. She closed her eyes and inhaled the unique smell of him, pine trees, fresh air and just a smidge of exhaust. The luggage turnstile turning on made them break apart so Zeke could watch for his luggage. Taking her hand in his, they got a spot right in front to wait.

He let go when an army green duffel bag came shooting out down the metal slide. It was the size of a hockey bag, and stuffed to capacity, but Zeke lifted it off like it was full of air.

"How long did you say you were staying?"

"I didn't, and since I didn't know, I brought a little of everything. Even shoes to go dancing in, if you wanted to. I mean, you probably won't because of what's going on with your dad, I only thought it might take your mind off-"

Sydney laid a finger on his lips. "I'm not offended. Thank you, but you're right. I really don't feel like dancing right now. Let's swing by my place and drop your stuff off, then you can either come with me to see my dad, or stay at my place."

"I'd like to stay with you, if that will be okay?" He asked, slipping her hand in his.

She smiled and nodded, and reveled at how perfect this moment felt.

As they went outside, Sydney pulled her note out, because sure enough, she had no idea where she parked. Seeing Zeke had made everything in her mind disappear. "Yeah, it's totally okay. Thanks for being here, Zeke. It means more than you know," Sydney said, squeezing his hand.

"There's no place I'd rather be than wherever you are."

Maneuvering her car onto I-5 was always tricky. Sydney punched it so she could zip in front of the semi that was already going 70 miles an hour. Looking over at Zeke's pinched lips and his death hold on the "oh shit" bar, she laughed.

"What's the matter tough guy? Scared?"

"What? No, I'd forgotten what traffic was like. Jesus, Syd, you think you could slow down a little?"

"I'm only doing 75. Calm down, we'll be at my place in a jiffy."

"I'm sure we will since you're driving at the speed of light."

Gripping the steering wheel harder, she took a breath and said in a rush, "Um, I talked to my dad's doctor, and he got me an appointment to get tested today. He said we'd have the results in about three days."

"It's not going to change how I feel about you, and I'll be right here with you."

"But, what if-"

"Nope, we're not even going there. There is no "what if's" about this. We'll figure it out as it comes, no need to borrow trouble before there is any."

Sydney didn't think he was being realistic, but chose to go along with him. Getting off the freeway, Zeke sighed in relief, so she gunned it down the off-ramp. He crossed his arms and gave her a dirty look, making her laugh.

"Serves you right for rocking your boat on purpose when you took me fishing. You so had this coming to you."

"Touché. But we're even now, so knock it off."

After dropping Zeke's stuff off, and keeping quiet so as not to wake up Mandy, who was asleep on Sydney's bed, they drove over to the hospital. Much to Zeke's surprise, they made it in one piece and without getting a speeding ticket. Sydney found Jess talking to one of the nurses. Seeing them, Jessica raised a finger, letting them know she'd be done in a minute.

"Does your dad do that too?"

"What?"

"The one finger thing, you do the same thing."

Sydney looked up at him, furrowing her brows as she thought about it. "Yeah, I guess he does, I never thought about it before."

"So, you must be Zeke." Jessica held out her hand, her smile reserved.

"Yes, and you must be the Army Sergeant. Sydney has told me a lot about you." Zeke said, returning the firm handshake.

"Sergeant Major, but you can call me Jess." Jessica smiled wider at him, then turned her attention to Sydney. "Dad has been being a pain in the ass all morning. He's all yours."

"What happened?"

"Where to start? First he wants the catheter out even though he can't walk. Then it was the tube in his neck he wanted removed, and they're actually considering it. Now, he wants the IV moved to his left hand so he can write better, which they're doing right now. He asked me to bring his laptop in so he can write easier, so I'll bring it with me when I come back tonight. I need to get some sleep, and since your man is here, Mandy and I are going to stay at Dad's."

"Sounds like fun. Dad never did have any patience with lying around. Do you still have your key or do you need mine?"

"No, I have mine. I'll be back around seven, and I'll bring dinner with me. Nice meeting you Zeke, and welcome to the madness."

"Glad to be here. Let me know if there's anything I can do to help."

"Just don't ask him to drive anywhere," Sydney said with a smirk.

"Why, think you'd get lost?" Jess asked, looking concerned

"No, I need a couple of days to get my bearings and I'll be fine." Zeke shot a warning look at Sydney to keep her mouth shut, which she did.

"If you need a map, I have several. I'm outta here, see you both later." Jessica gave her sister a hug, nodded in Zeke's direction and left through the automatic doors.

"Why don't you have a seat for a few while I get the lay of the land?"

"No problem, take your time. Smartass." Zeke kissed her on the top of her head and reached up to tug her hair a little, and then ambled into the waiting area. Sydney checked in at the nurse's station who buzzed her into the ICU ward. Hearing a crash coming from her dad's room she quickened her pace.

"Now, Mr. Myers I understand this is a very trying time for you, but really, you need to calm down so we can do our job."

Graham held up the notebook which only had one word, in capitals, on it. "NO"

"Hi Dad, I see you're back to your normal cheerful self. Is there a problem?" she asked the nurse who was bent over righting the bedside tray.

"Well, I know he wanted his IV changed, but now he wants it in his foot and that's really not our standard procedure."

"I see. Can you give us a few minutes?"

"Certainly." The nurse looked relieved, and harried, so it was no surprise to Sydney how fast the nurse left.

"Now Dad, what's all this fuss about?" Sydney asked, scooting a chair next to his bedrail.

Graham flipped the pages back, then handed the notebook to her. The page he flipped to said: "I read your "notes" to Zeke. I had no idea you were this serious about him. You should've told me. I do love you and want you to be happy."

"I thought about that last night, you reading those. I am serious about him, and just so you know, he's here. In the waiting room. I don't want you to meet him yet, we have a lot of other things to worry about, but he did come to be here for me. That should mean something." Taking a deep breath, she crossed her arms and looked sternly at her father. "Now, why are you being such a pain in the ass?"

Graham tried to laugh, which turned into a gurgle. Making the writing gesture with his hand, Sydney handed the notebook back to him. He wrote: "You sounded just like your mom."

"Good for me. Answer the question."

He blew his breath out through his nose, like a bull, and wrote: "I hate it here. Want to go home. Will hire a nurse. Make it happen."

"No. Once you're released from the ICU, then we'll talk. For right now, you're staying here until you can breathe on your own. Stop being so pushy."

Graham wrote again: "Natalie said I was staying here, not with her, so I'm not going to die. GET ME OUT OF HERE!"

Sydney laughed and shook her head. "No matter what Mom said, I'm not taking any chances, and neither are the doctors. You really are a pain in the ass when you aren't in control. Just let them do their jobs, and concentrate on staying calm or they're going to make you stay longer. Now, can I get you anything? Besides a get out of jail free card?"

Graham mouthed "Very Funny" and wrote: "Jess will bring the laptop, I'll just have to watch the idiots on TV until then."

Rolling her eyes, she pulled some magazines out of her purse. "Here, I brought you a Newsweek and National Geographic to read. I figured these would keep you out of trouble for a while."

Graham smiled and wrote: "NOT LIKELY"

Chapter Twenty-Four – Earrings and Forklifts

Later that night, Graham kicked everyone out for the evening. He wrote that there was no need for all of them to lose sleep, since the nurses would be waking him up every couple of hours. Sydney gave in, collected Zeke from the waiting room and went home.

Sydney was content to drive slower, especially since Zeke had been such a good sport about hanging out in the waiting room all day. Glancing over at him she was shocked to see the earring sparkling under his hair.

"Hey, when did you get that?"

"Oh, this?" he asked, flicking the underside of his ear lobe. "Earlier today when you and Jessica were in with your dad. Mandy came by and took me to some mall and I got it done. You once said it would make me even sexier."

Sydney remembered vividly, and blushed in response. "I, uh, wasn't wrong either. Thank you."

"I know you specified a gold-hoop, but for one, the girl doing it said I needed to have a stud first and two, I refuse to wear a hoop anywhere except our bedroom. I don't want anyone thinking I'm gay." Realizing what he said, he quickly turned to her, "Not that I have anything against gay people, I mean, Mandy and Jess are great-"

Sydney was laughing at his attempt to jump out of the hole he'd just dug himself. "I knew what you meant when you said it, and I think if you were truly homophobic it would've come out by now. But I'm relieved to see you're a little tense too. I thought it was just me."

"What do you mean, tense?"

"Well, c'mon Zeke, how long have we known each other? Sometimes it feels like forever, and then there are times like now it hits me that I've known you for under a month. Talking to you on the phone is one thing, but you tend to be more than a little intimidating in person."

"Really?" he asked, sounding pleased, crossing his arms while giving her a sideways glance.

"Yes! I mean, I look at you and can't believe you're here, with me."

"Yeah, I have some of that too, only for me, its relief. I never thought I'd feel this way, and now that I do, I have to remind myself it's real."

"Right, I keep vacillating between extreme comfort and extreme doubt."

"You can quit with the doubt, I'm not going anywhere."

Sydney smiled at him as she pulled into her apartment complex parking lot. Parking in her appointed spot, she grabbed her purse and they both trekked up the stairs. A wave of relief hit Sydney as she stepped inside her domain, her sanctuary. Having Zeke with her took a little of the relaxation away, not that she was going to be complaining about it. Here, alone with him, she was a little nervous.

"Do you want something to drink? Eat?" she asked, tossing her purse on the table.

"No, I'm good. I like the frame," he said, nodding at the picture of them with the fish.

"Thanks, made it myself. So, um, do you want to watch T.V.?"

"We can. Is there some reason you're being so skittish?"

"I'm not being skittish, I just don't know how you like to unwind."

"Come here, Sydney, I won't bite, well, not unless you ask nicely," he said, half smiling as he opened his arms.

Sydney walked into his embrace, the nervousness melting away. Normally, men in flannel were a turn off, but not this man. On him it seemed fitting, right. And the shirt was soft against her cheek. Zeke kissed the top of her head.

"We'll just stay like this until you're comfortable again," Zeke said, then his phone started ringing. Looking at the number he answered, "Hey Alex."

"Hi. How's Sydney?" Sydney didn't move, and she could hear every word.

"Right now, she's pressed up against me and feels rather good. But to answer your question, she's doing fine. Thanks for giving me the time off."

"Yeah, about that, I have a problem. One of the idiots, Tom, decided to play chicken in the forklift today and overturned both of them. He broke his leg, and Donnie got a concussion, so they are both out for a few days. I really need you to come back for a few days while I hire someone else."

"You have to be kidding me! C'mon Alex, I need to be here right now, I thought I explained that!"

Sydney stepped back, shook her head, and said, "It's okay, I'll be fine. He needs you."

"No, he doesn't."

"Yes, I actually do. I wouldn't ask if it wasn't absolutely necessary. That's why I waited until tonight to call. As it stands now, we are already backed up three days in the warehouse for deliveries, and I've got a delivery coming tomorrow I couldn't reschedule since the driver is already en route."

"Hold on a sec, Alex," Zeke said, putting the phone against his chest, "You sure you don't mind?"

"I'm sure. Go and come back when you can." Sydney said.

Zeke put the phone back to his ear, "Alright Alex, I'll be on the first flight tomorrow. But tomorrow morning I want you to call Bud Maynard and get him in there and hire him like I told you in the first place."

"I already called him. He'll be in at nine."

"Good, I'll see you when I get there." Zeke closed his phone and looked at Sydney, who was sitting on the couch.

"So, who's Tom the idiot?"

"He's a friend of Donnie's, who is the other idiot Tom hit in the forklift. My guess is Alex will pay both their doctor bills, because he's a sucker, and meanwhile, I have to go home for a few days. But I'll be back. In fact, I wanted to talk to you about our immediate future." Zeke went over and sat next to her. "I know you won't be able to move now, not with the shape your dad is in. How would you feel about me moving here?"

"No. You have a life you love out there, and if you move here you'll hate it here. I don't want you to resent me later because you're here."

"I won't, and no I don't love my life out there. I love you, and wherever you are is where I want to be. I've thought about this, and if you can't come to me, then I'll come to you."

"Let's just see how it goes. No need to plan everything out now. Besides, you're needed there." Sydney grabbed a throw pillow and hugged it to her middle.

"Are you saying I'm not needed, or at least wanted here?"

"No, don't put words in my mouth. I'm not saying that at all."

"You can trust me Sydney, I'm not going to hurt you." Zeke pulled on the pillow and dropped it on the floor. "You don't need to protect yourself from me."

"It just happened too fast, I can't catch up," she said, her eyes pleading with him to understand.

"I hear you, but I'm here to stay. Well, not here, at least for the next couple of days. The guy Alex is going to hire tomorrow will do a good job and he'll be able to replace me in a week. Then I'll be coming back. Here."

"Are you sure? I want to trust you, I really do. But I don't have a stellar track record with men."

"Have a little faith, Sydney."

"You're not going to start singing that George Michael's song, are you?"

"No, but thanks a lot. Now I'll have that stupid song stuck in my head for the next three days." Zeke picked up the pillow and threw it at her head.

"Hey!" she cried, laughing and snuggled the pillow to her chest. "I want one condition though."

"What's that?"

"No sex until after my results come back." Sydney held up a hand to stop him from talking. "No, I'm serious. I know too well how accidents can happen and if I am HIV positive, it would kill me if you got it too."

"Fine, we'll wait, but I'm not happy about it."

"I said no sex, but I've got a pretty fertile imagination so I'm sure I can think of other things to do with you, or to you."

Zeke pulled the pillow away from her, picked her up and she let out a screech. "So, where's our bedroom?" Sydney smiled and happily showed him.

Chapter Twenty-Five – Back At The Ranch...

Zeke got off the plane in Ruby Lake and walked into the airport feeling an ironic sense of deja-vu. His bag in hand he said hello to a few people he knew and walked out into the cold to find his truck waiting for him. He had called Alex when the plane got to Minneapolis and asked him to bring it over since Zeke had left his truck at Alex's house. He smiled as his thoughts went back to the previous night, and of just how creative Sydney was, and flexible. His thoughts warmed him more than the heater in his truck. In fact, the heater was just starting to shoot out warm air when he pulled into the parking lot at work.

Pulling his coat around him a little tighter to ward of the chilly morning, he walked towards the door just as it opened.

"Sounds good, Bud, we'll see you tomorrow. Oh, hey Zeke, Bud said he could start tomorrow."

"Great, how you doing Bud?" Zeke asked, shaking the older man's hand.

"Good, I hear ya got yourself a woman in California, and you're bent on pulling me outta retirement." Bud shook a non-filtered cigarette out of a pack and lit it.

"Well, I couldn't let you just wither away or start puttering in a garden; it wouldn't be good for your image."

"Ha! I figure I have a few good years left in me, and now I'll finally get to teach you how to do your job proper like." Bud left the cigarette dangling in his mouth as he stuck his hands in his coat pockets.

"I don't plan on being here long enough for anything you have to teach me to sink in. Maybe you can teach Donnie a few things when he gets back."

"Son, I've forgotten more about 'lift driving than you ever knew. I'll be seeing you boys tomorrow." Bud slapped Zeke on his back and walked over to his truck, which was more beat up than Zeke's.

"Think we could go inside now? I'm freezing my balls off out here," Zeke said to his brother. Alex held the door open and let Zeke go in first. "Before I get started, I need to talk to you about a few things."

"Sure, you want to go in my office?" Alex asked.

"Yeah, it's warmer in there."

"Look at you, one day in California and you've turned into a candy-ass."

"More comments like that are going to get you put on *your* ass, brother," Zeke said over his shoulder as he walked inside the main office.

Saying hello to the room at large, he was just walking into Alex's office as Annie came out of hers.

"You're back. What a pity, and here I was hoping you'd stay there."

"Alex called me back, so here I am. Don't worry little sis, I'll be outta here in a few days. Apparently, he couldn't make it more than one day without me."

"Could you two try to act civilly for one day? Is that possible?" Alex asked, pushing Zeke into his office. Alex shook his head as he shut the door. "So, what's up?"

"I wanted to let you know I'll be moving to Sacramento for a while. At least until Sydney's dad is better. He's in bad shape Alex." Zeke propped his boots, crossed at the ankles, on the big desk and leaned the chair back as Alex sat back in his chair.

"Oh man, I'm sorry to hear that. I figured this is what would happen, you moving I mean. When?"

"I plan on going out there just as soon as Bud has it under control. Which will probably be by the end of the day tomorrow, knowing him," Zeke said with a laugh.

"You should've seen him this morning. Walked into my office, said "So I hear you need a real driver around here. You want me to start tomorrow?" and that was the extent of the interview."

"He'll do a good job for you. Of course, good luck controlling him," Zeke said with a smirk.

"Yeah, no shit. So, by the way, did you see Illana while you were out there?" Alex asked, trying to sound nonchalant.

"No, didn't have time. We were supposed to meet for lunch today, but with me here, that's going to be a little hard to do. I'm surprised you didn't know about my missed lunch, with all the emailing you two do."

"You didn't tell Sydney about the emails, did you? She doesn't know and Illana wants to tell her," Alex said, running his hand through his hair.

"No, but I was tempted. Why keep it a secret? Sydney and I are together, and Sydney's not going to care now," Zeke said as he crossed his arms.

"That's what I said, but Illana wants to do this her way. Besides, Illana and I are just friends."

"Riiight, you keep telling yourself that, and maybe one of us will believe you." Zeke stood up, pulling his gloves out of his pockets. Putting them on, he looked back at Alex. "One other thing, and this is just between you and me. Sydney might be HIV positive, she'll know later this week."

"Oh shit. What does that mean for you two?" Alex asked sitting up against his desk.

"Nothing, it won't mean a goddamn thing one way or the other. If she does have it, well, it'll make certain things more difficult to be sure, but I know she's the one for me. I need your promise this will stay between us."

"You have it. Christ, who do you think I would tell?" Alex asked indignantly.

"Mom, and then I'll get a phone call I really don't want," Zeke said with an eyebrow raised.

"Zeke, I'm not ten anymore, it's not like I run to her with everything," Alex said, crossing his arms in front of him.

"No, but you tell her plenty. Have you mentioned Illana to her yet?"

"Yes, but only casually." Alex ran his hand through his hair and leaned back in his chair.

"She'll be reserving the country club for your upcoming wedding in July now."

"No she won't, don't you have work to do?"

"Don't like it when the tables are turned, do you? See you later." Zeke opened the door, making Annie jump. "Listening through keyholes again?"

"No, I was walking by and you startled me. Why would I care what you have to say?"

"I don't have a clue, but if you did hear something I'll expect you to keep it to yourself. If I hear otherwise, your life will become very uncomfortable." Zeke leaned against Alex's doorjamb, making sure his brother could hear every word.

"You don't scare me, and besides, I didn't hear anything. Like I said, I was walking by when you came out. I don't have time for this, I have work to do."

"Still playing catch up from your 'vacation' Annie?" Zeke asked with a slight grin.

She turned around, glared at Zeke, and then slammed her door. Smiling wider, knowing he had gotten her goat, he started walking out to the warehouse when Gina stopped him.

"Hey, just so you know, she stood right by Alex's door shuffling paperwork for a couple minutes before you came out."

"Great. I figured as much. Hey, can you do me a favor?"

"Sure, what do you need?"

"Can you monitor her email, and let me know if she sends anything regarding Sydney?"

"You bet. I'd do it for you anyway, but for Sydney I'd do just about anything. I owe her big."

"She'd never see it that way, but thanks. I'll be out in the warehouse if you find anything."

Cracking open a beer, he took a swallow and snatching the phone off the counter, went outside to sit on his deck. The sun was just going down, the fading light reflecting pink and purple hues on the still water of the lake. Zeke frowned thinking about Gina not finding anything, and he wondered just how much Annie had heard. He debated telling Sydney, but decided she had enough on her mind and he could handle his sister. With that settled, at least in his mind, he called Sydney.

"Hello?"

"Hi, how's your dad?"

"He's doing pretty good. He got the trach tube out today, so he's been trying to boss everyone around. It would be more effective if he didn't sound like Kermit the Frog."

"Any news about what's going to happen next?"

"No, they still want to keep him in ICU for the next couple of days, but he's on the mend. How did your day go? Did Alex hire that guy, Buddy?"

"Bud, and yes. He was just leaving when I got to work this morning. Wait until you meet him, he's old and crotchety, but he can handle a forklift like it's a beautiful violin. It looks like I should be back out there by this weekend."

"That will be great! But, seriously, if you need to wait a week or two, I'll understand."

"No, I don't want to take the chance that you'll change your mind," Zeke said, taking another drink of his beer. The doorbell chimed, pulling his attention away from his woman and the sunset on the lake.

"Sydney? Someone's at the door, can I call you back?" Zeke set his beer bottle down on the railing and walked inside.

"Actually, let me call you tomorrow. Jess and Mandy will be here soon and we've got a lot of planning to do."

"Sure, no problem. Tell them both I said hi."

"Will do. Catch ya tomorrow," she said, disconnecting.

Zeke set the phone down on the hall-tree and opened the door, more than a little surprised to see Michelle standing there.

"Can I come in?" she asked.

"No. What do you want?" Zeke asked, crossing his arms.

"Zeke, let me in, it's freezing out here."

"You come here uninvited that's what you get. Again, what do you want?"

"I want you to take me back. I'm sorry, and I've paid the price of living without you. How much longer are you going to punish me?" Michelle asked, laying her hand on his arm.

He yanked his arm out of her hand. "Don't touch me. I'm not punishing you, it's over. It's been over for a year. Go home Michelle."

"I know we can work this out, I love you and you said you loved me!" she said, tears filling her eyes.

"No, we can't. I may have thought I loved you, but now I know what love is, and what we had was a like a pale shadow of the real thing. I'm in love with Sydney and will be moving there soon to be with her. You need to move on Michelle, and find someone else. Maybe next time, you won't listen to every rumor that comes your way." He shut the door to cut off whatever ridiculous thing she was going to say next. But it didn't stop her from shouting through the door.

"At least I don't have HIV! How can you want her knowing that?"

He yanked the door open, cold fury in his eyes. "What did you say?"

"I said I don't have HIV like that whore does. Annie called and told me you told Alex about it."

Zeke stepped outside, startling Michelle into backing up, and shut the door. Quietly and through gritted teeth he said, "Listen to me very carefully. Sydney does not, I repeat, does NOT have HIV, and never call her a whore again. Annie got it all wrong, and as usual, you'll believe anything she tells you. I'll take care of my sister, but you need to leave right now, before my anger gets the best of me. Do not come here again."

Zeke was shaking when he walked inside and locked the door. He wondered how many other people she had told, and was tempted to drive over to her house and throttle her. Why Annie was so interested in getting Michelle and him back together was a mystery, but he'd have to set her straight. Right now, he was too mad. He walked into the living room and sat down in his easy chair, leaning it all the way back so the footstool popped out. He watched as the last of the sunlight faded, and suddenly smiling, came up with the perfect plan to end Annie's scheming with Michelle once and for all.

Chapter Twenty-Six – Self-Inflicted Wounds

Zeke had no idea of how long it took him to drive to work, he was too consumed by cold fury to allow the passage of time to register on his radar. His plan set in his mind, he found himself getting angrier and angrier as the night wore on. Slamming his truck door shut, he marched determinedly into the warehouse, prepared to do battle with Annie, once and for all. But Bud had other ideas.

"What the hell took you so long? I've been waitin' for you for almost twenty minutes. Got a bug up your behind this morning?"

"Yes."

"Well, let's put it to work. Here are them sheets for what we're supposed to be pullin'. Why doncha show me where they are now so when we're through, we can take a break and you can cry all over me?" Bud smirked at him, his lips pressed tightly around a cigarette.

"If you were anyone else, you'd be on the ground. All right, let's see the printouts," Zeke waved his hand towards the sheets in Bud's hand. Bud took the cigarette out of his mouth and handed over the papers, laughing quietly.

Zeke spent the next hour showing Bud how the stock was laid out, and due to Sydney setting up the reports so everything was printed out in the order it was on the shelves, Bud picked it up quickly. So quickly, that Zeke was sitting back relaxing with his forklift shut off or else he wouldn't have heard his phone ring.

"Hello?"

"Well, are you coming here or not? I thought we had an 8:30 meeting?"

"Doreen? Oh shit, I totally forgot, sorry. I'll be there in fifteen minutes."

"See you then." The librarian hung up on him as he was jumping down from his seat. He put his fingers in his mouth to whistle at Bud, who in turn shut off his engine.

"Think its break time already, pretty boy?"

"No, I forgot I have an appointment, I need to leave for about an hour. You okay on your own? Not going to have a heart attack or break a hip while I'm gone?"

"I haven't even worked up a sweat yet. You go on, I'll see ya later." Bud turned the engine back on, and whipped around the forklift like a ballerina doing a pirouette. Zeke shook his head, smiling, as he walked over to his laptop, and quickly sent a "good morning, miss you" email to Sydney. He didn't know if she was going into work, but he was sure she'd at least check her emails, and he was selfish enough to want her thinking of him. After telling Alex he'd be gone for a while, he headed towards the town library.

Sydney swung into her chair in her work cubicle, and booted up her computer as she tossed her purse on the counter of her desk. On her way to the hospital to visit her dad, she remembered a file she needed that was on her hard drive instead of the network, and therefore not accessible from home, so she took a detour to work first. Hopping up from her chair, she walked over to John's closed door and knocked. Looking through the square glass window in his door, she saw him wave her in.

"Yes, I understand, but I'm not sure we have time to bid on another contract. Um hm. Yes, well, since you put it that way, I'll type something up and email it to you today. No problem, I won't. You too, thank you." John replaced the receiver in its cradle and looked up at Sydney. "You do know when you take a week off it means you don't have to report in every morning, right?"

"You're very funny. I only stopped in to grab a file off my computer and thought I'd check in with you while I was here. Anything new on the big contract yet? Are you putting in another bid?"

"Yes, and I was specifically asked not to mention it to you, yet. As far as anything new I can mention, no. I imagine we'll hear something on the contract this week, and until then, everyone has small projects to work on. Except for you. How's your dad doing?" John asked, steepling his fingers in front of his chest while leaning back in his chair.

"They took the tube out of his throat yesterday, so I imagine he's regained his full voice today and is currently busy bossing everyone around. I'm headed over there as soon as I check my email and get that file. Call me as soon as you hear about the contract, okay?"

"I will, and I don't want to see you here for the rest of the week, got it? Go take care of your dad, family comes first around here."

"Will do, thanks John." Sydney was still smiling when she walked back into her little piece of heaven and opened up her email. Illana sashayed into her cubicle just as she was deciding on which email from Zeke to open first.

"Why am I not surprised to see you here? Oooh, two emails from lover boy. Open the one with the attachment first, it came in last."

"Holy shit, you are the nosiest person I've ever met. Go away and let me read in peace."

"No, I'm vicariously living through your romance, so open it already!" Illana said, planting her ass on Sydney's desk. Sydney let out a long suffering sigh, and clicked on the email Illana requested.

"Sydney, I'm sorry to tell you this in an email, but I've decided we won't work. You have too many problems, and I need someone a little simpler in my life that isn't carrying around so much baggage. Michelle came over last night, and we've decided to get back together. I've attached a picture we took this morning so you know I'm serious. Please do not contact me again, I'll be blocking all your calls and emails from now on. – Zeke"

Sydney's eyes welled up before she could catch her breath. She numbly clicked on the attachment, and sure enough, it was a picture of Zeke kissing Michelle.

"Bullshit, this is bullshit Sydney. He would never do this to you. Wait a minute, move your hand, I want to blow up the picture." Illana pushed Sydney's chair over so she could squat in front of the monitor. She zoomed in on the picture and smiling, turned back to Sydney. "Okay, now tell me what you don't see."

"Me and my happily ever after."

"Stop it, look at the picture, specifically, look at his ear."

Sydney leaned in to look closer, and because his hair was in a ponytail, she could clearly see his ear, which should've had an earring in it, or at least a hole where it had been. "This is an old picture, isn't it? Annie, you think?"

"Of course I do, who else would do this? Call him right now so you don't stew."

Sydney spun her chair and grabbed her cell phone out of her purse, pushing the "1" button as soon as her hand was on it.

"Hey, it's me. Did you send me an email with a picture attached to it?" Sydney asked, tucking a curl behind her ear.

"No, why would I?"

"Well, I got one from you. Are you at work?"

"I'm just pulling in the parking lot now, why? What was the picture I supposedly sent you?"

"One of you and Michelle kissing, and the email said you were breaking things off with me."

"This is the final straw, I'm going to fucking kill my sister. I'm sure she'll have deleted the email from my sent files, so send it back to me, I want to print it. You listen to me Sydney, I'm going to be with you until I don't have any breath left in my body, do you hear me?"

"Yeah, I do. Zeke, for a minute there my whole world crashed down around me. First all the shit with Sean, then my dad's accident, you know how trouble comes in three's, right? I thought you were the third," Sydney said, wiping the last of her tears away. Sitting up straight, she quickly said, "Don't tell Annie it got to me. Tell her I saw right through it." Sydney clicked on the forward button to send it back to him, smiling at Illana who was still sitting on the desk, arms and legs both crossed, her foot jiggling her shoe.

"How did you see through it anyway? You had to have known I'm not that much of an asshole, right?" Zeke asked, a slight note of worry in his voice.

"I was in shock and just reacted at first. Yes, I do know you aren't an asshole, and I really believe I would've gotten around to it not being from you, but I didn't at first. Luckily, Illana was standing here when I opened it, and noticed you weren't wearing the earring. That's when it all clicked." Sydney heard a door slam, and guessed he had just gotten out of his truck. "I'm sorry I didn't have enough faith in you at first, I'll try not to make that mistake again."

"You won't have any cause to make that mistake after I get done with Annie. She won't be bothering us anymore. I just got here, I'll call you back in a few." Zeke hung up mid-stride and Sydney was left listening to the dial tone. She recalled the time she had felt sorry for Annie when she was crying in her car, now Sydney wished she could revisit that moment again and this time she wouldn't feel any sympathy for her. After all, no one gets sympathy for self-inflicted wounds.

Zeke walked into the warehouse and went directly to his computer. He pulled up the email Annie had sent, and printed it. Bud drove over to him, and neatly did a 180 so the driver's side was positioned next to Zeke.

Zeke shook his head, but waited until the last rumble escaped the forklift before he said, "Show off."

"That sounds like jealousy. Just wanted to tell ya I'm all done with the morning orders. I had one of the girls bring me some more while you were gone, so I'm gonna take my lunch now."

"You're quick. Think you can handle this place by yourself for the rest of the day? You'll have company tomorrow, I know how you need an audience."

"Sheeit, boy, I've handled bigger warehouses than this. You taking off for good this time?"

"For a couple of months at least, and when I do come home, I won't be alone. I'll be seeing you, Bud."

"You take care, and don't fuck it up." Bud started up the 'lift and was off before Zeke could blink. Chuckling to himself, he went into the office. He nodded at the women who all appeared to be busy taking calls, grabbed the printed email and, losing his smile, let himself into his sisters' office. He pushed the door open, letting it bang against the wall, making Annie and Alex, who was leaning on her desk, jump.

"Can't you knock? We're in the middle of a business related matter, and I don't appreciate the interruption."

"Oh, I'm sure you don't," Zeke said, closing the door quietly. "However, I have a little matter that needs to be resolved. Alex, take a look at this." Zeke held out the email, and Annie stood up and tried to intercept it. Alex turned and raised the paper up higher to hold onto it, and his eyes narrowed in anger as he finished it.

"Annie, you just never learn, do you?" Alex asked, shaking his head.

"Oh really now, calm down, it was just a little joke."

"A joke? After everything that she's going through with her dad, you decided she needed this little pick-me-up? Even for you, it's pretty low." Zeke took the email out of Alex's hand, crumpled it into a ball and tossed it in the recycling bin by the door.

"What does her dad have to do with this? Is he upset that she might have AIDS? I can see how that might adversely affect him since he's so famous-"

"She doesn't know, Zeke. I didn't tell her why you left," Alex said as he sat down in one of the blue cushy chairs.

"Know what?" Annie asked, looking alarmed for the first time.

"Sydney's father was in a near fatal car accident and is still in ICU. That's why I flew out there. If you were even remotely caring, I would've told you myself, but I figured you'd just do something, well, something like this and make things worse for her."

Annie's face fell as stumbled into her chair. "I'll apologize right away. I really had no idea. Is he going to be okay?" Annie's hand was pulling on the pearls around her neck, turning her necklace and making the pearls clack together.

"Oh, so now you care? I only want to know one thing, why are you so determined to get me back together with the woman that had sex with my best friend?"

Annie's eyes widened as her face lost every ounce of color. "She slept with Tyler?"

"I see she didn't mention that part. Yeah, it was an interesting morning when she walked into my house and saw him sitting there. He had no idea I was seeing her, but she sure as hell knew who he was. I'd shown her pictures of him, so she damn well knew."

Annie's eyes started to tear up. "I swear to you Zeke, I had no idea. I believed her when she said you cheated on her, and you never said any different. Why would you let me believe that?"

"For the same reason you've believed every other bad thing about me, you never asked," Zeke said, his jaw twitching slightly. He turned to Alex, who looked dazed. "I'm leaving today, and I'll call you when I know what I'm doing. Thank God Sydney knows me better than our sister, and didn't buy into Annie's email, but she's still upset and needs help with her dad." Turning back to Annie, he leaned on her desk and with a lazy smile said, "Now, you'd better leave us alone, or I will make sure everyone knows who gave you, and why they gave you, the little fairy figurines you love so much."

Annie sat up, straightened her black tweed skirt and glared at Zeke. "You have my word."

Alex stood up, looking more confused than ever. "Do I want to know what the hell you two are talking about?"

"No," they both answered.

"Okay then. Zeke, do you need me to do anything?" Alex asked, ruffling his hair for the umpteenth time.

"Yeah, you can give me a lift to the airport. We can talk on the way."

Chapter Twenty-Seven – A Soft Place to Fall

"Dad, you have to be more reasonable," Sydney said, exasperation clear in her voice.

"I am," Graham croaked. "It's the rest of you who won't see reason. I'm fine. I want to go home. I can hire a private nurse. Hell, two nurses so someone is always with me. There is no reason to send me to physical therapy."

"Well, I must say, this would be highly irregular, but I cannot force you to go to a rehab clinic. If you can show me proof that you will be receiving quality PT care, then I can release you in a few days." The doctor didn't smile as he looked from Graham's smug smile to Sydney's outraged expression.

"You have *got* to be kidding me! He almost died! Am I the only one who remembers that?"

"No, but your father does have the means to hire around-the-clock care, and I have every confidence he will. Once I get a phone call from the party or parties who will be providing care, we can discuss when he will be discharged."

"I'm right here, I may not have full use of my voice, but I do have full retention of my faculties. I do not appreciate being talked about as though I'm not sitting here."

"I'm not so sure of your faculties being present, but your stubborn streak certainly is," Sydney stood up, put her hands on her hips and looked down at her father. "I can't force you, but at least let me move in for a while. I can work from there and make sure you're getting the care you need."

"We'll see," Graham said, closing his eyes.

Sydney rolled her eyes and looked back at the doctor. "Thank you very much for everything you've done, Doctor." Sydney shook the physicians hand and smiled when he nodded at her just before he walked out of the room. "Okay Dad, you can quit playing possum now, he's gone."

Graham opened one eye and saw Sydney smiling, albeit faintly, at him. "I knew you'd come around. Where are your sister and her lover?"

"Dad!"

"Oh please, like I didn't know? I've known since she was small, so did your mom and it didn't bother either one of us. Well, it did a bit, only because we were afraid of how other people would treat her."

"You should tell her that, she's afraid you'll be disappointed in her."

"Oh for heaven's sake! She should know better. I'll have a talk with her later." Graham held onto the bedrail as he pulled himself to a more upright position. "Now, regarding this business of you moving in with me. No. I want you to go to Wisconsin and stop worrying about me."

"Absolutely not, Dad it is out of the question. For one: family takes care of its own, two: Mom would kill me, three: I do love you."

"One: your mom is dead and won't kill you, two: what makes you think I want you seeing me in a weakened state? And yes, I love you too. Do you think I want *you* to help me into the shower? Don't you think that'd be a little embarrassing for us both? Did you think about that? Even if your mom were alive, I'd still be hiring nurses or physical therapists so I could get better without anyone watching me. Your mom would've understood, and so should you." Graham reached out his hand, and Sydney stepped closer to put her hand in his. "Go, and find the life you've always wanted. If it doesn't work, come home. I didn't mean any of what I said the other night, in fact, I was turning around to go back to your place to tell you when I got hit."

"Oh Dad, it was my fault!" Sydney tried to stop the tears from forming, and let go of her dad's hand to wipe them away.

"Don't be ridiculous, it was my fault for answering my damn phone. Stop it now, no more crying, I've seen you girls do enough crying in the past couple of days to last me a lifetime."

"Dad, I wouldn't feel right about leaving you like this. I can't just go and leave you to the care of strangers," Sydney said gently.

"I'm not asking you to. I plan on getting your cousin to come up from San Diego and see if she still has any friends up here that she went to nursing college with."

"So it's fine for Vanessa to see you like this?"

A nurse opened the door, and smile apologetically. "Sorry for interrupting, but Ms. Myers, you have a visitor."

"Ah good, tell him to come back." Graham said with a wave of his good hand. The nursed nodded and left.

"Dad, she said I have a visitor, not you."

"Yes, I heard her, nothing wrong with my hearing either. I got a phone call about twenty minutes before you got here this morning from your Zeke."

Zeke walked through the doors holding a bouquet of white lilies and another of white roses. Sydney stood there dumbly, with her mouth open as she looked from Zeke to her dad and back at Zeke. "What are you doing here?"

"Hi to you too. Hello Mr. Myers, it's nice to meet you, I wish the circumstances had been different. These are for you." He set the lilies on the table next to Graham's bed. He shook Graham's hand gently and turned back to Sydney, handing her the roses. "These, are for you. Sorry I was gone so long." He bent to kiss her, but glanced at her father and opted to give her a peck on the cheek.

"Thank you, they're lovely, and you were gone for like two minutes. Why did you call my father this morning?"

"Uh, well...you told her?" Zeke turned sharply to look at Graham.

"Not what we talked about, just that you called. Drop it Sydney, that's an order. Remember, you don't want me to get upset or I might relapse."

"How long do you think that gambit is going to work?" she asked wryly. Sydney sighed, loudly, and said, "Fine, I'll let it go for now, but one of you will spill it sooner or later." Sydney looked behind her, hearing the door open, and smiled as Jessica and Mandy walked in.

"Wow, nice flowers, when did you get in Zeke?" Jess asked, making her way over to her father, where she bent down and kissed him on his forehead. Mandy stood next to Sydney and leaned over to smell her flowers.

"Almost an hour ago. It took me awhile to get the rental car and find a flower shop."

"Sydney, why don't you and Zeke go get something to eat?" Graham asked, being his normal subtle self.

"Oh, sure. I'll be back later Dad. See you two tonight." Sydney bent down to hug her sister, who was sitting by the bed and whispered, "Listen to him."

"This can't be good," Jess whispered back. Standing up, she gave Zeke a hug too. "Sydney, just come back tomorrow morning, Mandy and I will hang out here and have dinner with the old man."

"Watch it, I won't be in this bed forever you know," Graham said, feigning a frown.

Sydney led Zeke back to her apartment, only slowing down after almost losing him twice in traffic. She tried not to smile as she got out of her car, but the glare he was giving her had the opposite effect he was going for, and she erupted into laughter.

"Oh c'mon, is it my fault you drive like an old woman?"

"We're going to see about that surgery for you."

"What surgery?" she asked still laughing.

"The one to remove the lead from your foot," Zeke said, shutting his car door. Loud.

"It'll never happen. Do you want to go out or stay in?" Sydney said, still standing between her car and the open door.

"I'd rather stay in. Do we have anything to eat here?"

Sydney caught the "we" and smiled. "There's some left-over Chinese food that should still be good. If not, we'll order a pizza." Sydney closed the door, clicked her new car alarm on and led the way upstairs.

"Haven't you ever heard of a grocery store? We could just go shopping and make something Syd."

"I do go to the grocery store, they have a great buffet where you can get Mexican, Chinese or prime rib. I do know how to cook, I just don't normally do it when it's just me." Sydney said over her shoulder as she let them both in to her apartment.

"Well, it's not just you anymore. So tomorrow, we hit the store."

She saw her voice mail light blinking and walked over to scroll through her caller ID. Zeke watched as Sydney's hands started to tremble.

"What is it?"

"The lab called. With my results I assume. Hold on, let me get the message." Sydney pressed the button on her phone as Zeke walked over to sit in a dining room chair near her.

Holding the phone away from her mouth, she told him, "They didn't leave the results and said to call back right away. That can't be good." Sydney clicked off after erasing the message.

"Don't go borrowing trouble, just call and find out. Either way, I'm going to be here. Not just today, but every day until you can come home with me."

"What do you mean? What about your job?"

"Working for family has its perks, they can't fire me. Alex knows what's going on and told me to take as long as I needed. I don't want us to be apart, long distance relationships have a very low rate of success. So, if you'll have me, I'd like to stay."

Sydney stood stunned, phone in one hand, with her mouth open. "I never really considered it, you'll hate it here. You said so yourself."

"Yes, and I also said if I had to I'd move here. If you'd be more comfortable, I'll get my own place, preferably in this complex." Zeke leaned back in the chair, raising the front legs off the floor. Crossing his arms, he waited for an answer.

"Shouldn't we see what the results of the HIV test are first?"

"I. Don't. Care. If you have it, you have it and we'll deal with it. I'm here to stay Sydney, one way or another. I love you." Zeke was up and pulled her in his arms. Sydney snapped out of it, and hugged him back harder.

"Yes, I want you to stay, I just can't believe it. I do believe you, I'm just overwhelmed. I love you too, you've become my soft place to fall in such a short time. It scares the shit out of me that I've come to depend on you so quickly." Sydney buried her head in his chest, breathing in the scent that was distinctively his, diesel and pine trees and all man, her body relaxing as she inhaled.

"I'll always be your soft place to fall Sydney. Well, at times it might be a hard place," Zeke laughed as she poked him in the ribs, "just a little levity. Make your phone call so we can figure out dinner."

Sydney squeezed him then let go. Taking a deep breath she dialed the number for the lab. "Hello, this is Sydney Myers, I'm returning your call to get my lab results."

"Just a moment, I have to pull your file." Sydney could hear the phone clunking down on something and closed her eyes in silent prayer as she waited. "You had the blood test for HIV?"

"Yes."

"Who is your regular doctor? I think you should be talking to him."

"I don't have a regular doctor there, besides you called me. Can't you give me the results?"

"Well, you really need to talk to your doctor. You're negative for HIV, but you do have genital herpes. We typically run a blood screen for multiple with patients who have been exposed to HIV, due to the fact they obviously had unprotected sex."

"Yes, they explained that to me at the lab. Thank you for giving me the results." Sydney sat down in the chair, smiling.

"You'll need to follow up with your doctor regarding the herpes."

"Yes, I will, thank you." Sydney hung up, set the phone on the table and looked at Zeke. "Well, you want the good news or the bad news first?"

Zeke stood a little straighter and said, "Give me the bad first."

"I have herpes, but not HIV." Sydney's eyes began to well up and she bit her lip to keep it from quivering.

"Herpes can't kill you, so I can honestly say I'm relieved. C'mere Syd," Zeke pulled her out of the chair and took her in his arms again. "We'll deal with it. I have an Uncle who's had it for twenty years, and my Aunt has never gotten it. Don't cry, it'll be fine, you'll see."

"I feel dirty, I don't know anything about it."

"We'll look it up online, and tomorrow you can call and get an appointment, and we'll go from there. Look at me, Syd," he said, nudging her chin up. "I'm still here, and this changes nothing. Okay?"

"Doesn't anything rattle you?"

Zeke let out a short laugh. "Absolutely. You scared the shit out of me earlier today about the stupid email my sister sent. Outside of that, as long as we have each other, the rest of the world can go to hell. Let's see if there's any Chinese food worth salvaging. Then I want to have a look at the Brazilian you're hiding."

Chapter Twenty-Eight – No Thought Required

Sydney rolled over to find Zeke looking at her. Smiling shyly, she stretched and said, "Good morning. How long have you been awake?"

"Long enough. You're so beautiful Sydney. Sometimes, I can't believe I found you." Zeke reached out and ran one finger down her cheek.

Propping herself up on her elbow, she turned her head to kiss the inside of his palm. "Actually, I found you. I still can't believe what an ass you were that day."

He scooped one arm underneath her and pulled her on top of him. "Well, when I'm looked at like a prize bull I tend to get a little cocky. Speaking of which, I do believe there are other parts of me awake now too."

Sydney trailed one hand down his ribs to rest on his hip. "I was hoping so. I'm happy to see you too." She bent down and flicked his earlobe with her tongue, and then kissed her way down his neck. Zeke growled and flipped them both over so he was on top of her.

Cupping her breast with his hand, he slid down her body never losing eye contact with her as he took her nipple in his mouth. Sydney arched her back as she gripped his shoulders. He raised above her so he could kiss between her cleavage down to her belly button, nipping softly at her skin as he went. Her breath expelled when his teeth grazed the inside of her thigh and his fingers slid just inside her. Feeling his breath on the most sensitive part of her body, she closed her eyes just as he flicked his fingers back and forth inside of her.

"I love that you're ready for me, but I want to see you come first." Sydney cried out as Zeke used his thumb on her clit, while still moving his fingers inside, bringing her to orgasm almost immediately. She grabbed at his arms as her hips rose off the bed. She tried pulling at him, but he wouldn't be budged. He brought her to the point where she was ready to orgasm again. Then he stopped.

"What are you doing?"

"Watching you, making you wait," Zeke said, his finger still slowly moving in a circle inside of her. He reached over to the nightstand and got a condom, ripping the paper with his teeth. With one hand he rolled the condom on his hard cock as she watched him through narrowed eyes.

"You're making me crazy, come here already," Sydney said, panting as she tried pulling him on top of her in earnest.

"Pushy, but I like that in a woman. Especially in my woman." Zeke raised his body above hers, so she could feel just of tip of him against her. Sydney tried to move down to take him inside, but he had her hands in his and pinned to the bed. "Open your eyes, I want you to watch me watching you come."

She opened her eyes and in one thrust he was fully inside of her. Never taking her eyes off of him, she matched his pace, raising her hips and using the muscles that were wrapped around the hard length of him, squeezed him tight as he pulled out. He made a noise deep in his throat, so she squeezed harder, rotating her hips as she raised them. He sat up on his knees and pulled her to him, pushing her legs up over his shoulders to get deeper. With his eyes locked on hers, he watched as he pushed her over the edge several more times until he finally found his own explosive release. Easing her legs down, he laid down next her while they both tried, and failed, to catch their breath.

"You're going to have to make coffee, I won't be using my legs for a while yet," Sydney said, wiping the sweat off her forehead.

"I'll wait. I'm in no hurry for coffee, and if you'll give me a few minutes, you won't be thinking about coffee." Zeke was lying on his back, his arm flung over his eyes, but she still saw the small smile on his face.

"I'll go make it. If I didn't know better, I'd think you're trying to kill me. But what a way to go." Sydney leaned over him, moved his arm so she could kiss him on the cheek, and bounced out of bed. She picked up his t-shirt she had thrown on the floor last night, and put in on before leaving the room.

"I liked the view better without the shirt," he called after her.

"I'm sure my neighbors would too, but I'd rather not give the ninety year old man across the way a heart attack," she yelled from the kitchen.

Zeke smiled as he rested his head on his arms and stared at the ceiling. He thought back to the night before, and was again impressed at just how flexible his Sydney was. He let out a short laugh remembering he had been the one to get the leg cramp, not that he said anything to her about it, even though she was doing all the contorting. Hearing her grinding the beans, he sat up and looked around for his pants, which had landed on top of her dresser. Taking some underwear from his bag, he rummaged until he located his toothbrush and headed for the bathroom.

"Come take a shower with me," he called.

"I'll be right there, I'm just checking my email for work. Two minutes."

"Hurry up, and I'm timing you."

"With what? You don't wear a watch."

"No, but I can count to 120."

"Oh shit. Hey Zeke, I need to call the office, can I take a rain check on that shower?"

"I'm sure sometime in the next sixty years you'll get another chance." Tired of yelling from the bathroom to the living room, he walked out to where she was. "Why, what's up?"

"Looks like we got the big contract, but John said we also got a smaller one I might be interested in, so he asked me to call him." Sydney already had the phone to her ear as she spoke. "Hey John, what's up?"

"Good morning, I take it you saw my email?"

"Yeah, just now. What's the small contract?"

"The library in Ruby Lake wants to hire you specifically to bring them into the digital age. Those were the librarian's exact words. Nice sum of money, plus housing. With the fee we'll be getting, you can rent a car for the whole six months. Oh, she also said no hurry, she knew about your dad, so the contract can start whenever you're ready to go. If you want it."

"Of course I do, there's no thought required on this one! Is this the contract you submitted and didn't want to tell me about?"

"Yes, she asked me not to say anything just in case we didn't get it. I didn't want to get your hopes up. So now you can go there and still work for me. This solves all my problems."

She looked over at Zeke who had a huge, and very satisfied, smile on his face. "Hold on a minute John," covering the phone she whispered to Zeke, "Did you know about this?"

He just nodded and waved his hand at her to finish her phone call. Shaking her head, she said, "I'm back. Let me talk to my dad and my sister. I'll call you on Monday, unless you need to know sooner?"

"Monday is fine. But, if you can swing it, can you come in today? Just to give Dan a run through since I'm going to make him point person on the large contract. Of course, now that you'll still be working for me, I want you to be the lead on it."

"Absolutely, thanks John. I can probably make it in an hour or so. See you then." She put the phone on its charger then whirled back to Zeke. "How in the hell did you know about that?"

"Well, here, sit down. I have a few things to own up to. Actually, let's get our coffee first, then I'll tell you everything."

Chapter Twenty-Nine – Lies, Secrets and a Male Chauvinist Pig

Zeke sighed, took a sip of coffee, and looked Sydney in the eye. "Remember your last day in Ruby Lake when I had to be somewhere else?"

"Yes, I never thought to question it though."

"Well, I wasn't completely honest with you, I do have a background in computers. I went over to the library to talk Doreen into hiring you. I didn't think you'd be happy working with Annie. Hell, no one is. So I gave her the idea of what could be done, and showed her some of the reports and screen shots from the database you did."

"Why didn't you just tell me? It's not like I would have been offended Zeke." Sydney sat back and crossed her arms, smiling.

"I didn't know if she'd really do it, and didn't see the point in getting our hopes up if it didn't happen. I was actually going to tell you last week, but with everything that's happened with your dad, and the Sean thing, I just kept it to myself."

"Even though I see your point, in the future, tell me. Especially when it might affect my future, deal?"

"Deal. There is one more thing." Zeke looked down at his hands, seeming nervous for the first time since, well, ever.

"What? Do you really think I'm going to get mad at you about anything right now? Especially after you were so patient with me last night while we did all the research on this stupid simplex problem I now have?"

"Well, I wasn't being completely selfless by helping with the research. You weren't going to have sex with me until you had some answers, so I figured the sooner you got them the better we'd both feel." His grin was infectious and made Sydney laugh out loud.

"Oh yeah, Mr. Selfish. Just spit it out, it can't be that bad." Sydney's foot was rubbing his ankle. She was finding it more and more difficult not to be touching him in some way all the time. It was a really good thing he had the same affliction.

"Now, on this one I did lie, not outright, but I let you believe something you shouldn't have. Remember the printer drivers that disappeared and you thought Annie did it? She didn't do it. I did."

"What? Why, how, why would you do such a thing? Both things." Sydney sat up straighter, not believing her ears.

"I didn't want you to leave. I really am that selfish, and I don't regret doing it. Only the lying and letting you believe worse of my little sister than you already did." Zeke reached his hand across her dining table and held onto her fingertips. "Can you forgive me on this one? I swear I'll never do anything like that again."

"Jesus Zeke, it really was a horrible thing to do. You almost gave your cousin a coronary!" Sydney laughed, remembering. "I can't say I'm mad about having my stay extended, which I was already thinking of doing by the way, but I wish you wouldn't have let me believe it was Annie. Not that I like her any better, especially after the last stunt she pulled. That one is going to take me awhile to get over."

"Me too. Can you forgive me?" he asked, gently squeezing her fingers.

"Yes, God knows I couldn't stay mad at you if I tried. You get that goofy grin and give me butterflies and it's all over for me."

"I don't have a goofy grin, but I'm glad I give you butterflies. I'm totally crazy about you."

"Right back atcha. I have to get ready for work, so quit looking at me like I'm prey. Do you want to stay here or come with?"

"I really want to go with. I'd like to see where you work, and maybe have a little chat with Dan."

"How do you know about Dan?" Sydney narrowed her eyes at him. She had intentionally not mentioned him so was immediately suspicious.

"Uh, well, I do know one other secret, but it's not mine to tell. Ask your best friend."

"Illana? Illana told you?" Sydney was more surprised than mad, and it showed clearly on her face.

"Not me, Christ, just talk to her. I'm not going to be able to keep anything from you. Now, are you ready to make good on the rain check for the shower?"

Laughing, she got up and let him lead her right where he wanted her to go, knowing all along it was exactly where she wanted to be.

It was more like two hours by the time Sydney finally made it into her office, with Zeke trailing slowly behind her. She slid into her seat, turning on her equipment and looking through her stack of folders when Zeke kissed her on top of her head, saying he was going to hang out with John.

Sydney peeked her head around the corner to find Dan's office empty. Hearing male laughter coming from the conference room, she gathered her folders and walked towards the sound.

"Well, I was telling John we should set up some kind of golf tournament, separate the boys from the men." Dan's chest was puffed out, hands in his pockets as he rocked on his heels. Sydney mentally grimaced at the smug, smarmy look on his face and had an overwhelming urge to head butt him in the nose to watch him bleed, or at least toss the files on the table and leave, but merely cleared her throat instead.

"Hey Sydney, glad you could make it in. Sorry guys, can't keep a pretty woman waiting." Dan smiled mischievously and winked at the two other men, Brian and Jeff, who in turn glared at an oblivious Dan.

"Nor should you keep your lead waiting. Sorry to break it up guys, but I need to get back to my dad, so I don't have much time." She smiled at Brian and Jeff, who both looked as if they'd like to do some damage to Dan. With her back to Dan, she rolled her eyes making her two friends smile as they walked out.

"Sure, sure, no problem, I understand, you're a good woman to take care of him. A lot of working women seemed to have lost that family connection. So, what did you bring me?"

Sydney set down the folders and pulled out a large stack of paper which had diagrams in black and verbiage in blue. "These are all the specs I drew up for the contract. I'm not sure how far you've gotten already, so why don't you pull up the dummy database and we'll go over it." Sydney waited as Dan sat in front of the laptop and moved her chair further away from his so she wouldn't be hovering over him.

"You know, I don't mind if you want to sit a little closer," Dan said, and then proceeded to put his hand on her arm. "I'll only bite if you ask."

Sydney removed his hand off of her arm, bending his fingers back and stood up. "Listen, I don't know where you worked before, but let's get a couple of things straight. I'm your lead and as such, will be treated with the same amount of respect you seem to reserve for men. Secondly, I don't like you looking at me like I'm a piece of meat, nor will I tolerate you touching me. Lastly, quit referring to my gender, it tends to piss me off and I seem to have developed a violent streak so God knows what I might do. Knock it off, and we can start over right now. Otherwise, I will go to John and you'll be out on your ass. Capiche?" She continued to bend his fingers back until she could see a little pain reflected on his face and let go.

He held his hands up and smiled, "Whoa, yeah calm down. I'm sorry if I offended you; I'll try to remember you're sensitive. I never knew a woman who wasn't flattered by an appreciative look at their assets, but it won't happen again."

"The only 'assets' I want you to look at are my brains. Let's get back to work," Sydney said as she sat back down and pulled the laptop in front of her.

John made the announcement about the two contracts to the rest of the staff later that morning, and told everyone Sydney would be going back to Ruby Lake to head up the small contract, and Dan would now be the main point person for the database part of the large contract, but Sydney would still be the lead and overseeing it from Wisconsin. Illana was sullen and Dan strutted around thinking he had somehow shown to John he was the right man for the job. It infuriated Sydney, but she kept her mouth shut, knowing she would soon be rid of him.

Sydney walked back to her desk with Illana marching right behind her.

"Great, he's going to be completely insufferable now! How could you let him think John picked him over you for this?"

"I told John to let him think whatever he wanted, I didn't care. But if I know John, he'll set him straight. Besides, I'm still the lead, just from Wisconsin. Hey, have you seen Zeke?"

"Yeah, he walked across the street to the mall, said he'd be back in a little bit. Oh and you're to call his cell if you needed him sooner."

"Speaking of phone calls, care to explain how Zeke heard about Dan? He said I should ask you since it wasn't his secret to spill."

Illana gripped the desk with both hands as she leaned back against it. "I didn't tell you because of everything that's been going on. I was going to tell you the night I came over with potstickers, but then with everything I just didn't. Look, it's not a big deal, Alex and I have kept in contact by email and a phone call now and then. We're just friends, and he makes me laugh." Illana tipped her chin up and pinned her brown eyes on Sydney, daring her to get mad.

"I trust you. And gee, like I'm in a position to talk right now? Good for you, if he makes you happy, I'm all for it."

"I never said he made me happy, we're just friends. It's not going anywhere, we just like talking. Don't make a thing out of this, just because you have one going with Zeke."

"Temper, temper. Who are you trying to convince, me or you?"

Zeke strolled into her cubicle, took one look at the situation and said, "I think I'll go talk to John again."

"Oh no, we're done here," Illana said as she pushed off the desk, glared at Zeke who gave her a lazy smile in return, and strode past him, barely missing his foot. He moved it just in time.

"I take it you know about the emails then?" Zeke asked, cocking his head in the direction Illana went.

"Yes, those and the phone calls, but nothing is going on, they're just 'friends' she said."

"I didn't know about the phone calls, but I'm getting the same line from Alex. You ready to go, or do you need more time?"

"Nope, I'm ready, let me just grab my stuff and we can head out." Sydney picked her purse off the floor and was just standing up when Dan appeared in the door way. "Need something Dan?"

"Um, no, I was, uh going to invite you to lunch," Dan said, his gaze going from Sydney up to Zeke.

"She already has plans," Zeke said, placing one hand on her shoulder.

"Zeke, stop it. As it turns out, I'm leaving and won't be back for a couple of days. Feel free to email me any questions you have."

Dan stood still for a moment, much like a rat caught in a snake's gaze. He shook his head slightly and smiling said, "It's pretty simple so I'm sure I won't." He almost ran into his cubicle.

Sydney narrowed her eyes at Zeke and pushed him out towards the door. He opened the door for her and put his hand on the small of her back. Looking back, he wasn't surprised to see Dan standing there. Zeke shot him a smile that didn't touch his eyes. Turning back around, he followed Sydney outside, feeling a little superior, and a lot more smug.

Chapter Thirty – Finding a Balance, With a Helping Shove

The sound of laughter met them at door to her father's room. Sydney walked in smiling broadly, letting the light mood lift her spirits. Still holding Zeke's hand, she grinned at her sister. "I thought we were supposed to keep him calm, yet I could hear you guys all the way in the lobby. What's going on?"

Graham pushed himself up straighter and motioned to Zeke to shut the door. "I got a call today from an old friend who wants to collaborate on a book. He just happens to be based in Madison, so it looks like we'll both be moving to Wisconsin."

Sydney stood stunned, the ramifications spilling over her like a sheet of ice. "Oh. Well. That's great! Really. I mean, after you get all your physical therapy taken care of you should be able to fly, right?"

Graham cleared his throat and crossed his arms. "Actually, I called in a favor and I've got a transport that can get me there in my present condition. We'll have to find a place to stay of course, but I'm sure your young man here can help with those arrangements."

"Actually sir, it's already been taken care of. Sydney, tell him about the library job. Remember, there's housing included."

"Oh! I almost forgot. I've been assigned another contract in Ruby Lake, at the library this time, and it's for six months. So we can live there Dad. Just you and me." Sydney was trying hard to keep the disappointment out of her voice, but failed as usual.

"Actually, as much as I'd like that, the friend I'll be writing with has offered to come up and stay with me. I called your cousin, and she's on board too. So you can quit looking disappointed Sydney, you won't have to live with me after all," Graham said with a chuckle.

"Dad, that's not what I meant-"

"Oh hush. As long as it's okay with the contract, I'll take over the housing you've been offered, since I assume you wouldn't be staying there anyway?" Graham smiled knowingly at the couple who were both blushing.

"Dad, leave her alone. For God's sake, you're making her face as red as her hair!" Jess playfully backhanded Graham's shoulder, who of course winced dramatically. Turning to Sydney, she said, "Dad will be released on Monday, so I figured we'd stay and help pack and then take off back to base on Wednesday. Mandy and I already called the moving company who can move both of you at the same time, all we have to do is supply them with the destination addresses."

Sydney could barely keep up. "Well, you all seem to have taken care of it. Might have been nice to have gotten a phone call and had a voice in it."

"Now Sydney, we're just trying to help. Besides, Dad is going to stay in his house for a week until the moving truck delivers yours and his stuff." Jess checked her watch and looked down at Graham. "I need to make some calls and take a nap, since someone got me up before the sun this morning."

"We had things to organize, quit complaining, Sergeant Major." Graham offered up his cheek as Jess bent down to give him a quick kiss. After saying their goodbye's Jess and Mandy scooted out, leaving the room much quieter.

"Dad, I wish you had at least talked to me first before you and Jessica arranged everything."

"Now you're just being silly, tell her Zeke."

Zeke approached the bed and saw Sydney's injured look. "No sir, I will not. I happen to agree with her, and I think you were wrong not to include her." He reached out and clasped her hand in his again.

"Son, I admire you for standing up to me and standing with my daughter, but you're wrong. Sydney's never been any good at the kind of organization it takes to do this kind of major move, whereas Jess is used to ordering troop deployments and the like."

"Again, I disagree. I watched her *organize* an entire group of people and assign out batches of work so the data could all be entered in an orderly way. Perhaps you've never seen her in action, but I have. I watched while she created an entire system from nothing in three days.

She had to analyze the data and make sense out of it, and did it with very little assistance from anyone." Zeke stopped talking when Sydney squeezed his hand.

"Dad, listen, next time just consult me first. That's all, okay?"

Graham cocked his head up and to the side, studying Sydney. "You know, I never thought about it that way, how you do your job. I'm sorry Sydney, Zeke's right. I should know better than to make judgments without obtaining all the facts. I promise I won't do so again." Graham reached out to clasp her other hand. She let go of Zeke and gingerly hugged her dad.

Standing back up she held on to her dad's hand and blew out a nervous laugh. "It'll be nice not being steamrolled all the time, and also to finally get a chance to show you I am more capable than you think."

"I should've given you the chance long ago. So, what are we having for lunch?"

Stretched out on her bed, lying next to an equally satiated Zeke, Sydney stared at the full moon outside her window. She couldn't remember a busier day. After conferring with Jess, Sydney left the moving details in her sister's capable hands, and thought about her conversation with Illana.

"I have a surprise for you."

"Another one? I don't think my heart can take it."

She hit him half-heartedly, and then turned on her side to face him, propping her head on her hand. "Not that kind. I realized I'm going to have a week in between moving and starting my new job, so I thought it might be nice to have a little vacation. How do you feel about the ocean?"

"Love it. Where on the coast do you want to go?" Zeke was lying on his back, his arm tucked under his head. The picture of male contentment.

"Not the coast, I was thinking an island. Illana's dad has a house he never uses on the west coast of Kauai and she said we could use it if you're interested."

Zeke turned over to face her. "Seriously? Just like that, we have a house to stay in the Hawaiian Islands?"

"Yep. If you're game," Sydney said with a grin.

"Hell yeah! When do we leave?"

"Tomorrow, if it's okay with you. I figured since the Haunted House got cancelled we didn't have to get back right away. I was almost all packed for the move and Jess said she'd take care of the rest of it for me so we can go. This is her way of trying to kiss up to me for always going along with Dad I guess," she added while twirling a lock of his hair around her finger.

"Did you get plane tickets already?"

"No, but I got us a plane. Illana's dad owns a couple Lear jets, so we'll be using one of those."

"Holy shit, we're going in a private plane? Have I mentioned lately how much I love you? What the hell does her father do?" He asked as he sat up, and untangled his hair from Sydney's finger.

"Yes, breathlessly not too long ago. He made it big during the dot com rush, and got out before it collapsed. He has houses all over the world, but Illana only uses this one. It's a long story, I'll tell you another time. What time do you want to leave?"

Rolling over on top of her, he asked, "Can we go now? Or, at least in an hour or so?"

Chapter Thirty-One – Never in a Million Years...

Sydney walked out the beach house door right onto sand. Breathing in the soft, tropical air, she smiled as she spotted a very relaxed Zeke snoozing in a beach chair. Sydney's colorful wrap flapped gently in the breeze and her feet sunk in the sand as she walked over to join him in the lawn chairs they had moved under a palm tree.

"Wake up mister. Do you want to check out the Na Lima Hana festival tomorrow? I have a brochure and it looks really fun. It's all about health related practices from several different cultures, and then tomorrow night there'll be an authentic luau." She bypassed using the other chair and joined Zeke on his.

"If you want to go, we'll go. You don't need to convince me, I still can't believe we're here." Zeke raised his sunglasses, resting them on top of his head so he could look at her as he wrapped his arms around her.

"It's magical isn't it? I've been here five times now I guess, no, six including this time. Every time is a little more magical. I already used that word, didn't I?" Sydney asked as she lay on her side, half on top of him, and half on the chair.

"It can't be used too many times, not for here. Do you think we'll see any humpbacks?" His blonde hair was getting even lighter, and the tan on his chest had already darkened a couple shades in the three days they had been there.

Sydney laughed. "Not unless they're lost, they usually don't come until late November, and I don't think we can stay the full month. Oh, I just looked at the weather in Ruby Lake, it's snowing there right now."

Zeke closed his eyes, smiling, letting the filtered sunlight warm his face. He pulled Sydney on top of him, and sat them both upright. "Let's go for a walk, and then maybe a swim."

"It's not dark enough for our 'swim' yet!"

"Fine, walk then." Zeke playfully slapped her butt, helping her get up. They strolled down to the surf and Sydney asked, "Which way?"

"South. Oh, sorry, left," he said with a playful grin.

"Keep it up mister. Making fun of me will get you nowhere," Sydney warned, kicking water at him.

"Hasn't hurt me so far," Zeke said with a half-smile.

They walked hand in hand on the edge of the surf, the warm water spinning around their feet. Sydney sighed, gazing at the crystal blue water which reflected the setting sun.

"Stop a minute, I have something in my shoe." Zeke pulled her out of the water onto dry sand and kneeled down just as Sydney realized he wasn't wearing shoes. Reaching in his pocket, he brought out a little black velvet jewelry box. "I know it hasn't been very long, but I feel like I've known you my whole life. I can't imagine my life without you in it; I want you with me forever. I never want to be apart from you again, and I promise I will love you every day for the rest of my life. Sydney Myers, will you marry me?"

Sydney raised her hand to her mouth in wonder, tears filling her eyes, as he opened the ring case. "Yes, oh my God, Zeke, yes. You're the most romantic man I've ever met, and still can't believe you're mine. You've become my best friend and my whole world. Never in a million years did I see you doing this, here, now."

Zeke took the square-cut diamond ring out of the case and slid it on her finger, wearing his half grin that made her insides do somersaults. He tugged on her hand, and she glanced, stunned, from the ring to his face before throwing herself into his open arms.

He laid her down on the soft, warm sand, and rolled over on top of her. When they kissed, about a mile offshore a lost humpback whale sang.

ABOUT THE AUTHOR

Sherrill Willis lives in Northern Wisconsin with her children and is currently at work on the second book in the Ruby Lake series. She loves to hear from her readers, so please contact her on Facebook. Please visit her website at SherrillWillis.com for more information and upcoming events.

Made in the USA
Lexington, KY
11 December 2019

58414547R00133